His smile was warm, but she had the strangest feeling he wasn't being sincere about this. He was asking for one thing, but looking for another. What?

"Well... you're obviously a college graduate," she began.

"Harvard Business."

"About twenty-eight, twenty-nine years old."

"Thirty. Not bad."

"I don't think you're married or have been married."

"Correct again."

"You're obviously physically active... you're ambitious, you have a clear value system, but you're a little bit intolerant of conservative attitudes. I'd say you're a firm boss, but well liked."

"Well, that's a pretty damn good analysis," he said finally, and sat back. "Even if it isn't true, I'm going to work on it to make it true."

Now she was curious.

"Which part wasn't true?"

She thought he looked very satisfied with her so much as he was satisfied with himself. Once again she had the feeling that he was testing himself. What did it mean?

ILLUSION

ANDREW NEIDERMAN

ILLUSION
ILLUSION

WORLDWIDE

TORONTO • NEW YORK • LONDON • PARIS
AMSTERDAM • STOCKHOLM • HAMBURG
ATHENS • MILAN • TOKYO • SYDNEY

ILLUSION

A Worldwide Library book

First published September 1987

ISBN 0-373-97044-7

Copyright © 1987 by Andrew Neiderman. All rights reserved.
Philippine copyright 1987. Australian copyright 1987.
Except for use in any review, the reproduction or utilization of
this work in whole or in part in any form by any electronic,
mechanical or other means, now known or hereafter invented,
including xerography, photocopying and recording, or in any
information storage or retrieval system, is forbidden without
the permission of the publisher, Worldwide Library,
225 Duncan Mill Road, Don Mills, Ontario, Canada M3B 3K9.

All the characters in this book have no existence outside the
imagination of the author and have no relation whatsoever to
anyone bearing the same name or names. They are not even
distantly inspired by any individual known or unknown to the
author, and all incidents are pure invention.

The Worldwide design trademarks, consisting of a globe surrounded
by a square, and the word WORLDWIDE in which the letter "O" is
represented by a depiction of a globe, are trademarks of
Worldwide Library.

Printed in U.S.A.

*For Diane,
because our love is no illusion.*

CHAPTER ONE

STANDING BY HER WINDOW in her office, Jillian Caldwell looked down at the commotion on Madison Avenue. A squad car had stopped at the corner of Forty-fourth Street and the two policemen had gotten out to spot-check a fruit peddler. Apparently he wasn't properly licensed and they were in the process of confiscating his goods when he went berserk and turned his table of produce out on the street, creating a considerable traffic jam.

Jillian thought that the bedlam that resulted was characteristic of the city she had come to love. It could be explosive; it could be mundane, even drab; and it could be elegant passed comparison. For her, New York was a city filled with contradictions. In a real sense, that made it a microcosm of life, for life itself was filled with paradoxes. Often things were not what they seemed to be, but to Jillian that made life exciting. She wasn't frustrated by the mysteries and the unknowns; she was challenged by them. She was challenged by New York, and she loved it.

Where else, beside Beverly Hills, could she stand on a corner waiting for a light to turn, look to her immediate right, and say hello to Robert DeNiro? Robert DeNiro, as big as life, looking as though he just walked off the screen! He gave her his famous cinematic smile and crossed the street when she did. All the while she tried hard to think of something sensible to say, but by the time she thought of something, he went left and was swallowed up in the mass of humanity that flowed up and down these sidewalks. The moment passed like a quick fantasy.

"It probably wasn't him," Betty Lincoln said. Jillian stopped at the reception desk to tell her, but the twenty-year-old black girl with dyed red hair just smirked. Jillian could never understand why Nelsen Grant ever hired such a petulant person to be his receptionist. Her smiles for the day could be counted on fingertips, and if there was one thing a public relations firm ought to be able to do, she thought, it was develop its own public relations. "There are a lot of look-alikes walkin' around the city. My boyfriend looks like Stevie Wonder. Sometimes he puts on sunglasses and puts people on."

"It was definitely Robert DeNiro," Jillian said firmly. "I think I know the difference between a look-alike and the real thing. Don't forget I peddle illusions," she added. She wasn't going to let Betty Lincoln steal away her moment. But the caustic receptionist was undaunted.

"Better than you have been fooled."

Jillian didn't reply. She didn't know why she had even bothered to tell her, except she was so excited she had to tell someone. She told Marlo Abromowitz, one of the secretaries, and Marlo had the expected reaction. Later, when Mike Shagger stopped to talk about the Rickle account, she told him, too, but with him she tried to make it sound nonchalant.

"I once sat behind Leonard Bernstein in a movie theater," he countered. He was the kind who was competitive about everything but the things that were significant, the things that really counted for something. "I didn't know who it was until the lights came on, and I didn't say much more than hello, either. So don't feel bad. It makes New York, New York," he added, and she thought yes.

Yes, it was that; and it was the mugging of the eighty-year-old woman a block down from her apartment yesterday, and the people babbling on the street about the coming of the end or the beginning of the beginning, and it was the break-dancers at Bryant Park, and the dope peddlers on Eighth Avenue. Yet she loved it—the danger, the excitement, the glamour and the turmoil.

"I'm involved in a romance," she told her mother, who was constantly waiting for such an announcement. After all, Lois, Jillian's younger sister, was married and living in Old Westbury; and Bradley, her younger brother, who had just passed his New York State Law Bar Exam, had just gotten engaged, as well. She was the only unclaimed Caldwell left.

"You are!"

"I'm having a romance with New York."

"Oh, Jillian, I thought you were serious. What happened to that nice young accountant you were seeing? Your father is always looking to bring someone fresh into the firm."

"He was interested in the wrong figures," Jillian said. She loved being clever and funny whenever she was under pressure, especially when her mother put her under pressure. It was the best defense mechanism.

"What's that supposed to mean?"

"Mother, when the right man comes along, I'll call to let you know, and if you're at school, I'll leave a message on your answering machine."

"There's no sense talking to you when you get this way," her mother said. It was the conclusion Jillian wanted her to reach. "Are you coming to Northport this weekend? Lois and Bradley have said they are, and your uncle Phil will be here."

"I'm not sure yet. Nelsen might get me a ticket to *CATS* gratis."

"A single ticket? You want to go yourself?"

"People do go to the theater alone, Mother."

"You're doing far too many things alone, Jillian," her mother said. "And in New York, that's not healthy."

"So long, Mother," she sang out, but after she hung up, she couldn't help feeling a little depressed because of the conversation. No matter how good she felt about herself and how proud of herself she was, her mother had a way of making her feel gloomy.

Jillian thought her parents' view of her was unfair, and she was tired of attributing it solely to the generation gap. True she was unmarried and living alone on the upper east side, but at twenty-six, she was also earning as much as her mother earned after twenty-eight years of teaching fourth grade. She had graduated Columbia with honors; she had gone quickly from one public relations firm to another; each time the change was accompanied by a significant salary raise and a significant addition of responsibilities. Now there was a strong possibility that Nelsen Grant would make her a vice president this year. Despite her unattached status, most parents would be proud of that, she thought.

It wasn't as though she avoided men. She had had two significant relationships since college, one with a doctor and one with a lawyer. Was it her fault that neither took the shape she thought? Her mother was more excited about her affair with Bart Fenton, the surgeon who was interning at Mount Sinai; but Jillian found his arrogance impossible to tolerate after awhile. She liked a man who had some subtlety. Maybe it was the detective in her, but she enjoyed the romance of mystery. There wasn't much mystery to Bart Fenton; he was boring because he was so unambiguous.

"He's in love with someone else," she told her mother after revealing that they were no longer seeing one another.

"Really?" she asked, the disappointment practically dripping out. "Someone at the hospital?"

"Yes," she said. "Himself."

"Oh, Jillian," her mother responded. "You're too unforgiving."

Jillian didn't reply to that. Maybe her mother was right. She was no longer sure about what she was looking for herself. What did she expect in a man? Did she want someone who would simply idolize her? Could it be that she was the one who had too big of an ego? Jillian had to admit that her mother wasn't totally off the mark. If she wanted to be truthful, she would have to admit that she was often flippant when it came to men.

But is it because of me or because of them? she wondered. A boyfriend she'd had in college told her, "You're too smart for me, Jillian. You know what I'm going to do before I do." It was the way he ended their short romance. Her attitude was that he was right—

she did know what he was going to do before he did. He was that obvious. I hate obvious men, she thought. Is that such a fault?

For a while she became defensive, believing that most men couldn't stand a woman who was more intelligent than they were. Dana Johnson, her roommate, told her she was too honest.

"You're too blunt. You say exactly what you think."

"I don't like pretending to be stupid just to feed some man's ego," she replied.

"Oh, just think of it as a game."

"This isn't a game; it's life."

"Life's a game," Dana said, and giggled.

It was for her, Jillian thought. Dana came from a very wealthy family who lay things out for her like pieces on a game board. Ironically, Dana's money took away from the seriousness of things, Jillian recalled. Yet it was Dana who married shortly after college. Of course, she couldn't say whether or not she was still married. By mutual consent they had no contact with one another now. It was that way with so many of her past acquaintances that it made Jillian wonder. Perhaps I am too demanding, she thought, and whenever she thought about it, it put an ugly, bruised cloud in her otherwise bright sunny sky.

She was feeling that way today, very anticipatory. She had no reason to feel insecure or tentative about herself. Everything was going rather well. She had just gotten off the phone with the advertising department at WOR radio, and when she added the cost of the spot commercials for the new Pooley shoe line, she saw that she had brought the media expenses in well under budget. She had done it by choosing the "at random" spots on the other three networks, reasoning that one "at random" spot on NBC was worth ten selected times on WOR. She could easily justify it by showing the audience share to the client. Nelsen would be happy about it.

As though he could read her thoughts, he buzzed her.

"How far are you along on the Pooley?"

"Just completed the media package minutes ago. Under budget."

"Fantastic. Send it in and I'll go over it with Jerry Thorton. We have a lunch meeting tomorrow. In the meantime I'm going to give you a milk run."

"Oh?" she said. Nelsen loved to use old World War II terms. A "milk run" was supposed to be an easy bombing mission, but more often than not, such an assignment from Nelsen did not mean an easy task as a reward for doing well with very difficult jobs; it meant doing something no one else was interested in doing.

"Yes. We have a prospective client coming in who has a chain of department stores located within three counties in upstate New York, apparently doing very, very well. He wants to franchise and expand into Jersey and Connecticut. He plans to build himself into another Caldor's or Penney's. You're familiar with the profile."

"Uh-huh. What are his immediate goals?"

"I haven't met him yet. Get to know him; get a handle on his objectives, and then start to layout a package. Don't throw anything important completely aside, you understand, but give him your best. Put everything up front as soon as you can, too. We'll see how serious he is. I happened to be talking to Stuart

Maletta over at Bronson's Associates and he mentioned the guy. It was his next appointment, so we know he's shopping around. His name is Ron Cutler.

"That's interesting," she said. What she really thought was interesting was Nelsen's talking to Stuart Maletta. Nelsen didn't talk to other public relations people unless he was looking to take on someone new or replace someone. She had been hearing rumblings about Nelsen being unhappy with Mike Shagger's last three assignments.

"He's an eleven-thirty, so if you want to take him to lunch..."

"Why, Nelsen, I thought you'd never suggest it."

"Just remember our budget," he said only half-jokingly as he hung up.

At exactly eleven-thirty, Betty Lincoln buzzed her.

"There's a Mr. Cutler here," she said in an uncharacteristically pleasant voice. "And Mr. Grant said you're to see him?"

"That's correct. Send him in, Betty, and please, show him exactly how to find my office," she added, remembering the advertising man from Dickinson's Hardware who got lost in the corridors and went around and around until he ended up going out a fire exit. He couldn't get back in that way so he'd had to go down two flights and take the elevator back to Nelsen Grant's.

Betty not only explained how to get to Jillian's office, she personally escorted the man. At first Jillian thought the receptionist was just being her sarcastic self, but a quick perusal of Ron Cutler and an equally quick read on Betty's reaction to him told her why she was being so extraordinarily nice.

Ron Cutler was a very handsome man. Tall and tanned, he had wavy dark brown hair, sparkling blue eyes, and a demeanor that radiated confidence and warmth. Just yesterday she was talking with Miriam Levy from Dewars about their search for a model who had such an executive look.

"We want someone who takes command right on the page," Miriam had said. How quickly she'd grab this man, Jillian thought, and made a mental note to analyze her own reaction.

As a practical public relations person, she had always ridiculed the concept of charisma. To her, charisma was something tangible and easily explainable. Simply put, it was something developed by good image-makers, given a certain amount of raw talent, of course; but to suggest that there was a mystical quality that would always come out was, in her mind, ridiculous. However, now as she looked at Ron Cutler, she wondered if she would have to revise her theories.

"Hello," he said. His smile made her feel foolish for gawking like an infatuated schoolgirl. Self-conscious about her own involuntary reaction, she blushed and stood up quickly. Betty Lincoln wore a look of satisfaction, as though she thought herself responsible for the man simply because she brought him to the office.

"Thank you, Betty," Jillian said, and the receptionist reluctantly left Ron Cutler's side. He thanked her for showing him the way and she shot a defiant glance back at Jillian. "Please come in," Jillian said. He was still standing in the doorway. "I'm Jillian Caldwell," she said, extending her hand. "One of Mr. Grant's assistants."

"Prettiest one, I expect," he said. He held her hand for an extra moment. She thought he might be inspecting it for an engagement or wedding ring.

There I go again, she thought, anticipating and imagining what they're possibly thinking. She could almost hear her mother chiding, "Why can't you let something happen spontaneously?"

"Well, since all of Nelsen's other assistants are men..." Jillian let the sentence trail off as Ron Cutler laughed.

"Smart man, this Nelsen Grant, not sending me to any of them." He winked and looked at the empty seat.

"Oh, please, sit down."

"Thank you."

She pushed the forms to the middle of her desk and sat down. Ron Cutler unbuttoned his sports jacket and crossed his legs. She could see that he was a firm, well-built man with athletic shoulders and a narrow waist. His light blue jacket and white and blue striped tie brought out the color in his eyes. At times her study of psychology, especially the powers of suggestion and color therapy, encouraged her to be an amateur sleuth. She enjoyed the discoveries.

Jillian thought she could tell a great deal about someone by the way he or she dressed, especially if that person evinced an awareness of the effects of color. A client who already understood the importance of visual suggestion had no trouble appreciating the significance of imagery in advertising.

It might be an old-fashioned idea to some, she thought, but she believed that the amount of ambition someone had was directly related to how well he or she presented himself or herself. This man looked like he had a clear concept of his identity. Without hearing another word from him, she characterized him as the well-organized, authoritative type. He liked to be in command and he liked an unambiguous picture of what had to be done and what he had to do. The fun now, Jillian thought, was to see how much of her initial impression was correct.

"From what Nelsen tells me, I understand you have a chain of department stores in upstate New York. Where exactly are they located?"

"We're not that far upstate, only a hundred or so miles northwest of the city. I have two in Sullivan County, three in Orange County, and one in Ulster County."

"What are these like...Penney's, Two Guys..."

"On that model, yes; but I like to think we have a lot more personality."

"That's good," she said. "We're going to have to explore ways to present your unique qualities. There are dozens of department-store chains. The question to answer is why should customers go to yours, aside from sales on different items, of course."

"Yes," he said. "That's cutting right to the heart of the problem. You see, mine is a family business in the true sense. My father started small; he never had great ambitions, if you follow my drift. I mean, he built a small business into a rather big one for where we are located, but he would have been satisfied with half of what we are."

"Well, it's only right," she said, "that the younger generation move onward and upward." Oh, God, she thought, I sound so damn ingratiating. Get hold of yourself, Jillian Caldwell.

He smiled, but she thought he was just being polite. Try hard, she thought, going back to her credo for success, but make it seem as though you're not trying at all. Never let anyone take you for granted.

"You don't know how difficult a time I'm having with my father convincing him of that."

"Our job is going to be to convince a great many more people of that," she said. He nodded. "Of course, my first job is to show you why we can do all this for you better than anyone else in the field."

"Uh-huh."

"I'm sure that you already know that we handle accounts for a number of department stores."

"Yes. I saw the list of your clients. Impressive."

"Thank you. Now in order for me to get down to specifics, I'm going to have to know a great deal more about your operation. What I'd like you to do is tell me as exactly as you can what your short-term and long-term objectives are," she said, hating herself for sounding so official. "In other words, what do you expect from a publicity campaign?"

"I understand," he said. There was a smile in his eyes. Did he find her seriousness amusing?

"Then, what I'll do is work up a program for you to consider, including the costs." She looked at her watch. "Do you have enough time to carry this on into lunch?" she asked. His eyes widened with interest. "I only ask so I can judge how much we can get down during this first session."

"Lunch, huh? Yes, I believe so." His smile widened, originating from his eyes and moving through his face to the lines of his mouth. He looked satisfied, like someone who had achieved something significant. It made her step back a moment and the first note of something mysterious was sounded. Perhaps this man wasn't as easy to read as she had first thought.

And then she had the weirdest sensation, feeling as though she were suddenly on a stage and this was all part of a performance. They were actors in a scenario written a long time ago.

"That's good," she said. "I hate having to rush important things." She sat back. She didn't know why, but her usual confidence was slipping away. She could actually feel herself slide into insecurity. It was as if this were her first interview with a prospective client. "Why don't you begin by telling me what your stores are like and why you think they're different."

He thought that was a good idea and began, but she found herself fighting to concentrate on what he was saying rather than how he was saying it. His smile, his eyes, the way he turned his head and gestured, even the way he sat back in the chair...everything about him conspired against her use of her intellectual powers.

It was eerie, almost as though he had a spiritual charm, not in the religious sense, but in the supernatural. She was mesmerized...hypnotized by the tone of his voice and the power of his demeanor. She was bewitched in the true sense of the word, charmed beyond reason, possessed by his good looks and personality. She was succumbing to the very thing for which she criticized so many other women: infatuation with the man as a man rather than as a business associate or client.

"Are you hungry?" she asked him when a pause developed.

"If you're ready to go to lunch, that's fine."

"I have a ravenous appetite today," she said, and then smiled. "Actually, I have a ravenous appetite almost every day."

"You don't look like a big eater."

"Looks deceive," she said, and for some reason, he blanched. She hadn't meant it as a reprimand. Did he take it as such?

She was afraid to stand up, afraid that she might tremble when she walked.

"There's this great Korean restaurant on Vanderbilt. Do you like Korean food?"

"Well, I don't mean to sound like a greenhorn, but the truth is I've never had any. But I'm willing to experiment," he added quickly. She laughed defensively and thought it was debatable who was really the greenhorn here.

She was comfortable standing beside him. At five feet ten, with long legs and a slim figure, she had the feeling she gave the impression she was towering above many of her escorts, whether they were the same height or an inch or two taller. High heels were deadly. She stuck to flats most of the time. But now that she was standing close to Ron Cutler, she realized he was even broader and taller than she had first thought. He even made her feel diminutive. It made her want so much to be graceful.

She slipped her pocketbook strap over her shoulder as he stepped back to let her pass through the door. She was glad that she had decided to wear something special this morning, something bright and expensive. She had put on her cotton-challis floral skirt, and a heavy-silk mauve-gray blouse with pleated sleeves. This year's early July weather had been running ten degrees above normal. Even the mornings were unusual. There was no need to wear a jacket to work.

Today there was even something special about her hair. The day before yesterday she had gone to Dawn's Salon and had her reddish-brown hair cut into a bob with a side part. The bangs were feathered. She had to agree with Daniel, her stylist. The cut did bring out the hazel-brown in her eyes and did make her face look brighter and younger.

Actually she had been hoping to go out to Northport for the weekend so she could show off her new look. Too often lately her mother had scolded her for her tired and drawn appearance. She told her she looked too serious most of the time, and she predicted it would prematurely age her.

Jillian didn't say anything to Ron Cutler until they got out to the elevator. Betty Lincoln glared with jealous eyes as they walked past the front desk.

"Tell me about that black book you said every salesperson in your stores keeps," she said after the doors opened. It was one of those rare times when the elevator was right there on the fifth floor and there was no one else in it.

"Whenever anyone in any department makes a sale, he or she writes down the name and address of the customer. From that day forward, whenever there are any specials or unusual sales within his or her department, the salesperson contacts everyone in his or her book. Often they make personal phone calls. We've had wonderful results with it. People feel they are being treated special and the sales reflect it."

"That's a great idea. When you think about it," she said, getting a little excited, "what is it we don't like about large department stores—certainly the impersonality. Most people today don't know what it's like shopping in a small town store where the owner knows you and won't push the wrong merchandise at you because some floor manager says he has to get rid of an item."

"Exactly. Cutler's is the big town store with the small town attitude."

"Is that your slogan?"

"No. Why? Should it be?"

"I wish I had thought of it before you did," she said, smiling. "Then I could have impressed you quickly."

"But in a way you did," he said, "by asking me the questions. You get co-authorship status," he added. He gestured for her to step out.

"Oh." People waiting for the elevator were staring in at them. "I get terribly absentminded when I'm thinking about something."

"You remember where you want to go for lunch, don't you?"

"Yes." She laughed nervously. "It's only a few blocks." *Why am I so nervous?* she asked herself.

As soon as they stepped onto the sidewalk, he took her arm. She couldn't recall any of her other male clients ever doing that, even the ones she had grown to know fairly well. There was always that wall between them, that professional business relationship. It permitted courtesies, but rarely familiarity.

"Just give me the directions," he said. "I know what it's like walking through the lunch-hour crowd here."

"Up two and over one," she said. Her first impression of him was right, she thought; he was a man who wanted to be in control. People did seem to step out of his way and there wasn't any of that usual people-walking-into-people activity because many pedestrians didn't stay to the right. No one walked into him, and because he was hanging onto her tightly, no one walked into her, either. She liked that; she liked being protected. The funny thing was she felt guilty about the feeling. It was as if she was violating some principle of woman's independence because she had this pleasure.

"You can't be timid in New York," he said when he stared down a taxi driver who wanted to turn before they crossed.

"Are you in the city often?"

"Often enough to know how to deal with it." He paused after they crossed. "There are some places up my way where you could take an afternoon nap in the middle of main street."

"You live there all your life?"

"From first breath on," he said.

"It's right over there," she said, pointing. "I hope you like it," she added, and she couldn't believe how worried about it she sounded. Was it because she thought of him as a potential client or a potential lover?

They were seated at a table in the far right corner. From the moment they sat down she was conscious of her mixture of personal and business questions. It was part of the "sell" to be that convincing, and she had been doing it so well these past few years that it was hard to break the pattern. She never let the conversation move too far from the point. After all, Nelsen Grant was paying for all of this.

Ron Cutler wore a half smile on his face throughout the preliminary conversation, and she wondered if he understood what she was doing and was amused by the way she shaped the conversation. She couldn't get away from the impression that they were both auditioning for parts in a play. She felt as though the rest of the restaurant were the audience. Indeed, it might have been only her imagination, but when she looked about, people did appear to be watching them.

"The main point is who will be your market," she said in the way of a summary. "The description we create for your stores will dictate our approach."

They paused as the waiter completed the cooking of the chicken dish on the small gas stove before them and served it. He waited for their approval of the taste and then left.

"Fantastic place," Ron said.

"It's always good here. You understand what I'm driving at, don't you?"

"Pardon?"

"The image of the store." Was she pushing too hard?

"Oh. Yes, yes, of course." He looked up at her and then sat back. "Well," he said, "why don't we try an illustration? Take me, for example."

"You?"

"You're trying to sell me on your company's ability to do a good job for Cutler's, right?"

"Yes."

"You've listened to me give you a general description of what I'm all about and what I'm looking to do; what did you pick out to determine your technique and direction?"

She winced at his characterization of everything she had done as a planned, structured presentation. She thought she had been warmer and more sincere than usual. Certainly she had told him more about herself personally than she usually did over three or four meetings with other clients.

"That's unfair," she said.

"Why? I've been exposing myself for the cause. What's wrong with Nelsen Grant Associates doing it?"

She sat back. He was serious.

"I'm not sure I understand what you want me to do."

"You're an expert at sizing up clients. Size me up. How do I come off to you?" He leaned forward, smiling. "Don't tell me you haven't been doing that."

His smile was warm, but as she looked into his eyes she had the strangest feeling he wasn't being sincere about this. He was asking for one thing, but looking for another. What?

"We've been together only an hour and a half or so," she said softly.

"I realize that, but you're a trained observer, a student of the image-makers."

"Oh boy."

"Be honest now," he said, sitting back. "Come on."

"You know why this isn't fair, don't you? You're not only asking me to reveal my own professional secret tactics, you're asking me to reveal my feminine perceptions, too."

"Now won't this make today's lunch memorable for both of us," he said. She laughed and shook her head. He was making her feel like a schoolgirl and she wasn't sure whether she liked it or not.

"All right," she said, "but if I insult you and you turn down the services of Nelsen Grant Associates because of that, you can't tell my boss."

"I'm not even interested in meeting him. Go on."

"Well...you're obviously a college graduate," she began.

"Harvard Business."

"About twenty-eight, twenty-nine years old."

"Thirty. Not bad."

"I don't think you're married or you've been married."

"Correct again, but how did you reach that conclusion?"

"Pure feminine instinct. Of course, you're not wearing a wedding ring, but that doesn't have to mean anything in today's society."

"Do you often rely on your instincts?"

"Not as much as I should," she said, and he laughed.

"Go on. I'm impressed already."

"Well, you're obviously physically active. Your build indicates that, but to me that also indicates a certain energy, a certain need to be a hands-on person. You don't strike me as the type who would be satisfied sitting back in his office, nine to five. You're probably out in the field a great deal, inspecting, overseeing. It wouldn't surprise me to see you with your jacket off and your sleeves rolled up."

"Anything else?"

She felt she was on a roll, so she went on. She thought he was enjoying it, but she also thought he was teasing her, or maybe—and she really didn't know why she should think of this—testing himself.

"You're ambitious, and that makes you willing to take certain gambles. I'd say you came from a rather structured childhood. You might even be an only child."

"Why do you say that?" he asked quickly.

"Well, for one thing you didn't mention any brothers or sisters in the business, and for another..."

"Yes?"

"Just instinct again," she said. She really wanted to say that she sensed an independence about him, an independence that left him somewhat alone. However, it was too abstract, too much of her own personal theory to mention it. "You have a clear value system," she went on, eager to change the topic, "but you're a little bit intolerant of conservative attitudes. I'd say you're a firm boss, but well liked. There's a calmness about you that comes from self-confidence."

She waited for his reaction when she stopped, but for a long moment he just leaned over the table and stared at her. It was eerie, but for a part of that moment she felt as though they were both talking about someone else. She half expected him to add to the description.

"Well, that's a pretty damn good analysis," he said finally, and sat back. "Even if it isn't true, I'm going to work on it to make it true."

"Which part wasn't true?"

"None. You didn't miss on anything," he said. She thought he looked very satisfied, but not satisfied with her so much as he was satisfied with himself. Once again she had the feeling that he was testing himself, not her. What did that mean?

Before lunch was completed, she began talking about ways to expand his present advertising and ways to reach potential investors. She kept the conversation strictly business. Back at the office she talked about the costs of a publicity package, pinning him down to a potential range.

"One of the first things I would want to do," she said, "is visit one of your stores." He nodded, but he didn't pick up on it. She had hoped he would offer some kind of an invitation. It was a good way to get him closer to a commitment. "Do you have any idea when you would be making a decision as to which firm would represent you?" she asked, a little more forcefully than she had intended, but she was aware that she had spent well over two hours with him.

"No." He didn't add to that for the moment and there was a long, embarrassing pause.

"Oh."

"To tell you the truth, I haven't been totally honest with you," he said. She smiled even though she didn't know what to expect. "I still have some selling to do myself. Selling my father," he said. "You understand I couldn't do it without getting all this information?" he added in an apologetic tone.

"I understand."

"He still holds the majority interest and he's become even more conservative in his old age."

"How old is he?"

"You couldn't tell from watching him at work, but he's seventy-five."

"No interest in retirement?"

"He believes in only one retirement plan—death."

"So that's where you get your energy?"

"I suppose so," he said, a dreamy, far-off look in his eyes for the moment. "Well," he said, standing. "I want to thank you for your time. If it's of any value to you at this point, this has been the best of all the presentations I've had."

"Thank you."

"I'll put that in writing and have it sent to Mr. Grant and you can fill him in on my temporary delay."

"Yes, I will." She wanted to extend her hand but he started for the door. She felt a great sense of disappointment thinking, I probably will never see him again.

"Thanks again," he said, and left.

She didn't sit down for a good few seconds afterward. When she did, she just sat there staring at the empty doorway. Almost as if she conjured him, he reappeared. The look on her face must have been comical because he smiled widely.

"Look," he said, "I don't know if this is off base or anything, but I'm going to be in town next weekend and I was wondering if it would be all right for me to call you. For purely social reasons," he added quickly.

"Yes," she said impulsively, but before she could add another word, he was gone again. Even so, she had such a clear image of him standing in the doorway, it was as if he had left a ghost of himself behind.

He was so attractive in every possible way, a made-to-order dream lover, but she felt this anxiety. Why?

Maybe because he is too perfect, she thought. She had learned to trust contradiction; she had learned to accept imperfection as a natural part of life. Look at the city. Look at its beauty and its filth, its richness and its poverty.

"Jillian Caldwell," she heard her mother say, "no matter what man walked through that doorway, you're going to find something wrong with him, and if there's nothing wrong with him, that's what will be wrong with him. The truth is there's something wrong with you."

She shook her head and laughed at herself. And then she put her anxiety aside and let herself look forward to next weekend and his call.

Later she would both reprimand and congratulate herself for doing so; but that was all just another contradiction out of which was to come the most astounding discoveries of her life.

CHAPTER TWO

RON CUTLER DID NOT wait until the weekend. His call came on Wednesday. It took her by surprise because she was in deep thought. She had just come from a lunch meeting with Jerry Thorton, a vice president at Pooley Shoes, and he had agreed with her concept of Pooley sponsoring the Bentons for the cross-country Walkathon for Cancer.

The Bentons were a married couple who were famous because they had both contracted and apparently beaten a similar form of bone cancer. It was believed that chemical wastes dumped in a nearby landfill had contaminated their land and ground water and so infected them. To dramatize the significance of the problem and the need for more public and government awareness, they had announced their intention to walk across the United States, following a route designed for them by environmentalists. The route crossed other potentially dangerous dumping sites.

The first thing Jillian thought after she had read the story was what an opportunity for Pooley and what a boon to the Bentons and the environmentalists because Pooley would underwrite all their expenses. All they had to do was reveal they were wearing Pooley shoes. She queried the Bentons and found them more than agreeable.

"Of course, if they develop blisters after the first ten miles, I'll kiss my job goodbye," Jerry Thorton kidded.

"Just provide them with the best you have."

"I'll do more than that. I'll have a podiatrist at their side the whole way. Jillian, this is a good piece of work. You're on the ball. It's one of those ideas from which everyone reaps rewards. It's good for the image; and it's good for the profits, and it's good for the battle against cancer."

"Thank you," she said. She was beaming all the way back to her office, so it was understandable that her mind was on nothing else. But she hadn't forgotten about Ron Cutler; he'd been on her mind throughout the past weekend.

She had relented and gone out to Northport, actually turning down Nelsen's offer to get her a free ticket to *CATS*. She didn't think she could face the guilt her mother would lay on her if she missed the family outing. It was the first time they had all gotten together since Bradly's engagement. She thought she would dread the way her single status would stand out, but as it turned out, she had a good time. It was mainly because of Uncle Phil.

Uncle Phil, her mother's younger brother, was one of those exciting and dramatic relatives every family had. He was surrounded by secrets and wore mystery like another set of clothes. His real means of making a living was supposedly hush-hush. Ever since she was a teenager, Jillian remembered her father's disapproval and her mother's anguish whenever Uncle Phil's name was brought up.

He owned and operated a car wash in Paramus, New Jersey, but her father said that was only a front.

Illusion

As far as she could make out, Jillian understood that somehow, Uncle Phil, an Episcopalian with a solid English ancestry, had gotten himself in with the mob and was involved in bookmaking, numbers, and even some loan-sharking for a sizable section of Jersey. Jillian believed that whatever success her Uncle Phil had in whatever he did was primarily a result of his personality.

Physically, he looked like any one of a half dozen currently popular movie stars. He had the same slim, but firm physique and an impish grin and twinkle in his eyes. She could never remember him unhappy or depressed. As far as she could see, he refused to take life seriously. His happy-go-lucky attitude was annoying to a man like her father, who was so serious and intense about everything. But what made it even worse, from her father's point of view, was that Uncle Phil was obviously very successful at what he did.

He wore the best clothes, drove expensive cars and wore expensive jewelry, especially whenever he visited them. He was often going or coming from some exotic vacation, and he had apartments in Florida and on the west coast.

Her father could only rely on a disguised wish. "One of these days your smart-ass brother's bubble's going to burst, Alice. Remember I told you. Remember I said it." Who could forget it? He never lost an opportunity to say it.

What Jillian especially liked about her uncle Phil was he was very good at breaking up the heaviness that often developed when families got together. When he sensed the conversation was getting too critical, usually at someone else's expense, he would turn everything into a joke. In fact, now that she thought about it, she understood why her mother often accused her of taking after him. She meant it as a criticism, but Jillian took it as a compliment.

Jillian anticipated that her career and life-style would become a subject for discussion before the weekend was over. It happened after dinner on Saturday. Friday night and most of Saturday had been devoted to settling in and getting to know one another better.

Lois's husband, Douglas, was a dentist. Jillian found him dull, even surprisingly withdrawn. She laughed when Uncle Phil compared talking to him to extracting a tooth. She saw the resemblance. Douglas answered her questions with single, undeveloped responses. The conversation between them was all her work.

She liked Bradly's fiancée because she was so much unlike him. Bradly was more a clone of their father—serious, even somewhat stuffy at times. His future bride however, Lisa Ethers, was flighty, almost disconnected. She couldn't stick to any topic of conversation long and wanted to bring any discussion back to one of three topics: clothes, soap operas or cosmetics. Jillian thought she was pneumatic and imagined that her head had been filled with different sorts of gases; she was a sort of Stepford Wife in the making. Bradly could pull her plug at any time and she would fizzle out and be folded up neatly into his pocket.

All of this caused Jillian to ponder her own state. She had a theory. My parents just don't understand, she thought. Life has become more complicated; therefore, living together has become more complicated. Her mother liked to talk about compromises, but Jillian didn't believe in marriage as a capitulation, a surrender of one's individuality. As far as she could tell, too many people, especially women, kept the best part of themselves subdued.

"I want a man who will bring out the best in me and let me bring out the best in him," Jillian had told her, but her mother simply shook her head. She believed Jillian was too intense about it.

"You can't fall in love with a man if you're constantly measuring assets and liabilities," her mother told her. Jillian thought that was ironic, especially as her mother was the wife of an accountant.

It was too difficult, maybe even embarrassing, to bring up these ideas in front of the others. She didn't want to create any bad feeling between herself and them. Her sister and her brother had a right to make their own decisions and decide their own lives; she wanted only to have the same right, and if that meant she would risk becoming an old maid, well, then so be it. She could voice none of this; she could only think it. Fortunately, Uncle Phil was there.

They had all settled in with coffee after Saturday night's dinner when her life-style became the subject. Her father wanted to know if she was in an area of such opportunity, with so many "big deals," why wasn't she meeting and dating some wealthy man?

"How do you know she's not?" Uncle Phil said. "What do you think, Teddy, she tells you everything? Those days are long gone."

"That's right, Dad. Besides, every date doesn't turn into a marriage," she added.

"From what I see of the modern world, the sooner you tie the knot, the better off you are," her father said. "A single woman in today's society... singles bars, computer dating. It produces aggressive women. Have you seen that commercial on television? The one where this girl calls the boy to invite herself over to his place with a bottle of wine?"

"How do you know I didn't help make that commercial, Daddy?" she teased. Uncle Phil laughed.

"You sound jealous, Teddy," Uncle Phil said.

"Phil," her mother cautioned, "you're not helping the situation any."

"What situation? There's a situation?" He looked to Jillian and she shrugged and then laughed. It was better to do that than cry or become angry.

"All I know," Lois said, threading her arm in and under Douglas's symbolically, "is I couldn't do what Jillian's doing. It takes guts."

"It's not as bad as you think," Jillian said. "I like having my own apartment in New York."

"But by yourself!" Her father's voice was a little louder now.

"If a man can live by himself, why can't a woman?"

"Because New York's a jungle," her father said. "Don't tell me about New York."

"So she'll meet Tarzan," Uncle Phil said. "What could be so bad?"

"It's easy for you to joke about it, Phil," her mother said. "It's not your daughter who's living alone and working in the city."

"I love her as though she were my daughter," he said, and Jillian and he hugged.

"Forget it," her mother said. "As long as you two are together, it's hopeless."

Bradly took that as a cue to change the topic. Jillian was grateful for the intermission. Round one was over. Of course, she knew that round two would be harder the next morning after Uncle Phil left. Before he did, she had an opportunity to have a private talk with him. They took a walk when the others went into the den to watch a movie on HBO.

Her parents had a beautiful home with access to the beach. Even as a little girl, she loved to sit by herself on the sand and become mesmerized by the refrain of the waves. The ocean had a magnetism that was medicinal. It washed her thoughts; it refreshed her mind. All the poetry in the world had its origins in the sea, she thought.

"They're getting rougher and rougher on you, huh?" Uncle Phil said. He had taken her hand just the way he did when she was much younger.

"I suppose it's understandable. They worry."

"What about you? You worry? You ain't met the man of your dreams yet, right?"

"Every time I think I have, something happens to change my mind. How come you never got married, Uncle Phil? Mother never mentions it. It's as if it's a foregone conclusion that you never will."

"Never stood still long enough."

"But you have a steady girl, don't you? You still see Joyce."

"Yeah, I see her from time to time."

"You think if you tied the knot, you'd be in some kind of trap."

"I don't know. I'd be responsible for someone else besides myself and I have enough trouble being responsible for myself."

"Is that a major reason why a man wouldn't get married?"

"It is for me. Why?" he asked, stopping and turning to her. "You trying to move someone into position and he won't budge?"

"No." She laughed and swung her arm so they would continue walking.

"Yeah, but—"

"But nothing. Oh, I had a new client come in this week," she said. "He's an interesting man."

"How do you mean, interesting?"

"Interesting," she repeated as though it would explain itself in repetition. "Anyway, his family owns a chain of department stores in upstate New York, less than fifty miles from Paramus. I thought you might have heard of the chain."

"What's it called?"

"Cutler's."

"Cutler's. Oh, yeah, I heard of that. Sure. Nothing like a Bamberger's or a Bloomingdale's. More like a Jamesway or Caldor's."

"You don't know anything about the family, do you?"

"No. Not my territory. Why?"

"Natural curiosity."

"Sounds like more than that."

"Well, we might see each other socially," she said. "Don't mention anything to my mother," she added quickly, "or she'll call the Huntington House and make preliminary arrangements for a wedding ceremony." He laughed.

"Jillian, anytime things become impossible for you, just come to me. Remember that."

"I will. Thanks, Uncle Phil."

He hugged her and they walked on in silence. From time to time she snuck a glance at him. Uncle Phil was a handsome man. There was too much softness in his face for him to be involved in anything really bad, she thought. Even so, he was a mystery. And she was glad he was. It was good for a man to have some mystery about him. That was probably why she was so attracted to Ron Cutler, she thought.

She thought a great deal about Ron Cutler that night and throughout the next day as she drove back into the city. In fact, he never really left her mind, so that even though the work had been exciting, it only took her moments to react when he phoned on Wednesday.

"I know I said I'd call on the weekend," he said, "but I figured I'd better not take the chance of being shut out."

"Well, I—I did keep my plans open," she confessed. She wanted to be encouraging and she didn't see any point in being coy.

"Good. Have you seen *CATS* yet?" he asked, and she laughed.

"No, but it was close."

"I've got seats in the second row."

"Fantastic."

He suggested dinner; she suggested he come to her apartment first for cocktails. Afterward, she laughed about that, recalling her father's outrage about the woman in the wine commercial. If only he knew...she thought.

When Nelsen Grant learned about her plans to bring the Bentons into a publicity concept that would help the Pooley account and the good reaction at Pooley to the idea, he called her in and offered her the vice presidency.

"It's not the result of this one thing," he said. "You've earned it with a series of successes. It's going to mean more of your time, Jillian. I'm not going to sugarcoat it. It's almost a total commitment, but since you're not married or presently engaged..."

"Don't give my mother any more reason to pressure me," she said. She was too happy to consider the implications of what he was saying, and anyway, she always found that other people exaggerated responsibility and effort. What was monumental to them was routine to her. She had no fears about developing a relationship at the same time she was developing a career. All she wanted to think about were ways to celebrate. Good things were happening; there wasn't a dark cloud in the sky.

"I HAVE TWO THINGS to celebrate," Jillian announced after she made her way to the back of Wine-O's, her favorite after-work spot, to meet Betty Dancer. Betty was the only one of her good New York friends who was able to meet her today. The others were too tired, had errands, or had to work late.

Presently an associate producer of "Day for Night," a daytime soap opera produced in New York, Betty had been producing commercials for Rawley and Wade. It was through her contact with them that Jillian and she had met. Right from the start they became good friends.

Betty was bright and intelligent, but she had a dry wit that could make her abrasive. Her often coldly surgical comments cut right through to the truth of things, even if that involved tearing someone's well manicured facade. Jillian imagined that Betty was not very popular in high school or in college, but her refusal to see things through rose-colored glasses gave her a certain edge in the business and professional world. She was truly executive material.

Jillian couldn't reconcile Betty's personality with the nature of the job she now held.

"After getting to know you, it's hard to believe you're working for a soap," she told her. Betty shrugged.

"It's just another job, honey. We're simply selling another product. In this case the product happens to be vicarious excitement and romance, that's all. We sell illusions. When you boil it all down, just about everything that is being sold either is, or is based on, illusion. You, of all people, should know that."

"Yes, but I bet you don't respect your product. At least I have a certain love for illusion."

"Oh, when you scratch this broad, deep down you'll find a throbbing, pulsating, damp, hungry romanticist," Betty said, and Jillian laughed. But when she thought more deeply about it, she realized Betty was probably telling the truth about that. All of them, no matter how well some hid it, had the same basic needs.

Betty was married, but her husband Roger rarely came into their conversations. He was a very successful corporate attorney; "criminally successful," Betty would say. They had met when he represented a firm that was suing Rawley and Wade. Jillian thought it was characteristic of Betty that she would meet, become romantically involved with, and marry a man suing the company for which she worked.

"At times we were like Furillo and Joyce Davenport on 'Hill Street Blues,'" she said the one time they talked about it.

Betty was good-looking, five feet seven with light brown hair and blue eyes. She had one of those figures that never seemed to need exercise or dieting to keep it shapely. Her metabolism enabled her to consume calories with a mindless abandon and not pay the consequences. She was two years older than Jillian, but at times Jillian thought there were ages and ages of hard experiences between them. Betty often had that tired look of familiarity characteristic of women nearly twice her and Jillian's age.

But what Jillian admired the most about her was the apparent success she was having managing a career and a marriage at the same time. And it wasn't only because she and Roger had no children yet. Whenever Jillian asked her about it, Betty would return to one concept.

"There's no secret about it," she would say. "I know some working women seem to have days filled with marital crisis after marital crisis. What makes us special, if you want to call it that, is that Roger hasn't set out to change me from what I was when we first met and I haven't set out to change him. In other words, we don't see marriage as a license to kill.

"Doesn't that just kill you when you think about it," she went on. "Two people get married, supposedly take on a lifetime commitment to one another, because of what they see in each other when they first meet; and then they spend most of the time trying to remake each other."

"But compromise," Jillian said, remembering her mother's viewpoint, "there has to be some compromise for it to work out, doesn't there?"

"There is, but on our own terms. It's not you do it my way now and someday I'll do it yours. Somehow, neither of us loses their integrity when sacrifices are made," Betty said after a moment's thought. "And I suppose, honey, that that is more precious to a relationship than all the so-called romantic love our viewers crave week after week after week." She laughed.

"Why is that funny?"

"I was just thinking about a conversation Roger and I had about this subject recently. You know, he actually respects what I do. He thinks soap operas have a place in our society."

"He does?"

"He calls them emotional management. Soap operas do for women what Clint Eastwood movies do for men—they provide the needed outlet and keep people sane. In Roger's view they even save marriages."

"Roger said that?"

"Uh-huh. So you see, we need our illusions in order to deal with our realities."

Yes, Jillian thought. That's it exactly. Betty and she both made their living off illusions, yet both liked truth and honesty. The balance was all that was important.

"Congratulations," Betty said, raising her glass of rosé. "As you can see, I started celebrating your good luck before you arrived. It's most chic. You look like you're about to explode."

"It's the way I feel. Thanks for meeting me. You're the only one who had the time or the energy apparently."

"That's because once in awhile I simply say, fuck it," Betty said, leaning toward her. Jillian laughed and then gave the waiter her wine order. "It's about time Grant recognized your true value over there."

"Oh, I haven't been there that long."

"Still, you competed with a man and you were promoted by a man."

"You sound like a feminist and I know what you really think of them. I don't think I'm ever going to be able to forget what you did to poor Clara Kaplow last Tuesday at the Hyatt. It was supposed to be a friendly little lunch. She'll never join us again."

"Well, I'm tired of hearing all this equal urinal crap. She had a real problem. I'm willing to bet a week's salary that she won't get laid unless she can be on top," Betty added just as the waiter brought Jillian her wine. His eyes widened and Jillian laughed.

"Maybe you're right."

"Of course I'm right. Have you ever known me to be wrong when it comes to other women? Now," she said, settling back, "I thought you said you had two things to celebrate. What's the other?"

"I met this new client last Thursday..."

"Don't tell me," Betty said, holding up her hand. "I heard the line on the show today. He's everything any woman would ever want," she said, raising her voice in pitch to satirize one of the soap stars.

"That's it. You stole the words from me." Jillian's smile faded. "I had a feeling you would think me silly."

"Absolutely not. I'm just teasing. I'm glad you feel that way about him," Betty added, with an uncharacteristic expression of warmth. "You don't deserve any less."

"What? No ridicule, no challenge?"

"How many times have you gone out with him since last Thursday?"

"None. That's just it. He told me he would call this coming weekend, but he couldn't wait and called today."

"I see. This does sound like potential material. Describe him and spare me no elaborate adjectives. I'm immune to anything else anyway," she said, leaning forward.

Jillian began her description, relating it almost as if she had memorized it as part of some dramatic script. Betty never broke her stoical expression.

"You want some advice?" she asked after Jillian finished.

"To tell you the truth, that's why I was glad you agreed to meet me. You know how I respect your coolhanded approach when it comes to men."

"When it comes to men, honey, I happen to have very hot hands. Just ask Roger. All right, I'll tell you what I would do now. I'd step back, take a deep breath, and when I met him this time, I'd open my most critical eyes. I know that sounds cynical, but you can't let yourself get swept off your feet just because some man is handsome, charming, personable, intelligent, debonair, gorgeous, exciting..."

"You told me not to spare the adjectives."

"Those weren't adjectives; those were prayers of worship. Listen, Jill, I see beautiful men every day over at the studio. Most of them are air heads, you know what I mean? If you have found a good-looking guy with brains, you're ahead of the game."

"Twenty years ago they would make that comment about women."

"So nothing's changed. Now, can you talk about nothing else but Mr. Perfect, or can you fill me in a little on your new responsibilities?"

"I'll try," Jillian said, and she did. But later on that night, and every opportunity she had on Thursday and Friday, she thought about Ron Cutler and about Betty's advice.

It was hard for her to open critical eyes. She found that a strange thing had taken place in her mind since she had seen him—the memory of his physical characteristics weakened until it was hard to recall specific images. It was as if he was made of some transient substance that faded with the passage of time. At times she substituted the faces of movie actors and other handsome men she had known or seen in her life, superimposing them over the recollection of Ron Cutler. He became more and more of a phantom, an actual "dream" lover.

In fact, on Thursday night she had a strange dream. In it Ron Cutler came back to her apartment after the show and they made love, but when she went to kiss him, his face began to slide off. There were other faces beneath it, but each one of them did the same thing. Some were the faces of old boyfriends, and some were just faces she had seen on advertisements and in television commercials. After awhile there was no face at all and she awakened feeling a little terrified.

I'm too uptight about it all, she thought. He's just another man...another man. She used that as a refrain to put herself back to sleep.

But all day Friday she had the jitters. She felt like an actress about to set foot on the stage in front of an opening night audience. It put her in a paradoxical state of mind because she wanted to be herself, to be natural; and yet, she wanted very much to impress this man.

Three times she changed the menu for the hors d'oeuvres to have with cocktails. When was such a thing like that ever so important to her before? Then she was worried she didn't have the right whiskey. When she saw she had everything but bourbon, she went out and bought a bottle.

The decision as to what to wear brought the most pressure. She didn't want to overdress and yet she felt it was important to show him that she believed the night to be something special. She settled on her new knit boat-necked sweater with the decorative stitching that ran down from the lightly padded shoulders. It was cream-colored, which she thought brought out the best in her complexion. She wore it with a red pleated skirt.

The outfit was completed when she decided she would wear a cream jacket over the sweater, and her matching red wide-brimmed hat with a white taffeta bow. She was going to wear the gold chain that Uncle Phil had bought her for her birthday last year, but she decided instead to wear a simple string of Majorca pearls because it gave her neck more of a bare and open look.

When Ron finally called up to her from the foyer of the apartment building, she nearly jumped out of her seat. She pressed the button to open the door below and waited with a thumping heart. Twice she checked herself in the mirror, each time thinking, What is wrong with me? What has come over me? I'm acting like a schoolgirl. She recognized what was happening, but she couldn't prevent it. She was under a spell, partially self-cast.

The door buzzer rang and she opened the door to greet him. The moment she saw him again, all the strange dreams and all of the nervousness faded. His smile warmed her heart. It was as though she had known him all her life. In a real sense she had, for to her he represented the man who had lived in her imagination for as long as she could remember.

"You're right on time," she said. In the back of her mind she heard Betty Dancer advising her to use her critical eyes, but she was intolerant of even the slightest cynicism now that he was standing here before her.

"Always been a fault of mine to be on time." He stepped into her apartment.

"It's not really a fault, is it?"

"You'd be surprised. You probably know how most people don't mean five-thirty when they say five-thirty. They mean around five-thirty." She laughed, thinking about one of her friends, Trish Hamilton, who was always saying "five-ish" or "seven-ish" to cover her own incapability of being on time anymore.

"You're right."

"You look very nice. In fact, you look quite beautiful. You sure you shouldn't be in modeling rather than in public relations?"

"I know my limits, thank you. Too many people make fools of themselves because they don't," she added. It seemed to strike a sensitive note because he nodded thoughtfully and looked around, obviously eager to change the topic.

"Nice apartment."

"It's adequate for a single woman in New York. You probably know what rents are like here."

"Yes. I was thinking of buying an apartment since I get into the city so often now. I'm finding out."

There was a long pause during which they just stared at one another. Once again she had the eerie feeling he was looking for something in her eyes, some recognition. He was almost like a man looking into a mirror. There was something about the way he turned his head and made his eyes smaller.

God, she thought, my imagination is running wild.

"What will you have to drink? I have...everything, I think."

"Bourbon and soda?" he said and she took a deep breath.

"I have it!" she replied in triumph. It made him laugh and lightened the moment. She was grateful for that.

"Well, that's great."

"Sit down," she said, indicating the love seat. "I have Wheat Thins and Brie on the table, and there's a new cheese and bacon dip I'm trying."

"Experimenting on me, huh?" She blushed. "That's all right. It's something we all do."

He came farther into the apartment and looked about, studying some of her family photographs and her paintings. He looked like a detective trying to determine her real personality on the basis of her taste in art and bric-a-brac. She wondered what part of herself was revealed in her choices. Was she obvious or subtle?

She wondered why none of the other men she had brought to her apartment had ever made her conscious of these things? What was it about the way Ron looked at her and her possessions that made her feel so exposed?

He had that piercing, intense look, which gave her that eerie sensation again. It wasn't unpleasant or frightening, but it made her feel that he had that supernatural air, some mystical quality that emerged from behind the face he presented to the public. She was intrigued by it, drawn to it in the same way she was the first time she had seen him standing in her office doorway.

"I like that picture of the beach and the ocean."

"I bought it because it reminds me of a poem I loved—'Dover Beach' by Matthew Arnold."

"I think I remember reading that in high school. A sad poem, wasn't it?"

"Yes. You remember that?"

"Some things stay with you. I suppose they appeal to an essential part of who or what you are," he added. She detected a note of bitterness.

"That's very true. I was brought up in Northport on the island. We have a beach by the sea."

"Ah, a child of the sea."

"Well, not quite. I never liked boating very much."

"Not even sailing?"

"To tell you the truth, I was always a little afraid of it, and my father wasn't into it and my brother never did it. My younger sister went sailing quite often. Still does. She's married to a dentist and they have a boat."

"Your family always lived here?"

"Uh-huh."

"Tell me about your family," he said, and sat back.

She began, but unlike other times when she had described her family quickly, she found she spoke of them in very honest terms, describing them the way she would if she were talking to another family member. He seemed to understand her feelings about Lois's marriage and Bradley's engagement, and he was particularly sympathetic when she talked about her father and mother and their attitudes about her career and life in New York.

"You never mentioned your mother," she said when they were both quiet again.

"She died of cancer a few years ago."

"Oh, I'm sorry."

"My father's more than a handful, anyway. Parents," he added, and then he sat back as though he was speaking to a classroom of philosophy students. At first she was amused by it, but then she sensed a bitter undertone that was uncharacteristic of the man she had met so far. "Parents have this need to ensure that their children will be like them. It's sort of a confirmation of their life, that they've done and do all the right things. I suppose there's no more difficult rejection to accept than being rejected by your own children."

"God, that's so true."

"I think so, but I wonder if it would keep me from being that kind of parent. The fact that I realize it, that is."

"I don't know," she said. "Maybe it's something that can't be helped."

He looked at her for a long moment and then shook his head.

"Damn, we're getting too heavy here and it's all my fault."

"No, that's all right. I don't mind having a serious conversation."

"I'll do anything, as long as you enjoy it," he said. It brought a blush to her face. "Now, I hope you like Italian food because I found this little restaurant off Seventh Avenue, family owned and operated. They're cut right out of the old country. I've been there so often, they're treating me like family."

"I love Italian food, especially when it's authentic."

"Great." He finished his drink. "You want to go soon? That way we won't have to rush dinner, curtain time being what it is."

"Yes," she said, "you're right."

After she went into the bedroom and put on her jacket and her hat, she came out to find that he had put everything away in the kitchen.

"Thank you," she said. "I've got to practice being a better homemaker." He simply stared at her, a big smile on his face. "What is it?"

"That jacket and hat does it all right. I was just imagining what it would be like if you appeared dressed like that at one of my hometown restaurants. Heads would turn, that's for sure."

"Oh, come on. You make it sound like another country."

"For me, it is," he said, the smile leaving his face for a moment.

"Shall we go?"

They left the apartment and stepped into the elevator. She wanted to ask him if he had found a parking spot because she knew how difficult that could be on her block, but when they walked out of the apartment building, she saw why that was not going to be a problem.

"A limo?"

"What other way is there to travel around this city?" he said, smiling.

"This doesn't turn into a pumpkin at twelve, does it?"

"Oh, Cinderella has grown with the times," he said. "Nowadays her beautiful carriage doesn't turn into a pumpkin until one o'clock."

She laughed. Betty Dancer's words of advice were all but dead and pressed into the morgue of her memory, but she didn't care. He was sweeping her off her feet. She knew it, but she liked the feeling; she wanted to be enchanted. It was time for a fairy tale. Right now she was willing to sacrifice whatever value reality had to offer and trade in the truth for "Once upon a time..." whatever the cost.

CHAPTER THREE

THE MELODY of "Memory," the most famous song from *CATS*, followed them through the city. Jillian never fully realized how bright and exciting the lights of Manhattan could be. She remarked about it in the back of the limo.

"I know what you mean," Ron said, gazing out the window and up at the skyscrapers. "Somehow things taken for granted or experienced often are transformed into things magical and special when you're with someone special."

Yes, she thought, but she didn't say it. The moment was as beautiful as fine china. She was afraid the mere sound of her voice might shatter it. So far the entire evening had been like that; so much so that she kept expecting something to spoil it. Jillian couldn't get away from her paranoia when it came to happiness. Sometimes she blamed that on what she did for a living. She created the illusion of happiness and satisfaction for her clients so well that she had come to distrust it when she found it herself.

Their dinner had been storybook romantic. He had surprised her with the restaurant because it was truly so unassuming. He hadn't exaggerated. It would have been very easy to ride past it without noticing it. Although it was clean and comfortable inside, it was also small and simple. The owner's wife was the maître d';

Illusion

the owner was the chief chef, and one of their older daughters was the cashier. There was soft music piped through inexpensive speakers and the menu was limited.

But the food and the wine were first rate. Everything had that homemade look and taste. Ron hadn't been kidding about the owners knowing him well, either. They greeted him as they would a relative. They had saved him the best booth and they provided warm and concerned service.

Probably because he leaves a big tip, she thought, and then she was critical of herself for concluding that was the reason. Why couldn't they like him for what and who he was and he like them for the same reasons? Where was the well from which she drew all these suspicions? Was it a result of a string of failed romances, or was it simply in her nature to be so insecure?

Ron was certainly easy to talk to. Their conversation had lightened up considerably the moment they left her apartment, but all through the small talk and the jokes she still felt there was something mysterious about him. Sometimes it came from half-completed sentences; sometimes it came from a cryptic remark or a vague allusion; and sometimes it came from that far-off look he took on for no apparent reason.

As the evening wore on she had the paradoxical feeling that he was with her and yet wasn't. She observed him as they watched the show. He was fascinated by the music and the lights and the drama, but he often looked away or looked down as though he were troubled and couldn't give anything its full concentration.

She noticed another thing. Although he seemed experienced enough when it came to traveling through the city and talking about it, there was that look of surprise and excitement in his face at times, a look she usually saw on tourists or visitors who came to New York for the first time. It was as though he had really just discovered the city and was continuing to discover it every moment they were together.

Maybe that's the magic of New York, she thought, and shrugged it off. After all, unless a person lived here day in, day out, he or she wouldn't have that urban indifference to things that shocked and excited most outsiders.

That was why she was so happy to find the lights and the activity especially exciting tonight; she realized she was still capable of new discoveries here; and then his comment about it while they rode in the limo restored her faith in his sophistication.

He took her to a little café in the Village where they had some espresso and listened to a jazz quartet. However, the longer they sat there listening, the more melancholy and withdrawn he seemed to become. Their lively and excited conversation slowed into short and occasional sentences. More and more he took on that far-off look.

A little after 1:00 a.m., her imagination began to activate again. She envisioned his identity slipping out of him. It had been happening little by little all night, and now it was happening more rapidly. Soon she would be left sitting here with an empty body. She looked around for the "body snatchers." Oh, God, if Betty Dancer could hear her thoughts now, she mused.

"I'm sorry," he said. "You looked bored."

"No. Just a little tired, I think."

Illusion

"Sure. Let's go." He paid the tab and they went out to the limo, but he didn't go right for it. "You want to walk a block or two. I'd like to air out my lungs. There was so much smoke in there."

"Okay," she said, even though his suggestion took her by surprise.

He signaled the limo to follow slowly.

"I guess the smoke has to go with the music. I mean, without the low lights and the smog, it wouldn't feel right, huh?" He sounded so sarcastic and disdainful, she wondered why he'd brought her there.

"Don't you like jazz?"

"I like it sometimes."

"What made you want to come down here?"

"I thought it might be a nice way to unwind. You didn't like it?"

"Oh, it was nice."

He stopped, took some deep breaths, and looked around.

"I don't think I could stand it," he said.

"What?"

"Living right on top of someone else and having someone else living right on top of me."

"You get used to it. After awhile you don't notice half the things you first noticed."

"You get kind of hard, huh? Kind of insensitive."

"Well, I don't know if I would put it that way, but..."

He stepped closer to her.

"On the street right outside my house, I could take you in my arms and kiss you and you would feel no embarrassment. The only witnesses would be a stray dog or two and some stray cats. All the birds are asleep and the owls could care less."

She laughed and then he kissed her.

The memory of her first real kiss burst out of storage to join itself with the reality of this one. Ron held the kiss a beat longer than she expected. She thought he was going to press on for a second surge of passion. It was as though the kiss had revived the real Ron Cutler and it was he who wanted to kiss her now. But then, as suddenly as he started, he stopped.

She liked the fact that he didn't try to apologize, even that he didn't whisper passionate words, words that could be thought automatic and expected. More was said in the silence. He put his arm around her shoulders and they walked on for another half block without speaking. Then he turned and waved the limo up. She got in and sat against him, hardly speaking until they reached mid-Manhattan.

"It's going to be beautiful tomorrow," he said. "How about us going for a picnic in Central Park? That's something I've never done."

"Neither have I. I usually go out to the island for my picnics."

"Oh, well, I suppose we could..."

"No, I want to go to the park."

"Good. I'll pick you up about eleven?"

"Fine."

She gathered from the tone of his conversation that this was it, the end of their date. He wasn't going to make any attempt to go up to her apartment. She had contradictory feelings again. She didn't want to be thought of as easy and yet she couldn't help wanting to spend the night with him.

But at the same time she had to respect his control. He seemed to have a firm grip on things now. She told herself this was a mature man, a confident man, a man who didn't need a conquest to prove to himself he was good with women. This was an ingredient she didn't see as clearly in the other men with whom she had developed relationships.

Of course, once again her old paranoia had its say. He knows what you're thinking, it told her. This is simply part of a calculated plan to make you believe he is different from other men and he isn't driven by mere physical attractions. Then, when your defenses are relaxed...

So what? she told herself. I'm tired of being so damn intelligent when it comes to men.

"Let me walk you to your door," he said when they came to her apartment building. She thought maybe she had come to the wrong conclusions. He might just be a lot more subtle in his approach.

"Thank you."

"I hope you had a good time."

"Oh, yes. It was wonderful."

"You mean, I match up to your New York men?" He smiled when he asked her, but she sensed that he really wanted to know. They stepped out of the elevator.

"Some of the New York men I know have a lot more of the hick in them than you'd think."

"You see any hick in me?"

"You're different," she said. "Wait a minute, are we playing that game again? You tricked me into this once, but you're not going to do it again."

He laughed.

"All right. I'll figure things out for myself." He leaned over and gave her a quick kiss on the lips. "'Night. See you at eleven," he said, and walked back to the elevator. She waited a moment before opening the door, looking after him; but he didn't look back.

After she stepped into the apartment and put on the lights, she looked at herself in the hall mirror. She thought her face looked flushed, but she also thought she looked terribly young for some reason. It was as if Ron Cutler had sent her reeling back through the years until she was a teenager again, overwhelmed by a crush on a boy and eager to fantasize a relationship.

She took off her hat and went into the bedroom to finish undressing. It wasn't until she had put out the lights and gotten into bed that she realized she had no idea where he was staying in the city.

Like a phantom lover, he had come into her life and gone out with the promise of return. This strange feeling she had... Was it the beginning of true love or was it a kind of warning? Why a warning? Why did she even think such a thing? A warning about what?

You always talk about how you want your men to have some mystery to them, Jillian Caldwell. Now that you've found one who has, don't start complaining about it, she thought.

She giggled at the way she was carrying on these conversations with herself and she turned over in bed. Through her side window she could see some stars tonight. She never looked for them or cared very much if she saw them or not before. Suddenly they were very important. It was reassuring to know that they were there; even behind the clouds, they were always there.

"RIGHT ON TIME AGAIN," Jillian said after opening the door. "You'll spoil me."

Ron stood there with a bouquet of red and white roses in his hand. Today his eyes looked more green than blue. He was dressed in a tight, short-sleeved turquoise shirt and jeans, and she was surprised at just how muscular and how tanned he was. His wrists were thick and his forearms looked hard. The shirt seemed strained at his shoulders. Oh, well, she thought, he must spend a great deal of time in a gym.

"There was this little old lady selling them on the street. I couldn't resist." He handed her the flowers.

"Thank you. Let me get them into water."

"I thought we'd stop and get a bucket of fried chicken."

"Oh," she said, "I just finished making sandwiches."

"Really?" His eyes widened, and she nearly laughed.

"Don't look so surprised. Anyway, I thought I had already impressed you with my hors d'oeuvres."

"You did, you did."

"What kind of an image do you have of a New York woman?" she asked. She was only half-kidding. Was she the first city girl he had ever known?

"Women are women," he said, raising his arms.

"Uh-huh. Scratch a man and you'll find the chauvinist underneath," she said. He laughed. "I have roast beef. You struck me as the roast beef type. Am I right?"

He didn't answer for a moment. The smile faded.

"What brought you to that conclusion?"

"I don't know. Intuition."

"You're right," he confessed.

"Give me a minute." She went into the kitchen to get things together and fill up her insulated picnic basket, a gift her mother had given her not so long ago. It was as though she'd had a premonition and wanted to lay things out neatly for Jillian to trap a man.

Trap a man, she thought. Her mother did use that image. How many times did she say something like, "You let him slip away?"

But trapping a man or doing something like that implied contrivance, planning, strategy. It took away from the excitement of spontaneity. Jillian was a great deal more romantic than she cared to admit. If something was to happen, it would happen because it was meant to happen, like the star-crossed lovers, Romeo and Juliet. The ingredients were there to make it happen. It didn't need the planning of mothers or other matchmakers.

"You didn't bring the limo again, did you?" she asked as they left the apartment.

"No. I thought we'd rough it with cabs."

"How did you get down to the city?"

"I drove, but I'd rather take cabs than take the car out of the parking lot and drive around myself."

"I don't know why anyone owns a car in New York," she said as they stepped out of the building. "It's so expensive to keep it and it's so hard to get about most of the time." Outside it was a beautiful day. Clouds looked like puffs of white cotton pasted on a light blue mural. There was a gentle breeze that lifted the strands of her hair off her forehead. Even the usual heavy and noisy traffic looked relaxed. The city looked in tune; everything complemented everything else.

"My nervous system rebels at the idea of sitting behind a line of traffic," Ron said. "Where I live it takes two minutes to go two miles."

"You make it sound like a rural wonderland."

"In some ways it is." He flagged a cab and the driver cut across a lane to pick them up. Once again she was impressed with the way he did things. He commanded obedience and attention. There was confidence in the way he held himself and moved. This is what we mean by executive material, she thought, recalling a meeting at the agency when everyone was arguing about a look for the Dewars advertisement. He held the door for her and she slipped in quickly. "Central Park," he told the driver.

"Any particular part?"

"Wherever you come to first," he replied. He looked to her to see if she approved. She just smiled. "Like pitching pennies with your eyes closed," he said, and laughed.

They entered the park off of Sixty-eighth Street. It looked like everyone in the city had come up with the same idea. There was an endless line of joggers, all sizes and shapes, their faces locked in serious intent, their eyes pointed with determination. As the line went by them, Jillian noticed Ron's smile of amusement. Once again she had the feeling he was seeing something for the very first time.

Off to the right they saw a group of men and women playing touch football. They looked upper middle class. The men were Kennedyesque, with their well trimmed bodies and wavy hair; the women were bright and colorful in their designer sweat suits. The shouts and the laughter revealed their comradeship. Other people who stopped to observe them wore the same half smile frozen in a look of envy. Jillian imagined they each thought the same thing: why couldn't we all be young, healthy and affluent?

Ron's attention went to a high-flying kite. He followed the path of the string until it disappeared behind some trees in the middle of the park. Just above it, a commercial jet was climbing in a turn, taking passengers south. It seemed to Jillian that everywhere around and above them there was life; there was movement; there was hope.

Ron took her hand and they continued walking deeper into the park. He found a spot under a big maple tree. From it they could look out at Central Park West and watch the traffic and movement, as well as the other couples and families crossing along the grass to find their own comfortable place.

"There's a never-ending show going on here," he said. "There's drama everywhere," he added in a deliberately deeper voice. She laughed and they sat down on a thick, grassy spot.

"I think I should have brought a blanket. I guess I'm not as rural minded as I would like to believe," she said.

"We'll take turns being pillows. Who's first?"

"I'll be first. I deserve it," she said. He spread himself out perpendicular to her and lowered his head to her lap. "Comfortable?" Jillian asked.

"Terribly. Maybe even sinfully."

She looked off across Central Park West and saw a hotel doorman arguing with a cab driver. It brought something to her mind, even though she had made a promise to herself that she wouldn't mention anything that could be construed as business.

"How do they get along without you on weekends? Aren't the weekends the busiest days of the week for your stores?"

Illusion

He had his eyes closed, but his face was still in a squint because of the sunlight. For a moment she thought he was simply not going to answer. Then he opened his eyes and looked up at her reproachfully.

"Are you trying to slip in some business talk?"

"No, no, honest. I was just curious."

"Uh-huh." He closed his eyes again.

"It's the furthest thing from my mind right now."

"Good. Keep it that way."

"Okay," she said. "Tell me about your childhood."

"What do you want to know?"

"What's it like being an only child? I used to wish I was."

"There's more pressure, for one thing," he said. "You feel it's all on your shoulders."

"What is?"

"Their hope. You're the future. You can't screw up. There's no second team, understand?"

"Yes. You have a close relationship with your father?" He sat up abruptly. "That wasn't a business question. You can't call it one," she said quickly and defensively.

"I know." He turned and looked out over the park. After a moment he said, "Do you think it's possible to be of the same flesh and blood and be strangers?" He didn't turn to her; he kept looking away.

"Yes," she said. "I think parents often forget that their children are individuals. I often feel like a stranger when I go home."

He turned to her.

"Really?"

"Yes, really."

He stared at her for a moment.

"You know, I have this theory about people. We're all on wavelengths, frequencies, and when you find someone who is on your frequency, you know it; you feel it. I think you're on my frequency, Jillian Caldwell."

She tilted her head expectantly as he leaned forward and kissed her. Behind them they could hear the sound of children shouting. Overhead, there was the sound of a jet beginning to descend, its roar like an afterthought as the plane sped onward.

Ron kissed her again, this time more passionately, the implied demand quite clear. One of her voices tried to remind her that they were in the park, that it was broad daylight, and there were people all around them. But she told herself this was New York in the 1980s. Most people would barely take note, and who cares anyway?

Somewhere in the middle of that second kiss, she abandoned all caution. She lowered herself into the car that would carry her over a roller coaster of emotion. She could already hear her screams of excitement.

She returned his kiss with even more enthusiasm than he had when he began it. I'm being swept off my feet, she thought. My God, it's really happening.

When they parted, he just lowered his head to her lap again and they were quiet. It was like that after he kissed her last night for the first time, too, she thought. What makes him so pensive? How would he be after making love? The questions made him even more mysterious.

Suddenly she had the idea that what was happening to him was something he couldn't help, either, but he didn't want. Perhaps it saddened him to fall in love.

Illusion

But why should it? She stroked his forehead and he opened his eyes.

"Something's happening pretty fast," she said.

"I know."

"Are you unhappy about it?"

"No. Just..."

"Just what?"

"A little confused. But that's not unusual for me. I always start out a little confused." He started to close his eyes again, but a Frisbee came floating down from the left and landed at his feet. "What the —" He sat up and took it in his hands. They heard some teenage boys shouting and he stood up. "Go for it," he shouted back and threw the Frisbee high and wide so the boy on the left had to run and dive to make the catch. There were shouts of appreciation.

"Very good," she said. He took a bow and she laughed. "What were you, football?"

"Mm-hmm. Quarterback, but only in high school."

"You haven't lost your touch."

"Some things stay with you." He looked after the boys longingly.

"You know," she said, "you have me at a disadvantage."

"Why's that?"

"Every time I ask you a question you don't want to answer, you claim I'm talking business."

"That's not true."

"Ever been married? Truthfully now, no games."

"Nope."

"In love?"

"Who hasn't?"

"Me," she said. He tilted his head and smirked with skepticism. "I mean it. Not the way I want to be anyway."

"And what way is that?"

"Completely, full commitment. No secrets," she said. She was testing and she could see he knew it.

"Sounds like...like you're a very serious woman."

"That scare you?"

"A little," he said. "So go easy on me, will you?" He teased her with a smile and she had to laugh. "I didn't really eat breakfast," he said.

"I get the hint."

He sat beside her and she broke out the sandwiches.

"This is good, but I'm no longer surprised," he added quickly. She laughed. "Look," he said, "at least for a while, let's not try to analyze each other. I know that's the modern way of romance, but..."

"Oh, I don't like that, either."

"Good. Like I said, we're on the same frequency. Just keep tuned in."

"I'll try. As long as there's no static," she said. He laughed, loud and hard as though she had just said the most truthful thing of all.

After they ate, they decided to walk through the park. Once in awhile he stopped to watch some children playing or observe another couple. Whenever he did that, she studied him.

"You like children, don't you?"

"I envy them," he said, a half smile on his face.

"Why?"

"Because they're carefree, innocent. It's better not to know what's ahead," he added, sounding his first strong note of pessimism. "I wouldn't mind being six forever."

"I guess my first impressions about you were more off than you admitted."

"Why do you say that?" he asked. He wasn't smiling and his gaze was so intent, she hesitated to reply.

"You struck me as one who sought challenges."

"Yes," he said, relaxing. "I'm full of contradictions."

"We all are."

"Then maybe we don't have a real identity. I mean, our identities change so often, it's impossible to be sure," he said.

"Dr. Jekyll and Mr. Hyde."

"Exactly," he said. "Here, let's play a game."

They broke out of the park and crossed to the Plaza Hotel. There he picked out individuals who were walking in and out of the hotel and then he challenged her to take guesses about what kind of people they were and what they did for a living. He asked her to support each comment by describing what brought her to each conclusion. She was amused by it at first, but after awhile, she grew tired of it because it was too much like being at work.

He moved back into an impulsive, light mood and they walked down Fifth Avenue, window-shopping and joking. They went over to Rockefeller Center where they enjoyed the beautiful display of flowers and looked down at the people having lunch or late snacks at the tables set up where the ice-skating rink was located during the late fall and winter months. After that they walked for another block before deciding to stop.

"I've got tickets for the Yankee ball game tonight," he said after he had pulled over a cab to take her back to her apartment. "Care to join me?"

"Well, I'm really a Mets fan, but..."

"Right. I should have asked you about that first." He looked upset.

"I'm just kidding. I don't follow baseball that closely. In fact, I hate to admit this, but..."

"You've never been to a ball game?"

"Uh-huh. Look," she said, "it's the old story. You'd be surprised at how many New Yorkers have never been to the top of the Empire State Building, either."

"Just lucky for you I arrived on the scene. Maybe by the time we're finished, you'll see the city."

She laughed, but she wondered what made him say, "by the time we're finished." Why was she hanging on his every word so closely?

"I know this great hero sandwich shop right near the stadium. How about me picking you up at six-thirty?"

"Six-thirty?" She felt as though she were on a roller coaster all right, with barely a chance to take a breath. She shook her head, but she agreed.

When she got into her apartment, she collapsed on the couch and looked up at the ceiling. Her mind was like a video machine replaying scenes and words from the afternoon. She paused over glimpses of him caught in a certain look or demeanor. She listened to the sound of his voice, noting how he could move from a light tone to a deeply pensive one so quickly. She hadn't spent so much time thinking in such detail about a man since...actually, she couldn't remember when she had done it like this before.

Illusion

The phone tore her away from her introspection. It was her mother, and like all mothers, her mother instinctively sensed something different about her.

"You sound excited. What's going on?"

"Nothing, Mother."

"I tried to call you all day. Where were you?"

"Shopping," she said quickly.

"Guess what. We're in New York. Your father splurged and bought tickets to a show, *A Chorus Line*. I know you've seen it, but we thought it would be nice for you to join us for dinner."

"Oh, I can't."

"Why not?"

"I—I've already made plans."

"For what?"

"I'm helping Trish Hamilton paint her apartment," she said, the lie coming easy.

"Oh."

"Now, Mother, just enjoy yourself. I'll call you tomorrow."

She hung up as quickly as she could. It reminded her of when she was a little girl and she had done something she knew her parents wouldn't approve. Why did she feel so guilty?

And why in heaven's name did she lie? It came so instinctively. It made no sense. If Ron Cutler was anything, he was what her mother would want for her.

She looked at the clock. There wasn't time for all this self-analysis, and besides, that was what got her into trouble whenever she had a relationship with a man. She was determined not to let that happen this time.

CHAPTER FOUR

THERE WAS SOMETHING about rushing around the city with Ron that made Jillian feel like a teenage girl again. Their cab got caught up in traffic about two blocks away from the stadium, and Ron decided they would get out and walk to the restaurant. It turned out to be nothing more than an opened window at the sidewalk, and the idea was to get to their seats and eat at the ballpark. She was glad she had dressed very casually.

Jillian had always found that regardless of where she had to go, she spent serious time and thought on what she would wear. Choice of dresses or outfits for a formal occasion did not take more time than an outing at the park or attending a baseball game. It was the result of her belief that she, as well as everyone else, was always on display, always in a performance. She had to be organized and prepared.

Ironically it was Betty Dancer, someone who was really involved with performances, who said, "You need to be more impulsive, Jillian. Be more spontaneous. Don't worry if a strand of hair is out of place or a color doesn't quite match. There's something attractive about imperfection, too, you know."

Maybe so, she thought, but right now she was with a man who seemed to enjoy perfection. Maybe he even expected it.

She had chosen a milk-white cotton shirt with an attached hood that lay over the back. The front of the shirt read Esprit. The shirt was cut just a little too tight. Usually, whenever she wore it, she wore a bra; but something about Betty Dancer's advice was still appealing. She wanted to be more reckless and more daring.

Besides, the memory of Ron's unusually passionate kiss in the park returned with an erotic vividness right before she took her shower. It remained with her throughout her preparations. She was standing naked in the bathroom and thinking about him when she actually closed her eyes and pursed her lips to relive the kiss. When she looked in the mirror afterward, the surprised expression on her face made her laugh.

But everything she did with and to herself after that had a sensuous feel to it. Her body tingled under the shower spray as she washed her hair. Even the electric motor of the blow-dryer took on a soothing rhythm. She felt caressed by it. These thoughts and feelings brought a flush to her face that still hadn't left by the time Ron buzzed up.

"Every time I see you, you astound me," he said when she opened the door for him.

"Why?"

"You look like a high-school girl."

"I look the way I feel," she said, and the mood remained with both of them right up to the first pitch in the first inning.

Jillian thought that Ron was even more relaxed and more natural at the ballpark. He was involved with the game almost immediately, shouting and clapping, standing and waving his fist at the umpire and cupping his hands to blast instructions to the players. At times he was so involved she thought he had forgotten she was with him. From time to time he would poke her or ask her opinion, but for the most part, it was as though he were with one of his pals.

Who were his pals? she wondered. He hadn't mentioned even one friend during all their conversations. With what kind of people did he socialize? Were they all business people and professionals? There were things about him that suggested a more democratic spread, and yet she also had the sense that he was quite a loner.

It was a close game and during the latter innings, Ron's activity grew more and more intense. She was surprised when he shouted profanities in the last half of the ninth inning after a particularly close call at third. He didn't apologize, even after he realized what he had done. His face was bright red with anger, his eyes blazing. She was actually a bit frightened by his vehemence. For a few moments she felt as if he had become someone else and she was reminded of his statement about contradictions. Was this the Mr. Hyde coming out of his Dr. Jekyll? she wondered.

The Yankees lost by one run in the last inning on an error by the shortstop. She understood that the runner on third had been harassing the infielders by pretending to tear down the baseline and then returning to the base. As soon as the player had come to bat, Ron muttered something about the man being a great base stealer, and sure enough, he stole his way from second to third after hitting a double.

The hometown stadium crowd groaned in unison when the shortstop's throw went beyond the first baseman. Ron was part of it. He sat back in disbelief, his hands clenched into fists, his fists pressed against the tops of his thighs. People began to leave in disgust, but Ron didn't move.

"Did you have money on this?" she asked as gently as she could.

"Huh? Oh, no." He saw the look on her face and sat up. "I get a little overenthusiastic. Been a Yankee fan all my life. You either love 'em or hate 'em."

"I don't think I'm that passionate about anything," Jillian said, sounding regretful.

"Oh, I can't believe that. Come on," he said, taking her arm and standing, "let's make our way out of here with the rest of the mourners."

"We'll get them next year," she said, and he laughed.

"It's all right. They're still three games up."

"Are all your friends Yankee fans?" she asked as they made their way down the aisle.

"My friends? No, most of them hate the Yankees and love the Mets. They got this idea that the Yankees are a rich man's ball club."

"Aren't your friends well-to-do?"

"Huh? Yeah, some of them are. Boy, it's hot, isn't it? Let's go somewhere for an old-fashioned, ice-cream soda, okay?"

"You know how much weight I'm going to gain hanging around with you?"

"We'll work it off...somehow," he said, and smiled at her in a rather suggestive way, but a way she thought was out of character. Nevertheless she couldn't help being titillated by it.

She noted that he knew his way around the stadium area very well. There was no indecision, no look of novelty on his face. Everything was familiar to him.

He took her right to an all-night luncheonette and they sat in a booth near the front window.

"You've attended a number of games, I take it."

"Off and on," he said. "I was here the day Mantle almost hit that ball out of the park," he added proudly.

"Your father take you?"

"No, I came with friends. My father...my father doesn't relax very much. Actually, we didn't have that close father-son relationship. You were right when you said I am someone who has a great deal of independence. Had to, if you know what I mean."

"You regret it, too, don't you?"

"Sometimes." He hesitated, sat back against the booth and smiled. "Actually, most of the time I feel as though I've grown up in a kingdom like a little prince. You know, maids, servants, chauffeurs. You grow up making friends with the gardener."

"I was thinking about your father's age. He had you quite late, didn't he? And with no brothers or sisters..."

"I had a brother," he said quickly, and sat forward. He folded his hands and looked down at them for a moment. "Although I never met him."

"Never met him?"

"He died before I was born."

"Oh, I see."

"And then they had me." He looked up, his eyes blazing with emotion. "Second team, so to speak."

"They wanted only one child?"

"Yes."

She was encouraged by his candor, but she felt she had to tiptoe through the information and take great care in the way she phrased her questions. He looked so tense she was afraid he would actually get up and leave her if she asked the wrong thing or made the wrong statement after he answered her.

"How old was your brother when he died?"

"Nearly ten."

"Oh, so then...then there's little doubt they wanted only one child."

"Exactly."

"But why? I mean, your parents were well-to-do, right?"

"My mother...my mother was not supposed to have another child. She had had breast cancer and the doctors advised against it, but when my brother died, they went for it."

"And then the cancer returned," she added, as if she was helping to write a scenario.

"Now you got the happy ending."

"I'm sorry." She was afraid to say anything more because he was looking at her so intently.

"I can see your mind going a novel a minute. You think my father resented me because of it," he added, but there wasn't any bitterness in his voice. If anything, he sounded tired, defeated.

"I wasn't thinking anything like that. Is that what you believe?" she asked softly. He looked like he would say no more. Then he sighed and nodded.

"Sometimes."

"Did you ever talk it out with him?" She hated the tone in her voice because she thought she sounded like some high-school guidance counselor having a "pal" session with a problem student. But Ron didn't seem to notice or care.

"You don't know my father. If I brought it up, he would call it nonsense and start talking about something to do with the business."

"It constantly amazes me how parents often forget what it was like to be younger, to be impressive and sensitive."

"Does it?" he asked, this time sounding bitter.

"I was thinking of my own situation, my own parents," she said, and his face softened. "I don't mean the problems are as complex as yours seem, but you don't know what I'm going through being career-minded more than marriage-minded. I really think my father feels I betrayed him by going through college without getting engaged."

Ron laughed and she felt the moment lighten.

"I bet he does."

He reached across the table and took her hand. For a few moments they simply sat staring at one another. It ended when the waitress brought their sodas. They were both double scoops with small mountains of whipped cream.

"Oh, God," she said. They laughed at each other when they both got whipped cream on the tips of their noses. Afterward they walked back to the stadium because Ron thought it would be easier for them to catch a cab. She sat snugly against him in the back. Neither of them said very much during the trip, but she felt his lips press against her hair and then against her ear and neck.

Nothing was said when they reached her apartment building. Nothing had to be said. Ron paid the cab driver and they got out. He took her hand and they walked into the building. When the elevator door closed, he took her into his arms and kissed her. She clung to him until they reached her floor.

Jillian couldn't believe how nervous she felt when she took out her apartment key. Her fingers wouldn't close tightly around it and she had difficulty inserting it into the lock. He had to help her. When the door opened, she looked up at him. The longing she saw in his eyes thrilled her. It was good to know she was the object of such desire.

"You want something to drink, or coffee?" she asked. It seemed necessary to ask, even though she hoped that he wanted nothing to slow down the passion that was building between them. He didn't. He barely shook his head.

She went directly to her bedroom. He followed her and she turned on the small lamp on the night table. It projected enormous silhouettes of both of them on the far wall. For a moment she thought she was watching a film about two other lovers. Ron's silhouette moved closer to hers. His arms embraced her and the two silhouettes melded into one.

The gentle way they had touched and kissed one another up to this point dropped away as quickly as did their garments. Every touch, every look, every word had been made tentatively, carefully. They had handled one another as they would handle fine, fragile china.

But now the demands they made on each other intensified through every kiss. A new confession was made with every advance. He wanted her and she wanted him to touch her, but to touch her in such a way that he would find the truer version of her. Inherently she felt that if he did so, she would find the truer version of him, as well. In her mind that would make their physical love more significant and more meaningful.

Jillian had made love before, but there was always an exploratory air to it. She was trying to discover things about herself and the man she was with; namely was there really something significant between them? She had the notion, romantic perhaps, that it was only through the act of love that she would be absolutely sure about her feelings for someone.

Consequently she made love almost as though she were a scientific observer. It resulted in her being somewhat detached. Maybe that was what the men in her life up to now had felt. Maybe that was a turn-off for them. Her mother could be right, she thought. A good deal of all this was partly her fault.

Almost from the start with Ron, she didn't have the old feelings about lovemaking. She didn't have the time for it. She was lost in the passion and the need to drive herself and him into the high of their own physical pleasure. She kissed him as hard and as long as he kissed her. She stroked him and pressed herself to him as intently as he stroked and pressed himself to her.

It seemed that they were just suddenly naked and in her bed. The preliminary moves were lost in a haze. In a frenzy, she seized on details—the strength in his arms, the thickness of his shoulders, the firmness in his waist and legs. He was hard in places other men had been soft, and that made her feel totally vulnerable. She expected this feeling of helplessness would frighten her, but it had an opposite effect—it excited her, but only because she had faith that he would make love in a most satisfying and affectionate way.

He did. He never pressed too hard or nibbled too sharply. He fit himself to her gracefully, but unlike any other man she had been with, he was intent on her looking at him, kissing him, and reaching for him just as much as he reached for her. He wasn't making love; he was making love with her, and that was all the difference.

She thought he said her name a hundred times, confirming each time that she was really there or that she wouldn't drift away from him. She had the strange idea that he thought she might be an illusion. Any moment she would disappear and it would all be lost. She confirmed her presence with her yes, each yes more endearing than the one before.

When it was over and their breathing slowed, they lay side by side, her hand in his, and stared up at the ceiling. The aftermath was never as satisfying before. Maybe it was corny to think she was fulfilled, but she was. For the first time she felt she had reached her full female potential. She started to laugh, thinking about Betty Dancer's reaction to these thoughts, should she ever tell her.

"You found it funny?"

"Oh, no," she said, turning to him. "I was just thinking about this friend I have. She has a very dry wit sometimes, and she does a great job on these other friends of mine whenever they describe their love life."

"Is that what you plan to do now?" he asked. She didn't like the sharpness in his tone of voice.

"Of course not. I don't follow the reveal-all, expose-all crowd. What's personal to me is personal."

"Good," he said. He turned to her. "That's what makes it special." He kissed her and then sat up.

"What are you going to do?"

"Why?"

"You might as well stay here tonight."

"Is that so? What about the neighbors?"

"This is New York. There are no neighbors," she said. He laughed.

"All right. Maybe I will. I think I need a cold drink, though."

"There's soda and juice in the fridge," she called as he started away. "Get me a glass of cranberry, please."

"Right away, ma'am."

She pulled her blanket up around her. Is this all really happening? she thought, or is this the middle of a dream? The sounds he made in the kitchen reaffirmed the reality. She had met a handsome, charming man. They had gotten to know one another very fast, perhaps too fast for some; but nevertheless they had found out enough about one another to know that they wanted one another. Of course it was too soon to think of anything long term, but in the back of her mind she wondered how anything so perfect could be for anything else but forever.

It was good to be so happy and so content. She refused to think anything but good thoughts. There was a sign up on the door of her mind: No Dark Possibilities Permitted. She giggled at her own foolish musing.

"Laughing again?"

"It's just because I'm happy," she said. She took the glass of juice. "Thank you."

"I don't know. You sure you're not some kind of pervert, some city slicker taking advantage of a country hick?"

"You'll never know."

"We'll see," he said, and crawled under the covers.

They made love again, slower, but just as intense. This time when it was over, she turned off the lamp.

She fell asleep in his arms and drifted into such a deep repose that she never felt him release her and turn away. Nor did she hear him get up and get dressed.

He slipped out of her apartment so quietly that when she awoke in the morning, it was she who had to wonder if it had all been an illusion.

JILLIAN HAD FOUND no note. In fact she found no trace of him except for the juice glass on the kitchen counter. As she looked around the apartment, she indeed had the eerie feeling she had made love to a ghost. Usually she was a fairly light sleeper. How did he get up and get dressed and go out without her hearing him? she wondered. Most of all, why would he do that?

Dressed only in a bathrobe, she sat on the livingroom couch, half in a daze, half expecting him to appear any moment with a bag of breakfast goodies. It would be like him to do that, she thought, or rather, she hoped. Finally, when it was apparent to her that he wasn't going to do that, she looked at the phone and hoped for a call. That didn't come, either.

She got dressed, made coffee, and tried to eat some toast and jelly, but she had a sick feeling running through her. At first she had felt confused, then hurt, and then angry. She didn't want to be angry so it wore on her until she fell into a depression. She was like that when Betty Dancer called.

"Are you able to talk?" Betty asked.

"Why do you ask?"

"From the way you sound, I thought you might be still in bed, and if you were still in bed, I imagined you might not be there alone."

"No, I can talk," she said.

"I'm disappointed."

"So am I."

"Oh? It wasn't a good weekend?"

"It was. That's what makes it so...so frustrating."

"Now you've got my interest."

"We went to dinner in this romantic little Italian place; we went to *CATS*; we went on a picnic in Central Park; we even went to a Yankee ball game. And I enjoyed every minute of all of it."

"So? Why so glum?"

"And he was here last night," Jillian went on, "but when I got up this morning, he was gone. He snuck out."

"Snuck? You mean as in tiptoed through the door and was gone?"

"Didn't leave a note or anything."

"Not even slam, bam, thank you, ma'am?"

"Not even that. I wish he had left that," she added quickly. "At least then I'd know something."

"Maybe it's the new chic; maybe you just don't say goodbye. I've been out of circulation for a while, so I can't help you there."

"Oh, Betty, this was more than that."

"I see. Well, then, why don't you call him?"

"I thought of that."

"And?"

"I don't know where he's staying. I never asked him and he never said."

"This does sound more and more like two trains passing in the night."

"It's not. At least, it wasn't for me."

"Well, try not to let it get you down. Actually I called to see if you wanted to go to a movie matinée. Roger has to go to the office today. Some brief he must get done. There's that new French film at Cinema One, the one that got that great write-up in *New York* magazine."

"Yes, I remember."

"So go with me. It will do you good to get out for a while. You shouldn't sit there waiting by the phone."

"I don't want to wait by any phone."

"Good. Just meet me in front of the movie theater at twelve and we'll get a bite first."

As soon as she agreed, she regretted it. She knew that Betty would want to hear about the events of the weekend in detail and she wasn't in the mood to talk about it. Not now anyway, not until she knew why he did what he did.

Betty was sensitive to her feelings, though, and she avoided asking any questions about the weekend. And then the movie was fascinating and did take her mind off everything else. It was about two sisters who fall in love with the same man. The man lets each sister believe he is in love with her. Finally he is murdered and until the end, it is unclear who committed the crime. Each sister is a suspect. In a delicious twist at the end, the audience learns that both partook in the murder, after they learned what their lover had been doing.

It wasn't until Betty summed up her feelings after seeing the film that Jillian thought about Ron again.

"So much is not what it seems to be," she said to herself.

Jillian left her, promising to meet for lunch some time late in the week. When she got back to her apartment, she was excited to discover she had had a phone call. Her answering machine's little red light flashed on and off. Her finger actually trembled as she rewound the tape, but when she played it back, her anticipation deflated like a punctured balloon. It was only her mother.

Jillian called her back, even though she wasn't in the mood to talk.

"We had such a wonderful dinner and loved the show. I wish you could have joined us," her mother said.

"Me, too."

"Did you finish helping your friend?"

"Friend?"

"You said you had to help your friend paint her apartment."

"Oh. Yes, we finished."

"What's wrong? You sound sick. Aren't you feeling well?"

"Just a little tired."

"Maybe you inhaled too much of those paint fumes. It's not very healthy, and especially with this kind of humid heat."

"I'm all right, Mother."

"Nevertheless I want you to call me tomorrow night. Will you call?"

"I'll call."

After she hung up, she collapsed on the couch. She had little appetite and no desire to make supper. Instead she placed a pillow behind her head and closed her eyes. She was sorry she had done that because she fell asleep for a good two hours.

She awoke abruptly when she thought she had heard the phone ringing. It hadn't. Perhaps it had been part of a dream, she concluded. She forced herself to make a salad and sat chewing lazily on the fresh vegetables. After she watched some television, she tried reading a new novel she had bought at the beginning of the week, but it was difficult to keep her attention on anything.

"It's not fair," she muttered to her stuffed Snoopy dog. It was on the rocking chair facing her. This wasn't the first time she had had a conversation with it. "People shouldn't play with each other's feelings like that, should they?" Snoopy seemed to sympathize. "I feel so...so violated," she concluded, and returned to strong feelings of anger.

As she expected, all of this kept her from falling asleep for most of the evening. She tossed and turned until the wee hours and finally drifted off out of exhaustion. She felt terrible when she awoke, and the shower didn't have its usual powers of revival.

Despite the extra pains she took with her makeup and coiffure, she thought she looked pale and tired. Even her favorite pink cotton blouse and cream-colored skirt didn't brighten her outlook. Nothing seemed to build her confidence, which to her was disastrous on the first day she was officially to begin work as a vice president.

And then Nelsen unknowingly added to her panic when he called her into his office without warning to meet Bob Geldorf, the mayor's public relations officer. Geldorf had heard about her idea for the Pooley Shoes' Walkathon for Cancer and thought that whoever had come up with it was someone they could use to help with the upcoming I Love New York winter campaign.

She stood there stuttering like a girl just out of college facing her first big assignment. She had met Geldorf before at a cocktail party for the new Duffy Tower Enterprises, but she didn't expect he would remember her.

Geldorf had been a very successful public relations man himself before joining the mayor's campaign four years ago. He was recognized as one of the country's foremost media consultants, and for Jillian, he was something of a cult hero in the business. In his midfifties, Geldorf was a stout, six-feet-three-inch man with graying hair and a lightly freckled face that belied his age. He looked more like a prematurely graying forty-year-old.

"Jillian is a vice president here," Nelsen said as if she had been a vice president for years. "But she's a hands-on executive. You can be sure she'll be directly involved with anything that comes out of her office."

"Good. I'll lay the challenge at your feet, Jillian," Geldorf said. "You know how successful we were using Broadway stars for the I Love New York commercials."

"Yes, I loved them." She thought she sounded inane and told herself to just sit quietly and listen.

"We need an idea that's just as dynamic and just as original. Use the city to sell the city. You understand?" She didn't say anything for a moment, nor did she nod. Geldorf looked to Nelsen.

"I'm sure she does," Nelsen said. "If anyone does."

"Good. Call me in a week and we'll talk."

"I'll get right on it," Jillian said. She got up abruptly, as if she were looking for an excuse to escape, and fled to the sanctity of her own office. She closed the door and sat down, aware that she had broken out in a terrible sweat. She had butterflies in her stomach. When she gazed at herself in the makeup mirror she carried in her purse, she thought she looked even paler than she had after she had first gotten up. Maybe her mother wasn't so wrong; maybe she was coming down with something.

Nelsen had noticed something different about her, too, because he called her as soon as Geldorf left his office.

"You all right?" he asked

"Yes, sure."

"You looked a little peaked. I know there's a summer flu going around."

"No, I'm okay. I was just very excited about the possibilities of the New York campaign."

"I thought you would be. When you come up with something you think worthwhile, stop in."

"I will," she said. After she hung up, she straightened herself in the chair and took on an attitude of determination. She would put Ron Cutler and the weekend out of her mind if it was the last thing she did. She had the mental power to do it. She certainly wouldn't let it ruin her chances for a successful major promotion, not now, not when opportunity was really knocking.

She did get into it, combing through files and setting up concepts with a maddening pace. Rarely had she pursued something as aggressively as she pursued this. The first two days were filled with research and investigation, phone calls and discussions with media people and artists. She brought the work home with her at night. She ate and slept it, until she came up with three possibilities she felt were good enough to present to Nelsen.

Of course, Ron Cutler came to her mind often, but she pushed him out as quickly as he came in, treating his memory and his image as though they were poison. It worked; it was all going well until her phone rang late Wednesday afternoon and she heard his voice.

CHAPTER FIVE

JILLIAN'S FIRST IMPULSE was to hang up on him for a number of reasons. Of course she was angry with him for the way he had treated her, and her pride demanded she be stern; but she also felt threatened. She thought he would take her attention away from the project. She was afraid he would drain her imagination.

She had submerged herself in her work with both a passion and an abandon because she wanted to be possessed by it. In many ways she saw herself the way she saw an athlete. She needed a professional athlete's dedication and determination. Most of all, she needed the same kind of self-sacrifice in order to succeed.

Ron would interfere with her concentration. During the last two days she had almost been grateful for what had happened. In a strange way, she saw it as protective fate. Just at the time she was handed this challenge at the firm, her potentially all-consuming love affair came to an abrupt end. She was, in a sense, free to pursue career objectives without distraction.

But she couldn't hang up on him. It was as if there were another hand pressing down on hers and keeping the telephone receiver at her ear. His voice was captivating, and like some powerful magnet, it was drawing bits and pieces of the past weekend back up to the surface of her mind. The subdued warm images returned. She softened.

She closed her eyes, pressed her hand against her forehead, and listened as attentively as would someone who had had some verbal message implanted in their subconscious mind, a message that triggered obedience.

"I know you must hate me for running off like that, but you were sleeping so soundly."

"I would have been glad to have been awakened."

"I know. All I can say is I'm sorry."

"You can say more. You can start by explaining why you did it," she said in as hard a voice as she could muster.

"I remembered something terribly important and I called my answering service. There was a serious problem up here, one that required my immediate attention."

"In the middle of the night?"

"I'm sorry to say, yes."

"But it's been nearly three days."

"Unforgivable, but you have to believe me. If I could have gotten to you, I wouldn't have been good company and I wouldn't have made good conversation anyway. I wasn't in a good state of mind," he added in a tone of self-pity.

"Is your father all right?"

"Yes. I could lie and say that was it, but it wasn't. For now, I'm just going to have to ask you to forgive me. Think that's possible?"

"I felt pretty bad. I thought…"

"I know. God, I'm sorry. The last thing I want to do is hurt you. I won't do it again, I swear."

She was quiet for a moment. She wanted to be harder and more demanding, but she was unable to phrase the words. Another part of her was overcoming all that. This part of her did not want to drive him away, not even for the sake of her work.

And then, of course, she was curious about him, more curious than ever. What was he up to? Was he sincere? Did something unavoidable really happen and should she be more understanding? How would she feel if it had been the other way around and something to do with her work or her family had caused her to treat him in a similar way? Wouldn't the first thought to come to her mind be something like, if he really cared about me, he'd be understanding?

"Are your problems over?"

"For now. How are you doing? How's the new vice president?"

"Neck deep. I have a chance to do a major project for the city of New York, part of its promotional campaign."

"Sounds heavy."

"It is."

"Is it going to take up your weekend?"

"I don't know. I'm about to make a presentation to Nelsen and if that goes well, I might have some breathing room. What did you have in mind?"

"Provincetown."

"Pardon me?"

"Cape Cod. I thought we'd fly up to the cape and spend two days eating lobster, sailing, walking through the street and looking at the artists."

"Are you serious?"

"Deadly. Will you do it?"

"I—I told you. I'm making a presentation and..."

Illusion

"I know. If it goes well?"

She was surprised by her lack of hesitation. It seemed to come impulsively, as if there really were an entire other person within her, a person who could take complete control at will.

"Yes," she said.

"Good. I'll call you at your apartment tonight about eight, okay?"

"Okay," she said.

"Jillian?"

"Yes?"

"Last weekend was a dream. I have never been happier. The memories helped me overcome my problems."

"I'm glad," she said. She felt tears coming to her eyes. Since when am I so emotional? she wondered.

"Go get that boss of yours. You have an added motivation now," he said, and hung up.

She sat there for a moment with the receiver still pressed against her ear as if there were an echo to his words. Finally she put the phone down and sat back.

Had she gone mad? How could she ever explain this to anyone? Certainly Betty wasn't going to believe it. But she would have to tell someone and get some other reaction, just to be sure she wasn't completely out of her mind. Maybe this was what love did; maybe all those romantic ideas weren't so corny after all. People did act as if they were in a daze.

The buzzer snapped her out of it.

"Jillian, Mr. Grant's back and wants to see you now," Nelsen's secretary said.

"I'll be right there." She looked down at her proposals and suddenly she felt what Ron had suggested she should—she wanted to sell him on her ideas as much for the free time it would buy her as she did for her own career interests. The worst thing that could happen was for her to be sent back to the drawing boards and thus to have to spend the next few days, including the weekend, on coming up with alternatives.

She got up with a sharp look of determination in her eyes and headed for Nelsen Grant's office, carrying her portfolio under her arm and moving truly like a woman possessed.

WHAT SHE THOUGHT was her best idea was the one in which she proposed using ordinary people and avoiding celebrities. The lower cost factors were obvious, but more important was the thrust of what she was trying to say. In a real sense, she had to thank her parents for this one.

"Sure, New York is glamorous and exciting," she told Nelsen, "and the past campaigns have done a good job of using and selling that fact, but you know what makes a great many people in the hinterlands anxious about the city? Its largeness and its apparent impersonality. In their minds people don't live and work here; buildings live and work here. It's cold concrete and metal, and the people in the cabs, in the offices, in the stores and on the streets are just as concrete and impersonal."

Nelsen Grant stared at her in his usually uncommitted fashion. He was a slim, fifty-one-year-old man, who had a mannequin-perfect clean and neat look. His clothes were never uncoordinated; his hair was never untrimmed. Even during the more humid and hot days of summer, Nelsen looked cool and comfortable.

Perhaps his appearance and demeanor were unconsciously designed to compensate for his rather nondescript face. He had a narrow forehead, dull, light brown eyes, sharp cheek and jaw bones, and a small mouth with thin lips. His chin curved under abruptly, making his neck look a trifle long.

His face was rarely animated, and so Jillian often found it difficult to read his thoughts and feelings. If anything, he personified objectivity through that blank but attentive expression. Sometimes she felt she was looking at a mask. Whenever she did see an excitement in his eyes, she was intrigued; and if she saw that she had caused it with one of her ideas, she became even more excited herself. In a way, because of his attitudes and reactions, Nelsen made her strain to go that extra mile and find that special concept or angle.

"You know, my parents, who really aren't what you would call rural people, are somewhat terrified every time they come into the city. They expect to be mugged; they expect problems; they expect people to be nasty to them. They rush in and rush out, grabbing up a dinner or a show and feeling as though they've accomplished something significant by enjoying a part of the city and getting out with their lives and fortunes intact."

Nelsen nodded. His lips tucked in at the corners, the first sign of a positive feeling. He was moving toward a smile, she thought.

"You want to bring this city back to life, you've got to show that it is filled with life, not in the extraordinary sense with which few people can identify, but in the ordinary sense. People who live in New York enjoy New York, so you can enjoy it, too. And safely."

"Uh-huh."

"Geldorf did say he wasn't interested in only filling up theater seats."

Nelsen nodded and his eyes narrowed to focus on the displays she was presenting.

"I've chosen spokesmen and testimony from every socioeconomic level and every significant age group. In this way every advertisement would have maximum reach. Of course, locations are important. I want to show how the city can be many things to many different people and in a true sense is everything anyone would want.

"For example, here you have a senior citizen in one of the senior citizen clubs and..."

She went on and on through her examples. Nelsen began leaning over his desk, the movement in his face becoming more and more emphatic until he broke out in a wide and excited smile. Then he sat back and held up his hand.

"Don't go into detail with the other two ideas," he said. "This is it."

"You want to go with only one?"

"Let's show him how confident we are and how much faith we have in this. Remember old man Goodman when we gave him the concept for his new canned chicken soup? Everyone he saw brought him half a dozen approaches. He was getting more and more confused and then we came with that one, simple concept. 'This is it?' he asked, and I said, 'If something's right, that should be it.' He looked at it again and looked at us and then bought it on the spot. When we're not sure, they're not sure."

"I don't want to go to Las Vegas or Atlantic City with you, Nelsen," she said, and he laughed.

"We'll go see Geldorf tomorrow," Nelsen said.

"You don't want me to change anything or build anything more, get better artwork or..."

"We go just the way it is."

She took a deep breath. Nelsen folded his hands and sat back.

"Okay."

"Jillian, I knew you would throw yourself into this completely. It's obvious that when you make up your mind to do something, you don't let anything interfere. That's what makes you special. You're like a shark, a monomaniac, intense and determined. You seize upon everything with a scientific scrutiny, going right to the heart of the matter. Don't ever change."

She stared at him for a moment. She believed what he said because she knew he could be just as objective and impersonal about people as he could about advertisement. There was no doubt that what he saw in her was really in her. What she questioned now was whether or not she was happy about it.

"A shark," she said.

"Jaws of the advertising world," Nelsen said, and smiled. She shook her head, gathered up her materials, and went back to her office feeling both triumphant and anxious. She wanted to be successful; she wanted to have a good career, but nothing in Nelsen's analysis of her suggested the warm femininity she wanted as well.

She had once had a discussion about this with Betty Dancer. They had been talking about Clara Kaplow, whom they both described as lacking that warm ingredient characteristically feminine. Of course, they recognized that Clara, an orthodox feminist and something of a fanatic at times, wouldn't recognize the existence of such an ingredient. Nothing was characteristically male or female; all was socially, politically, or economically implanted.

"Do you think it's possible for Clara to fall in love in any traditional sense of the word?" Jillian wondered aloud. Betty thought a moment and said she believed it was possible.

"If the right man comes along, he will bring out her femininity."

"If she heard you say that..."

"Why? What's so terrible about that idea? People act upon one another, affect one another, stir things to life that might be dormant in one another. That's what significant interaction means," Betty explained, and Jillian thought she might have a point.

Now she wondered if this was why she was so attracted to Ron. Was he stirring dormant things to life in her and thus in a sense helping her to become a complete woman? Was this why she felt as though another person was living within her? Being different things to different people was an old idea, but what about really being more than one person? Was it schizophrenia or was it normal?

Damn it, she thought, as though she were a reformed nonsmoker catching herself reaching for a cigarette, when will I put a stop to all this self-analysis? When will I stop distrusting good feelings?

That night she looked forward to Ron's phone call. But Betty Dancer called before he did and confirmed their lunch date for the next day.

"I ran into Trish and she said she'd meet us twelve-ish," Betty said. "Of course, we'll start without her. Anything new?" she asked, teasing with musical tones.

Illusion

Jillian described the New York City campaign, but she did it too quickly and nonchalantly. Betty sensed there was something else.

"I'm expecting a call from Ron. Plans for the weekend."

"Oh?"

"I'll tell you about it at lunch."

"Good narrative hook, darling. I'll be on time."

Jillian laughed and hung up. Ten minutes later, Ron called.

"I'm holding my breath," he said.

"Nelsen loved one of my ideas. Actually he didn't even bother examining the other two. We're going with it tomorrow."

"Does this mean what I think it means?"

"Knowing the bureaucracy, we won't get any definite reactions until next week at the earliest, so I'll be free for the weekend."

"How early can you leave?"

"I'll bring an overnight bag to the office. How about three-thirty?"

"Perfect. There's a five o'clock flight we can easily make. The limo and I will be out front. I can't wait to see you."

"I'm looking forward to it, too," she said, but she had that feeling again. Something within her was trying to make her hesitant. Was it just because things were moving so quickly?

They didn't say much more to one another. For some reason he was calling from a pay phone and the operator interrupted.

"See you three-thirty on Friday," he concluded. She went immediately to her closet and dresser and began to consider the things she would pack for the two-night trip.

First she took out the leather moccasins she had bought from the Ixtapa street vendor in Mexico last year. She hadn't really gotten much use out of them, but she couldn't pass up the bargain. She expected she would wear them constantly at the cape.

For the two evenings, she decided on a wraparound blue denim skirt with a light blue bodysuit one night, and a brown cotton skirt with a beige rib-knit top for the other. She debated awhile about her bathing suit and finally determined she would wear the candy-apple red two-piece and go for as much of a tan as possible. The sun was always better at the ocean. She took a lime-green hooded sweatshirt in case the days were cloudy, and decided on the Jordache jeans because they hugged her hips so sensuously. Except for a pair of gold leaf earrings, she took no jewelry.

She had been to the cape only once before. It had been a family trip, but they spent most of their time at a hotel in Hyannis and never really got to see much more. She was in her first year of college and she had heard about Provincetown, but her father said it was filled with queers and hippies and he wasn't about to submit himself to that kind of thing on a vacation. She spent most of her time playing Backgammon with Lois on the hotel veranda or walking with her mother and Lois through the village, waiting to catch sight of one of the Kennedys.

Even so, the cape still held a romantic charm for her because of one afternoon on the beach. She had gone off alone and walked a good mile or so down the surf when she caught sight of a couple, both probably no older than their mid-twenties. They were a good hundred yards or so ahead of her and there was scarcely anyone else on the beach. She felt guilty spying on them, but she was envious of their intimacy and the obvious joy they had in each other's company.

They were as playful as two puppies, gently touching, pulling and pushing on one another, teasing one another with the tide, jogging after each other on the beach, and then stopping to catch their breaths and hold each other closely. After a while they settled into a slow stroll hand in hand. They stopped by a large rock and stood staring out at the ocean, silhouetted against the horizon. She thought she had been vicariously part of a special moment because the image of them standing there remained with her so long. Of course she turned and ran back to the hotel before they saw she had been following.

She remembered that the seemingly insignificant incident left her flushed and excited. She had a hard time falling asleep that night; the sound of the surf was so haunting. The next morning and all the next day she was unusually quiet. Her mother thought she was getting sick, of course; and she finally had to play tennis to get her off her back. She thought she saw the couple one more time walking through Hyannis, but she wasn't sure.

Now the memories returned vividly, and even though she took a book with her to bed and tried to get her mind off the anticipation of the upcoming weekend, she was unable to concentrate on the words. Her eyes kept moving off the page. She saw herself on that beach again, only this time the couple turned around to look at her. Of course, it was Ron and she. Who else could they be? She tried to chastise herself for being so imaginative, but after she had put the lights out and lowered her head to the pillow, she could swear that she heard the sound of the surf. She let it be and eventually fell asleep to the rhythm of the conjured waves.

BETTY WAS LATE for lunch and very apologetic, but they laughed when they realized that Trish had not yet arrived.

"Her 'ish' is becoming longer and longer," Betty said. "She'd be late for her own orgasm," she added, and Jillian laughed. She liked Trish; they all liked Trish. She was so doll-like in looks with her tiny nose and sweet blueberry-colored eyes. Even Betty once said that Trish had a face of confectionery delight: cherry vanilla cheeks and raspberry lips with teeth as white as sugar lumps.

"She's the kind who'll be eighteen forever," Betty said, not without a note of envy.

It was true. Trish had the look of eternal youth. Her features were so small and dainty; her dark-blond hair so thick and soft. She looked synthetic, created by some toy company and made of durable materials designed to stand the test of time and constant use.

Betty thought it was characteristic of Trish to be working for a novelty company.

"Even though it's her brother-in-law's."

"Who else would put up with her lateness?" Jillian asked.

"To this day I don't understand what Trish does there. Whenever I ask her, she always says she's in charge of incoming, whatever that means."

They both laughed and then Betty explained why she almost had to cancel the lunch appointment.

Illusion 103

"We had a crisis on the show," she said. "Chardine Paul and Curt Johnson were having an affair. No secret, it was in *Soap Digest*."

"So?"

"Chardine found out Curt was still seeing his wife. As they say, the separation wasn't working out. It wouldn't be anyone's problem but theirs, of course, if it wasn't for the new script."

"I must confess. I haven't been following the show."

"In the next episode, Chardine, who as you know plays Donna Wild, was supposed to fall in love with Curt, who plays Tony Marco, and, after a rather steamy love scene, she is supposed to leave her doctor-husband and three children. In fact, her opening statement to her husband announcing her departure is the hook at the episode's end. Sometime down the road, that separation doesn't work out, either."

"And when they found out what they had to do?"

"Chardine stormed off the set. Somehow, it fell to me to smooth things out."

"What did you do?"

"I took her aside and we had a long talk about the differences between illusion and reality. I swear to God I felt like I was in a freshman psychology course. I must say I was rather good," Betty said.

"I bet you were. What did you tell her? I'm interested," Jillian asked, leaning forward, but just then Trish arrived.

"Am I late?" she asked as she rushed to their table.

"Just a little-ish," Betty said.

"I told Jimmy's secretary to keep me abreast of the time. She's such a dingbat," Trish said. As usual, she looked out of breath. She unpinned her blue beret and brushed her hair back with the palm of her hand.

"She's a dingbat but you have to be kept abreast of the time," Betty said dryly. "Did you ever hear of something called a wristwatch?"

"Of course, but I get so wrapped up in things. How is everyone? Oh, congratulations, Jillian," Trish said, as if she first realized Jillian was there. "Betty told me about your promotion." Trish bounced in her seat. Jillian smiled at her animation. She was so bubbly it was impossible to be depressed around her.

"Thank you."

"You'll be running your own agency in no time. What's the special today? I'm famished." Trish looked at the menu. When the waiter returned, she ordered a glass of white wine. "There's less of a chance of getting a headache from white wine than from red. I just read that yesterday," she explained, her eyes widening emphatically with the revelation.

"Why don't you just drink club soda if you're so worried about it?" Betty said.

"Oh, I need a pickup. What's happening on the show? I've actually been following it."

"I was just telling Jillian about that."

"Oh?"

"We're having, or rather we had, the intrusion of real life into our world of illusion."

"Yes," Jillian said. "Betty was about to tell me how not to confuse the two."

"That's exactly what I told Chardine. I said if you permit reality to intrude on the illusion we create for our viewers, they'll sense it immediately. They're tuning out reality; they're as sensitive to it as they would be to an orchestra playing off key. They're so into it."

"Why?"

"Pardon?" Betty said.

"Why do you think they're so into it?" Jillian asked.

"Because they can't stand their own boring lives," Trish said. "Everyone knows that. It's why I watch it, too."

"Is that what you think, Betty?" Jillian pursued.

"It's part of it, certainly," Betty said thoughtfully.

"But there's more?" Jillian asked.

"I'm starving. Where's the waiter?" Trish asked.

"Yes, there's more. I think everyone is somewhat schizophrenic; everyone wants to be someone else, actively wants it, I mean, and so they're willing to accept fantasy, suspend disbelief, pay whatever price is necessary to step outside themselves from time to time."

"Hey, I thought this was only a soap opera," Trish said. They both turned to her. She wore a confused expression—her head tilted to one side, her forehead wrinkled, and her mouth pulled in tightly at the corners. Betty and Jillian burst out laughing simultaneously. "Well, what's so funny?"

"Nothing. You're right," Jillian said. She patted Trish's hand. "I forgot how delightful it is to have lunch with you, Trish. You're a welcomed relief. Believe me, I need it," she said, and filled her in on the New York City project and the pressure she had been under.

The waiter returned and they ordered their food. When Betty asked Jillian about Ron Cutler, Jillian had to fill Trish in on that, as well. She brought it all up to date, including his asking her to go to Provincetown.

"I guess I ought to meet you more often. This is turning out to be a saga," Trish said.

"So you told him you would go?" Betty asked.

"Yes. And I'm not sorry I did, either," Jillian added quickly.

"Why should you be?" Trish asked. "He sounds like a wonderful person, and I'm sure he had a good reason for doing what he did."

"I'm not," Betty said. "I'll reserve judgment."

"Oh, Betty, everything is a soap opera to you," Trish said. "There always has to be intrigue."

"How often there is," Betty said. "Sometimes people don't step back into reality when they cross over into illusion."

"Well, if they don't, it's your fault," Trish said. "You produced it."

Jillian laughed.

"*Touché*, my dear," Betty said. "And now fill us in on your love life."

"What love life? I'm married," Trish said. Betty laughed, but Jillian leaned forward with interest.

"You're not serious, are you, Trish? You and Billy still have romantic times, don't you?"

Trish looked at Betty.

"Is she kidding?"

"I don't think so."

Trish stared a moment and then smiled.

"We do, but you know what? We feel silly about it when we do. It's like we're too old to be playing games."

"That's very sad," Jillian said. "I don't want to ever be that old."

"You can't help it. It just happens," Trish said. "Maybe that's why shows like Betty's are so popular."

"That's very good, Trish. Very perceptive," Betty said. "She's right. The women who watch my show can be romantic for a half hour every day and not feel guilty or silly."

"Then illusion is dangerous," Jillian said.

"Why?"

"Because it's a substitute for the real thing; in the long run, it prevents you from experiencing your own real romance, your own adventure, your own life," she added, a lot more dramatically than she intended. Betty and Trish stared at her. "I mean..."

"It's all right," Betty said. "I know what you mean. Be careful, Jill. You're ripe for something now. Make sure it's the right thing."

"How can you ever be sure of that?" Trish asked.

There was a silence. Neither Betty nor Jillian had a good reply. They were grateful for the arrival of their food and the change in topic of conversation it presented. But before they left, Jillian's prospective weekend came up again.

"I've been trying to get Billy to take me to the cape for the past two summers," Trish said.

"It is exciting," Betty confessed. "I hope you have a good time, Jillian. I really do."

"Can't say I'm not nervous about it. I think I'm more nervous about it than I was about the presentation I made to Nelsen."

"Maybe the stakes are higher," Betty said.

"Of course they are," Trish said. "How can you compare success at work with success in love?"

"Hey. That's a great line," Betty said, and winked at Jillian. "Mind if I give it to the writers?"

They all laughed. Jillian thought it was a good omen that their lunch ended on such a happy note. They parted on the sidewalk outside, both Trish and Betty hugging her and wishing her good luck again.

Then she was alone, rushing ahead to the weekend and the mystery and romance of Ron Cutler.

CHAPTER SIX

JILLIAN PAUSED in the doorway of her office building. She leaned back so that no one sitting in the limo parked right outside would spot her. She could see the driver through a portion of the windshield, but Ron was hidden in the back behind the tinted windows. For a moment that seemed symbolic, even prophetic. Whatever it was, it caused her to hesitate, to step aside and take a breath so she could reconsider what she was about to do.

Of course, it wasn't going to be the first time she had spent a weekend with a man, even though she hadn't done it that often; but always before, in the back of her mind, she had the sense that she wasn't making a total commitment, despite the intimacy and despite the intensity of the time she shared with someone. A part of her held onto escape or rejection; there wasn't a feeling of an inevitable future.

But her romance with Ron had been different from the start. She was literally falling into it, sliding down a smooth warm tunnel in which there was nothing to grab on to, nothing to prevent her continuous descent into a relationship that would demand the surrender of some of her freedom, some of her individuality, and some of her private dreams. Compromises, although not necessarily painful ones, had to be made.

She knew this, and knowing this, she had come this far.

For the truth was, she wasn't sliding down that tunnel so much as she was permitting herself to fall. Her passion surprised her, even frightened her a bit. She hadn't thought herself capable of it, and for the longest time she believed that gave her an added advantage whenever it came to relationships with men. Jillian, she told herself as if she could judge herself objectively, always keeps her head above water. Jillian's too sensible to make a fool of herself over a man.

Was she doing this now? Was that what she had seen in Betty Dancer's eyes when Betty said she would reserve judgment about Ron? Maybe Betty was just jealous. What woman could really be trusted when it came to advice about men? Even mothers had clandestine motives whenever they offered opinions or made suggestions.

Trust yourself, trust your own instincts and go on. They haven't disappointed you in the past, she thought, and then she thought, but it was her instincts that were making her so indecisive and demanding that she be so cautious. She made a promise to herself that she would be careful, at the same time recognizing how difficult that might be once she got into the limousine.

She stepped away from the wall and pushed open the door determinedly. It was as if she had crossed a boundary and had made an irrevocable decision. But she moved without regret. The traffic, the noise and the activity around her were invigorating. After all, things were going her way. Nelsen and she had gone to Bob Geldorf with her proposals, and although Geldorf made it clear that everything would be strained through the bureaucracy and take time, he was favorably impressed. He gave them enough of a positive indication to make Nelsen optimistic. Afterward Nelsen suggested that she take a breather, but only because when she got back, she would be heavily involved with the Pooley Walkathon. "Among other things," he added ominously.

The moment the limousine chauffeur spotted her, he was out of the car and around to open the door. She thanked him and peered in. Ron was sitting back comfortably and coolly, even though he was still dressed in a three-piece suit and looked as though he had just walked out of a meeting. He held up a Tom Collins.

The driver took her bag to place in the trunk and she slipped in beside Ron, taking the drink from him at the same time.

"What is this?" she asked, smiling.

"Hi," he said, and kissed her quickly. "From this moment on, you're on vacation. Sit back and forget everything else."

She sipped the drink.

"If I finish this, I won't be able to think," she said.

"I made it too strong?"

"It's all right. I didn't have much lunch and on an empty stomach... Besides, you don't look so casual yourself."

"Sorry I'm still in formal clothes, but I had a meeting in Jersey on the way down."

"Oh?"

"No business talk." He loosened his tie to emphasize his command. She laughed. "I never even asked you. Have you ever been to Provincetown?"

"No. I've been to the cape, but we didn't make it up to the end." She decided against going into the reasons.

"Good. Then everything will be brand new for you, which will make it brand new for me."

"How's that?"

"When you see something familiar through the eyes of someone you care a great deal for, it suddenly becomes brand new for you, too."

"Where did you read that?"

"I didn't read it," he said. He blushed as though she had caught him in some deceit. How sensitive he could be at times, she thought.

"You're a conspirator, Ron Cutler," she said, deciding to tease her way out of it.

"Conspirator?"

"Look around us. A limo, a Tom Collins, a trip to a romantic place, and poetry. I'm in great danger. Don't deny it."

He laughed and the moment was firmly seized. It remained with them all the way. They had another drink at the airport, after he had gone into the men's room and changed from his suit to a pair of designer jeans and a V-neck dark blue Italian knit. It fit him snugly, emphasizing his muscular physique. It was something she sensed he liked to do. He was obviously proud of his body.

"Just got these in the store. What do you think?" he asked, joining her at the bar. She couldn't resist running the palm of her hand over his shoulder and down his arm.

"Soft," she said. "Very nice. You must have pretty good buyers."

"Good people, good people," he said.

"You never get involved in the buying yourself?"

"Yeah, sure, final cut, so to speak. My father has relinquished that area to me."

"Do I detect a note of resentment?"

"No, you do not, and even if you do, we're not getting into that. I told you..."

"I know," she said. "Okay."

They finished their drinks and then boarded the plane. The flight seemed short and smooth. She didn't even think about where they would be staying until the plane touched ground at the Provincetown airport.

"It's really what you would call a rooming house," he said. "It's not fancy, but it's quaint and clean and the woman who runs it, Mrs. O'Shane, is a fixture up here, almost a tourist sight in herself. Don't get into a discussion about where the pilgrims actually landed first."

"How often have you been here?" she asked, not disguising her suspicions and jealousy too well.

"Oh, at one time I did a lot of fishing."

"For what?"

"Hey, take it easy. This is not a trap, believe me."

"I'll reserve judgment about that," she said, and then realized she had used Betty Dancer's words. It brought her down from her excitement for a while, an excitement that wasn't revived until they took the cab to the Portuguese House.

"She's Portuguese, but her husband was Irish," Ron explained. "The house was hers."

"Oh, Ron, this is beautiful," she said when she stepped out of the cab.

The house was located on the north end where the beachfront cut in abruptly, thus giving it something of an isolated look. To the left were the dunes, the national parkland, and although there was a public beach area about a half a mile to the right, the location captured privacy because the house was built on a small rise and surrounded by a picket fence.

The Portuguese House was a long, two-story wooden structure with a single, small, third-story attic apartment facing the ocean. The apartment looked as though it had been constructed as an afterthought. It had a widow's walk built out from it and on the roof. Although the blue shutters on all the windows had been recently freshened, the siding remained a salt-weathered gray. All the front windows were paneled, but as their cab had approached the house, Jillian had seen the large bay window in the dining room that faced the ocean.

There was only a small area of lawn in front of the house and a parking lot on the right and to the rear, in which Jillian saw half a dozen cars.

"That's where we'll be," Ron said after he paid the cab driver. He pointed to the attic apartment. "There's a story about that apartment and why it was built."

"I'll bet." She smiled skeptically.

"You'll ask Mrs. O'Shane, if you think I'm making this up." Ron took their suitcases and started for the front door.

"How do I know she isn't party to all this?"

"Mrs. O'Shane? When you meet her, you'll see she's not the kind of woman who's party to anything she doesn't believe in."

Almost on cue, Mrs. O'Shane opened the front door to greet them. She was a tall woman, standing close to six feet, who wore her silver-gray hair in a tight bun. The hairdo emphasized her large earlobes, each of which had a red tint running through its peak as though she had just come in from a very, very cold day.

Her face was full of color. Her eyebrows were a very dark brown and her eyes were bright almond. There were small apricot-shaded freckles dotted over her emphatic cheekbones. Her cheeks were almost as rosy as the tops of her ears. She wore strawberry-red lipstick. There was a gold chain with a cameo around her neck and a thin gold chain bracelet on her right wrist.

She was dressed in a pair of men's overalls and wore what Jillian thought was a rather heavy, dark blue sweatshirt for this time of the year, even here at the shore. The sleeves had been rolled up close to her elbows, making it look as if she had just interrupted some heavy housework.

Mrs. O'Shane was a full-bosomed woman who looked like she once had had a magnificent figure. Her waist had thickened and her thighs had become heavy, but there was still a very feminine look to the curves in her neck, the smallness in her shoulders, and the way her buttocks turned into her legs. Jillian imagined her to be a woman in her late fifties, but she also had the feeling Mrs. O'Shane was the kind who didn't show her age. It wouldn't be surprising to discover that she was in her late sixties, Jillian thought.

Although there was a warm smile around Mrs. O'Shane's eyes, Jillian recognized the look of someone taking measurements. It gave Jillian the distinct impression that she wasn't the first woman Ron Cutler had brought to Mrs. O'Shane's Portuguese House. As they drew closer, Jillian thought she saw a conclusion. Mrs. O'Shane had an expression of approval. Jillian hoped she wasn't flattering herself.

"Mr. Cutler, right on time. Smooth trip, I take it."

"And quite right you take it, Mrs. O'Shane. This is Jillian Caldwell."

"Welcome to the Portuguese House," she said, and reached out for Jillian's hand. Jillian thought she smelled brandy on her breath, which might explain the flush in her cheeks.

"Thank you. It's so beautiful. I don't think I'd get used to it if I lived here a hundred years."

"That's true, my dear. I never grow bored with the view, but then the ocean has its own mystery and it is never really the same from day to day."

Ron's eyes twinkled with pleasure. Jillian couldn't help feeling that Mrs. O'Shane was a character in a play Ron had constructed. Everything was prerecorded, even the sounds of the surf.

"I suppose I could say the same thing about New York," Jillian said.

"I haven't been there in years," Mrs. O'Shane said. "Come in. Come in." She stepped back to let them enter.

The alcove was small. They went directly into the hallway, which led to a stairway on the right. To the left was the wide entrance to a large sitting room. Jillian saw an elderly Oriental couple seated on the settee that faced a thick-cushioned, Colonial-style couch. The bottle of peach plum brandy and three glasses were on the long dark oak table before them. They both smiled and bowed slightly.

"Mr. and Mrs. Kurosaka," Mrs. O'Shane said. "This is Ron and Jillian."

"How do you do?" Mr. Kurosaka said. His wife smiled.

"Great, now that we're here," Ron said.

"Hello," Jillian said.

She looked quickly at the blue and white wallpaper and the paintings on the walls. Two were of whaling ships and one was a seascape. There was a portrait of what looked to be a very young Mrs. O'Shane hanging over the fireplace, the white marble mantle of which was covered with knickknacks: small pewter figures, some pictures in frames, and an assortment of sea shells.

"The Kurosakas have been here a week," Mrs. O'Shane explained. "They usually come in the fall, but this year decided to try the summer."

"Oh. Which do you like better?" Jillian asked.

"Both have much to recommend them," Mr. Kurosaka said. "The seasons are like fruit. There are times one favors an apple over an orange, but who is to say which is better?"

"I like the summer better," Mrs. Kurosaka said quickly. Jillian and Ron laughed.

"We better go up and get showered and dressed," Ron said softly. "I made reservations at the Beach House."

"Reservations?" Jillian looked to Mrs. O'Shane.

"It was a good idea," she said. "There are a lot of people up here now and the Beach House is not a big restaurant. He couldn't have picked a more romantic spot," she added, "especially with the moon we have tonight. Candles on the table, the lights down low..."

"Hey, don't give it all away," Ron said. Mrs. O'Shane laughed. They started up the stairs.

"I can't believe you called a restaurant from New York," Jillian said.

"Couldn't risk potluck," Ron said. "I want this to be the best weekend you've ever had."

Jillian didn't reply. Mrs. O'Shane led them down the second-floor corridor to a door on the right. The door was so narrow it looked more like the door to a linen closet, but it opened to a short stairway running up to the attic apartment. Walking up to it reminded Jillian of when she once walked up into a small loft in SoHo. The loft served as both a studio and an apartment for a free-lance artist she was using on a project.

They came up right into the middle of the small bedroom. The brass double bed was just about at the center of the room, and the caramel-colored bedspread was folded back to reveal two large fluffy pillows.

Jillian looked about quickly. Except for some small shelves on the far right wall, the walls were bare. It looked as though the dark wooden slats had never been covered with wallpaper, pictures or paintings. Her first impression was that it made the room look cold and barren and she wondered why it had been left this way. Perhaps there was a story to it after all.

Although there wasn't much furniture in the room, what was there looked crowded. There was a big pinewood dresser to the left of the bed, and although the dresser appeared recently polished, it had the look of a worn antique. Maybe it had been left there to give the room authenticity, Jillian thought, because to the left of it was a small table with an attached oval mirror in a hand-carved, white-pine frame. Both pieces looked well over a hundred years old.

The patio door opening to the widow's walk that faced the ocean was on the far left. There was a sheer ivory curtain drawn across the door. Inexpensive and obviously more modern cabinet closets had been placed against the wall to the right of the door. Jillian saw the bathroom was adjacent to the closets.

There was a large, oval, tightly woven, brown and white rug under and around the bed. Other than that, the apartment floor consisted of bare hardwood slats. A small electric heater next to the bed was visible when she walked to the right of it.

"It's not the coziest room I have," Mrs. O'Shane said quickly. She saw a look on Jillian's face. "But it's what Ron wanted. It's what he always wants," she added.

"Now Mrs. O'Shane, tell me honestly. Which room gives a better view than this?"

"This has the best view. I'll grant that."

"And which room has the history this has?" he asked, putting the suitcases down.

"You told her, did you?"

"Told me what?" Jillian asked quickly.

"I said I'd leave it to you."

"I'll bet you did," Mrs. O'Shane said. She narrowed her eyes. "Making me party to something, Mr. Cutler?"

"Oh, no. Honest, all I wanted was for her to hear it from the source," Ron said, raising his hand to take an oath.

"What's this all about?" Jillian asked. Mrs. O'Shane shook a finger at Ron and then turned to Jillian.

"This room was built at the turn of the century for an aunt of mine who went mad when her husband and child were lost at sea. She never accepted it. Kept the table set for them and talked about them as though they were away for only a short while. Finally my grandfather took her back into this house and had this apartment built. The widow's walk was to keep her happy. She could sit out there and wait for the boat to return. Understand?"

"What happened to her?"

"One day she just walked into the ocean and drowned. Maybe she finally realized they weren't coming back."

"How sad."

"Yes it was, but it's the only sad thing about this house and my family. We're a strong people normally." She paused and looked about. "You have towels and washcloths in the bathroom. There's shampoo and soap. Just yell if you need anything else."

"Thank you," Ron said.

"I hope you enjoy it," Mrs. O'Shane said, smiling, and then went back down the stairs. For a moment Jillian just stood still, embracing herself.

"Was that all for real?"

"Who knows? It makes for good local color. I told you."

"It gives me the chills," Jillian said. Ron smiled.

"Good. You'll need to be warmed, then," he said, and he embraced her. After they kissed she shook her head.

"You're a pretty complicated man, Ron Cutler."

"Makes it more interesting, doesn't it?"

"Yes and no."

"Ready to shower?" he asked before she could pursue it any further. "I don't want to be late for our reservations. This restaurant is unique."

"What on this trip isn't?" Jillian went to her suitcase and then in to shower. After she came out of the bathroom, she decided to wear the brown cotton skirt and the beige rib-knit first. She dressed while Ron went in to shower. She sat at the vanity table and brushed her hair quickly, thinking all the while about Mrs. O'Shane's distraught aunt.

Perhaps she had sat at this table night after night, preparing herself for the return of her husband and child. What did she see when she looked in the mirror? Certainly not reality. She projected an illusion into herself. Maybe she wasn't so mad after all, Jillian thought. So many people were doing it. How many people saw the truth when they looked in a mirror? Did she see the truth? she wondered.

Ron emerged from the bathroom fully dressed. He wore another Italian knit. This one was black, which she thought made him look very sexy. For a long moment they just looked at one another.

"If this dinner wasn't so special," he said, "I'd want to spend the whole night locked in here with you. I wouldn't care about eating or seeing other people."

"We could have done that anywhere."

"Maybe. But sometimes I think doing things that are illogical or impractical is what makes a relationship special. Love should leave you a little crazy," he added. She started to smile, but stopped because he looked so serious and he wasn't relinquishing the expression.

He kissed her, but when they parted she thought she saw a look of confusion in his face. There was something in his eyes that suggested reluctance. For a few moments he didn't move or say anything. It was as though he really didn't know what to do next.

"Is this the effect my kisses have on you?"

"Huh? Oh, I was just trying to remember if I had specified the right table at the Beach House," he said quickly.

"There's a right table?"

"You'll see. Come on."

Mrs. O'Shane was waiting for them when they came down the stairs. Two other couples were in the sitting room: Ted and Alice Hickman from Old Westbury, Long Island, and Ralph and Jan Glick from Scranton, Pennsylvania. Both the Hickmans were well into their fifties, but the Glicks looked about Ron's and Jill's age. The Hickmans said they were on something of a second honeymoon.

Ron ended the conversation abruptly by pointing out that they had to make a dinner reservation, but Jill sensed that he wanted to avoid conversation for other reasons, as well. She assumed that one of them was his desire to be alone with her, but there was something else about the way he talked and looked at people. He made her feel he was a fugitive, afraid of having his real identity discovered. There was a sense of urgency to their exit.

Mrs. O'Shane had given him the keys to her Jeep, which looked like World War II vintage. The cloth top was down and the seats felt damp. Ron wiped hers with a towel left draped over his.

"Nice of her to let you use it," she said, even though she was a little afraid of what the ride would be like.

"It's part of the arrangement I have with her whenever I come up here. I pay her a rental. I thought you might enjoy this, even though it's roughing it a bit." He started the engine and it sounded as though it might explode. "I see she still hasn't fixed that exhaust pipe."

"Sure this is safe?"

"Yeah. But hold on," he said, shifting into first. They pulled out of the driveway and headed down the beach road. He wasn't driving fast, but the openness made it feel that way.

"So much for my hairdo," she said.

"What?"

"My hairdo!" she shouted. He looked at her and nodded.

"Nice."

"No. Oh, what's the difference," she said, laughing, and settled back to get a glimpse of the ocean whenever it came clearly into view.

The Beach House did look like something cut out of a dream when it first appeared before her. Built out on a cove, it was literally draped in moonlight. She had the feeling that if she came here in the daytime, she wouldn't find the small restaurant there. She thought it must appear magically when the sun went down and the silvery lunar corridor appeared over the glassy surface of the ocean.

The restaurant had a maximum capacity of about seventy guests. The walls were covered with the seaworn wood of old ships, or at least that was the story the owner related. There were fishnets on the ceilings, but no overhead illumination, the primary lighting coming from oil lamps on the small, round tables that looked cut out from the decks of sailing vessels.

Beside the main room, there were three small separate areas, each housing a table for two, on the north end. Obviously it was for one of these that Ron had made his long-distance reservation. Jillian was glad about it. Cut off from the main dining area, they sat in what was an especially private and beautiful part of the restaurant. It provided an unobstructed view of the ocean and consequently, was, as Mrs. O'Shane had suggested, awash in the evening's moonlight.

Ron smiled at her reaction.

"This is special," she said. He took her hand and when she looked at him, the warmth in his fingers moved up her arm with an electric speed that brought a flush to her neck and face. My God, she thought, I've fallen in love so quickly.

There was something about the intimacy of the restaurant that kept the conversations of people subdued. The waiters and waitresses moved on what Jillian fantasized to be a shelf of air. They glided in between tables and around one another with a minimum of conversation. Even the clatter of dishes and silverware was muffled. Opened windows, especially where they were sitting, permitted the sound of the surf to become the background music.

It was easy to feel she and Ron were alone, cut off from not only the rest of the Beach House clientele, but from the real world, as well. Her attention was drawn between Ron and the moonlight on the water, each pulling her with its own magnetic power. She grew dizzy on the wine, the quiet words, the good food, and the softly illuminated sea.

There wasn't all that much conversation between her and Ron. It was as though every word carried such significance that they had to weigh each syllable carefully for its phonics as well as its meaning. There was a rhythm and a music to everything, whether it be the passing of the salt shaker or a laugh or simply a long moment of silence while they ate and stared at one another.

At one point toward the end of the meal she looked up at him and thought his face was unusually luminescent. His eyes absorbed the moonlight and there was something both fascinating and eerie about his look. The feeling passed quickly, but it was part of the emotional high that left her drunk on the sound of his voice and the feel of his fingers pressed against hers.

He drove back to Portuguese House much slower than he had driven to the restaurant. She was able to lean against his shoulder and close her eyes to enjoy the cool breeze blowing against her face and through her hair. They said little to one another, both realizing that words now had the dangerous capability to shatter the moment that was as precious and as fragile as thin crystal.

The house was quiet when they entered. There was no one in the sitting room and Mrs. O'Shane wasn't about. They glided like ghosts up the stairway to the attic apartment, saying nothing, moving through gestures rehearsed a thousand years before. Their clothing fell away quickly but softly, peeled like rose petals off each other's bodies with gentle hands.

Jillian thought that even their lovemaking was dreamlike because of the subdued manner in which they touched. Each time he kissed her, he paused as though to see if the spell would be broken. It wasn't.

They pressed onward, finding each other's sex not with novelty and the excitement of discovery, but with a quiet awareness that gave Jillian a feeling of mystery as well as passion. For a moment she had the vision of two lovers from a previous existence finding each other once again centuries later, their love reborn in new bodies, but not in new souls. The wild fantasy gave credence to the whispered words of love: "I have waited for you all my life."

There was something holistic about their lovemaking now. It was impossible to isolate any part of it from the entirety. Every kiss, every touch, every moan and word melded. The impact was total, carrying her in smooth undulation up and out of her body.

When it was over, they lay silently together. The breeze made the curtain on the doorway to the widow's walk dance. She felt an urge to say something, to tie their physical communication together with some words of great significance. She hoped Ron had the same need, but when she turned to him, he looked distant. She decided against breaking the silence.

Instead she closed her eyes and let the breeze continue to caress her body. It was as though the room had powers of mesmerism. Its smallness, its aged furniture, its view over the moonlit ocean hypnotized her. Indeed she had fallen into a spell of sorts. She closed her eyes.

Perhaps she only had been asleep or perhaps their lovemaking had bewitched her and caused her to lose a sense of time and place, but when she opened her eyes again, she was confused and disoriented. Ron was no longer beside her on the bed and low and fast-moving clouds had all but blocked out the moon. It took a moment for her eyes to get used to the darkness.

She sat up when they did. The door of the widow's walk was open. She rose from the bed and walked to it. Looking out, she saw Ron standing by the railing, gazing intently into the darkness as though he could see something clearly in the night. She didn't understand why, but that frightened her for a moment and she uttered a small cry.

He turned, but she was unable to see his face in the shadows. For a long moment he said nothing. Then he seemed to finally realize she was there.

"Are you all right?" he asked.

"Yes. What are you doing?"

"Just getting a little air. Might be cloudy in the morning, but it's going to clear."

"Then we won't get up until it does," she said.

"Oh, no. We're going to have one of Mrs. O'Shane's famous early breakfasts and then I want you to see the fisherman." He walked back in and embraced her around the waist. "Let's go back to bed. It's been a wonderful night, hasn't it?"

"Yes," she said. He kissed her on the cheek.

Afterward, when she was lying down again, she turned away from him and for a moment thought about him standing out on the widow's walk looking into the darkness.

What did he see out there? She fell asleep in the grip of the question.

CHAPTER SEVEN

THE MOOD for the remainder of the weekend changed dramatically. Instead of things being dreamy and sensual, they were jolly and upbeat. It began with a hearty breakfast. Mrs. O'Shane had prepared something she called flippers, a deep-fried dough served with syrup. There was also Portuguese bread, eggs, juice and coffee. Everything was served on hand-painted heavy china, the work of a local artist. Even the table and chairs had been built by a Provincetown carpenter, a man Ron claimed had also been one of Mrs. O'Shane's many lovers.

The Kurosakas and the Hickmans joined them. Ron's conversation with them was quite lively compared to the way he had been the night before. He spoke enthusiastically about his department stores, exhibiting a great deal of family pride. He even jested about being one of Jill's potential clients.

After Mrs. O'Shane served the food, she joined them and made all sorts of suggestions as to where they should shop, what artists to seek, what galleries to visit, what scenery to experience, and what restaurants to go to for dinner. Jillian thought Ron had been right about her—she was a one-woman chamber of commerce for Provincetown.

But Jillian admired her for her passion. It was good to have commitments; it was good to feel strongly about something, she thought. Too many of the people she knew were committed to nothing but themselves.

Ron surprised her again with his planning when they went down to the dock. Many of the boats were in final preparation for a day's deep-sea fishing. Tourists were everywhere, some loud and boisterous about their expected accomplishments, others a little terrified at the prospect of seasickness.

After they watched some of the departures, Ron walked her toward the end of the dock where a beautiful sailboat named *Phantasia* was moored.

"So you lived in a Long Island sea town and you never got hooked on sailing, huh?" he asked as they both stood looking at the boat.

"Like I told you, my family wasn't into it."

"No boyfriends that were?" he asked playfully.

"Sorry to disappoint you."

"You don't know what you missed." He looked up at the sky. "Clouds are breaking up, just as they predicted. It's going to be gorgeous. Let's take a closer look at this boat." He walked over the gangplank and stepped down to the deck.

"Ron? Should you do that? I mean, I don't think people like strangers on their boats. I know they didn't like it where I was."

"Nonsense. New Englanders are more hospitable."

He reached up for her. She looked about and then reluctantly permitted herself to be pulled forward and onto the boat.

"Ah, what the hell," he said as soon as she was aboard. He pulled off the gangplank and undid the docking.

"Ron!"

A moment later he started the small outboard and then smiled at her.

"Take a seat."

"What are you doing?"

He laughed and shifted the engine to drive the boat away from the dock. She sat down quickly in shock. A moment later the ship's owner stepped out of the cabin. She looked up at him expectantly and then at Ron, the smile widening on his face.

"You no good son of a..." He laughed.

"This is Captain Carter," he said, and the fifty-two-year-old sailor tipped his hat. Jillian thought he had the weathered look of Spencer Tracy in the film of Hemingway's classic, *The Old Man and the Sea*. There was a twinkle in his eyes. He obviously enjoyed being part of the ruse.

"Once around the block, sir," Ron said, and Captain Carter went about the business of hoisting the sails and getting under way. Jillian joined Ron at his bench seat and they both sat back, his arm around her, as the wind gathered in the sails.

"This was very deceitful of you," she said.

"I knew if I asked, you might chicken out," he said. "And I didn't see any sense of coming all the way to the cape without going for at least one sail."

"Last night you didn't want to leave the room."

"Call me unpredictable. It's undeniably true," he sang. "That I am simply mad about you."

"Serenaded on a sailboat. What chance does an innocent, young girl have?" she asked. He kissed her cheek. The sailboat picked up speed and the spray showered them. She screamed with delight and excitement as the *Phantasia* dipped into the oncoming waves and sent them rolling toward the horizon. Ron tightened his embrace. A rather heavy sea spray splattered them, soaking both their faces in the warm saltwater. "Ron Cutler, I'm going to kill you," she said, but despite her initial fear she couldn't remember enjoying anything as much as this surprise ride on the *Phantasia*.

Ron had been right about the weather. The sky cleared and became a soft blue with lazy, fluffy, custard clouds. After they returned from sailing, they walked down the narrow streets window-shopping and stopping to observe various artisans at their craft. Ron bought her a bracelet made of sea shells and a hairband with a blue and white design she admired. She bought him a hand-carved leather key case. The gifts were ways of capturing a happy moment.

They had lunch out on the dock and watched some of the boats returning with good catches. There was an endless parade of tourists, yet the activity, the crowds and the noise did not detract from the warmth developing between them. It amazed her how she could feel so alone and private with Ron, even though they were seated in the midst of so many people. Whenever they wanted to, they could turn everything off around them by merely taking one another's hand or gazing intently into each other's eyes.

Ron bought them tickets for a tour of the dunes and during the early part of the afternoon, they sat in a dune buggy with a half a dozen other tourists and bounced over the hills of sand and down long stretches of undeveloped beach. Occasionally they came upon a shack or two, but other than that, Jillian was fascinated with the raw, natural state of the land. They could see where the ocean during particularly vicious storms had clawed out gaping holes in the coast and where the timeless and constant waves stroked the large rocks into glistening jewels of the sea.

After the tour ended, they returned to Portuguese House and put on their bathing suits for an ocean swim. Mrs. O'Shane provided them with a beach blanket and they spent the remainder of the afternoon sunning and swimming.

When Ron put on his bathing suit, Jillian's impressions about his physique were reinforced. His shoulders gleamed in the sunlight and his arms looked thick with muscle. There was a tightness in his body that seemed more than the result of frequent fitness workouts. He had a hardness about him that suggested long hours of manual labor.

When they lay together on the blanket, she traced a thin scar down his left thigh. He was oblivious of the touch of her fingertip, so she asked him about it.

"Oh, that. Bicycle accident."

"Bicycle?"

"Well, not exactly a bicycle. A motorcycle. Haven't flipped since."

"Don't tell me you still ride one."

"Why not?" He propped himself up on his elbows.

"I don't know. I just didn't think of you as the..."

"The type? Why, do you think it's low class or something?" he asked with uncharacteristic bitterness.

"No." She retreated to her back again. "I was thinking about the danger, that's all."

"Yeah, well, sometimes you need a little danger in your life," he said. There was a silence between them for a few moments and then he laughed and got up to coax her into the ocean for a final dip.

When they returned to the rooming house, Mrs. O'Shane invited them for cocktails. They showered and dressed, Jillian putting on her wraparound denim skirt with the light blue bodysuit. She put on the hairband he had bought her and her gold leaf earrings. Mrs. O'Shane thought she was dressed perfectly for P-Town.

"So many of the women who come up here overdress," she added, glancing toward Ron. Jillian assumed she was referring to one or more of the women he had brought to Portuguese House before. "There's something about simplicity."

"Thank you."

They were joined by the Glicks. The Hickmans had gone off to an early dinner, and the Kurosakas hadn't returned yet from an all-day excursion. As they sat around talking, Jillian couldn't help but compare herself and Ron to Jan and Ralph Glick.

The Glicks said they had been married for three years. They had no children and from the way Jan Glick spoke, Jillian thought they would never have any. They struck her as a couple who were quite engrossed in themselves, but not in themselves as a couple so much as in themselves as two distinct individuals. In fact, their individuality was so important to them that they took pains not to give the impression that either spoke for the other, whether it be merely an opinion about wine or a place to spend a lifetime.

Jillian thought they had a marriage of convenience. She would have almost called it a partnership. They were so intent on finding ways in which they could be of use to one another; their conversation was filled with examples of their trade-offs. From just this relatively short conversation, Jillian learned of a number of crises their marriage had endured. Perhaps it is a good thing that they have no children, she thought. They measure everything they do for one another too accurately, and children know no limits when it comes to the demands of love.

What was missing the most was the passion. Did they, could they have once had it? And to the extent that she and Ron seemed to have it now? True passion meant true sacrifice, she thought. These people didn't know the meaning of the words. They couldn't have ever been like the way she and Ron were now.

She was glad when they excused themselves to make their dinner reservation.

"I wonder what surprise Mr. Cutler has in store for me tonight," Jillian said to Mrs. O'Shane.

"Nothing special. Just a little steak and lobster place I know in town," he said.

"Brando's?" Mrs. O'Shane asked. He nodded. "It's the best steak and lobster restaurant on the cape," she told Jillian.

"I believe you."

"You can spare a moment," she said to Ron. "I want to show Jillian something special myself."

"Sure. I forgot something up in the room anyway. I'll give you five minutes, but that's all," he said. They watched him go and then Mrs. O'Shane took Jillian onto the back deck.

"The weather has been wonderful," Jillian said, taking in the warm night air.

"Yes, it has. You remember when you first came and we joked a bit about never being bored with the scenery? Well, look out there toward the lighthouse. See the lights of those ships?"

"Yes. How beautiful."

"It's fun to wonder who they are and where they're going. My husband used to make up so many stories about ships in the night. He had a telescope mounted on the railing here and he would fill me with fiction after fiction. He knew this one and that one. He was a lobster fisherman when we first met."

"How long has he been dead?"

"Nearly fifteen years, and you know, sometimes, I get the strange feeling that he's going to come out of the house or walk up the beach. Maybe I'm coming down with the same mental illness my aunt suffered," she said, and she laughed.

"I don't think I'd be any different about it," Jillian said. Mrs. O'Shane nodded softly.

"It's nice to see a couple enjoying themselves as much as you and Ron are," she said suddenly. "It makes me feel young again."

Jillian hesitated for a moment. She didn't want to sound like a detective, but she felt Mrs. O'Shane would understand her curiosity.

"Ron has been here often, hasn't he?"

"Oh, he's been here every summer off and on for the last five years. He's a very handsome, self-confident young man. He reminds me a great deal of the way my Kevin was. There's an earthiness about him that makes you feel he's true. I've not often seen it in New York executive types. He lacks the slickness, if you know what I mean? Of course, that might just be some of my New England prejudice showing itself."

"No, I think I know what you mean," Jillian said. "It's what I admire about him, too."

"I hope you'll be back here again," Mrs. O'Shane said. She smiled gleefully.

"So do I," Jillian said.

"Hey." Ron was standing in the doorway. "That's five minutes."

"Heaven forbid I steal another second," Mrs. O'Shane said.

"Thanks for the cocktails," Jillian said, starting back to the house.

"My pleasure. I enjoyed your company and the way you baited that other young lady, too. Don't deny it," she added before Jillian could speak. Jillian laughed.

"What's that all about?" Ron asked.

"Never you mind. Just go have a time of it while there's still time to have it," Mrs. O'Shane said.

"Okay, but next time we come up here, I hope you have that exhaust pipe fixed on that Jeep."

"What, and take away the Jeep's character?" Mrs. O'Shane asked. Everyone laughed and then Ron and Jillian left for the trip into Provincetown center.

"She's a remarkable woman. I like her," Jillian said after they got into the Jeep.

"Somehow, I knew you would."

"I'm having the best time of my life," Jillian said impulsively. She leaned against Ron's right shoulder and he smiled widely. "Don't look so darn awful proud of yourself, Ron Cutler."

"Why not? I got me a New York woman, don't I?" He laughed after he said it, but there was such a sinister sound to his laugh that Jillian didn't join in.

"I hope you're doing more than gathering trophies, Mr. Cutler," she warned. He looked down at her and saw she was serious.

"Much more," he said. "Much more."

She felt herself relax again. He was such a paradox, but she was falling deeper and deeper in love with him despite it. Maybe that was a truer test of sincere feeling. Somehow she knew it wouldn't be long before she knew for sure.

JILLIAN THOUGHT THE DINNER at Brando's was as good as Mrs. O'Shane had suggested it would be. But then again, she knew that in the state of mind she was in, anything and everything that happened on this weekend was beautiful or wonderful. Her senses were running at such a high intensity, she was afraid she would burst with happiness. Every sound she heard, whether it be the tinkle of glasses or laughter from a couple at another table, was melodious, a part of a symphony created by Venus herself.

Vaguely she understood that her judgments were unreliable. She was inebriated, drunk on the moment, on the sound of Ron's voice, on the look in his eyes, and on the way she felt whenever they touched. Catching a glimpse of herself reflected in a mirror on the wall of the restaurant, she thought she looked different...not distorted like one really intoxicated from booze, but instead, changed into someone even younger and more radiant. Perhaps it was true: the right man could bring the full woman out of you. She imagined telling this to Betty Dancer. Knowing Betty, Jillian expected she would tease her and threaten to turn it into a plot for her soap.

She giggled on the thought and Ron looked up expectantly. They were having coffee and he had become quiet and pensive, which had permitted her to dwell on her own thoughts for a while.

"What's so funny?"

"Nothing."

"Come on," he said. "It's not fair."

"Well, I was laughing at myself. I feel like such a...such a schoolgirl."

"Why?" The smile faded from his face. "You regret what we've been doing?"

"Oh, no. *Je ne regrette rien.*"

"Huh?"

"French. Edith Piaf. I regret nothing."

"Who's Edith Piaf?"

"A famous French singer. You never heard of her?" she asked. He bristled.

"I wouldn't have asked if I had."

"There was a Broadway show about her a few years ago. *Piaf.* It was wonderful."

"I see. So, then, why did you laugh?"

"I don't know. The unexpected way I feel, I guess. It makes me giddy."

"I was hoping for more," he said sadly.

"Oh, there's more." She reached across the table and took his hand. "Believe me. I meant it when I said this is one of the most wonderful weekends of my life."

"Good. Then maybe you won't think it too wild of me to propose another idea."

"Not going back tomorrow?" she asked. "I can't. I just have to..."

"No, nothing as serious as that."

"Then what?"

"This," he said, and opened up his closed hand.

For a moment she thought it might be part of some new ruse. She half expected the waiter to arrive with a bottle of champagne from the owners and an announcement to be made so that the other customers would offer a round of applause. Then she would take the ring out of his palm and discover it was a toy.

But this didn't look like any toy; it looked like the real thing...at least a karat and a half set in white gold. The stone glittered in the candlelight. She didn't reach for it, but she didn't take her eyes from it. He moved his hand closer and she backed away instinctively.

"Ron?"

"I know it seems fast, but when something feels as right and as good as we do together, why wait? We're inevitable."

"I don't know what to say."

"Just take the ring. That says it all."

"But...it is fast, and such a big step. You went and bought a ring," she said, as though to drive the fact home to herself.

"Well, actually, it was my mother's. She gave it to me a long time ago with instructions to give it only to the one woman I knew would make my life complete."

"Oh, God, Ron." She plucked the ring from his palm carefully and held it up before her as though the jewel were a miniature crystal ball and all the answers for the future were soon to be revealed. "I can't give you an answer to this now. I mean...it's not fair. I'm drunk on all our happiness. That's why I was laughing at myself. A decision like this has to be made sensibly, carefully, soberly. Do you understand?"

"I don't want to understand." He looked as if he would turn angry, but then his face softened. "But I do. All right, don't give me an answer this weekend, but take the ring."

"But why?"

"I want it to haunt you. At least grant me that."

"It will. That's dirty pool," she said, but she held onto the ring. "It's beautiful and beguiling, as beguiling as you are with your Portuguese House and your Mrs. O'Shane and your romantic restaurants."

"Don't fault me for being a good planner," he said, smiling. "Anyway, I'm in love with you, Jillian. Hopelessly in love. There wasn't anything else I could do." He leaned forward and kissed her. Her eyes were still closed when he sat back. She felt tears come to them and she wanted to keep them within.

"Let's go," she said. "Let's just walk through those charming streets and not talk."

"Okay."

They did just that and for a good twenty minutes or so neither of them spoke. The sounds of a guitar and a banjo and some singing drew them to a small café. They stood in the doorway awhile, looking in and listening. Jillian quickly realized that the crowd was gay. There were only two women and both of them looked like lesbians.

"You want to have a cup of coffee here and listen?"

She studied him a moment. He didn't realize what the place was. She would have thought him more sophisticated. Maybe his mind was concentrated too hard on other things. In any case she understood he might resent her pointing out the obvious, or at least what she thought was the obvious.

"No. Let's just head back."

"Fine."

They returned to the Jeep and started for Portuguese House. Along the way Ron pulled over so they could sit and admire a particularly scenic view of the ocean and shore. Jillian saw the lights of the ships on the horizon and thought about Mrs. O'Shane and their conversation. For some reason it left her feeling sad. Right now it was as though she were coming down from a particular high. The excitement of their activity, the intensity of their contact with one another, and all of it climaxing with Ron presenting her with the ring suddenly became emotionally exhausting. She half wished she could go off by herself for a while and just think.

"I guess you think I'm crazy," he said softly, not turning away from the ocean, "offering you a ring so fast, but it seemed to be something Ron Cutler should do."

"If Ron Cutler feels it's right to do it, he should. I don't think it's crazy. A bit impulsive maybe." She laughed. He looked at her and then shook his head.

"You don't have to hold onto the ring if you don't want to."

"Getting soft or having second thoughts?" she asked.

"Oh, no. I just don't want to hurt you."

"I'm a big girl now," she said. "If I hold onto the ring, it's because I want to. Don't worry."

"Okay, but don't say I didn't warn you."

He backed onto the road again and they continued on to Portuguese House. The Kurosakas were in the sitting room talking to Mrs. O'Shane, relating the details of their excursion. She and Ron resisted the invitation to join them.

"Lovers," they heard Mrs. O'Shane say after they excused themselves and started up to the attic apartment.

They did go up to make love, but Jillian found Ron was different this time. He was more aggressive, more demanding, almost as though he were making love out of frustration and anger. He behaved like a man trying to prove something to himself. When he saw that he was frightening her, he calmed down and became more like the Ron with whom she had first arrived. Afterward, he fell asleep before she did.

For a long time she tossed and turned in the bed. Her mind was filled with so many conflicts. Maybe it was because of the cocktails and the wine, but at one point she looked up and thought she saw someone out on the widow's walk. She started to laugh at the power of her own imagination when she saw the curtain on the doorway flutter. She slipped out of bed quietly and went to it. The door was opened slightly. It was only the breeze.

Nevertheless she stepped out on the walk, intending to go to the railing. She had taken only a few steps when Ron came up behind her, approaching so silently she nearly screamed.

"What's wrong?"

"My God," she said. "You scared me, moving so quietly. I just wanted to... I thought I saw someone out here."

"What?"

"Don't laugh. It's your fault, bringing me to a haunted room."

"Okay, okay, but if there is a ghost here, it's a good ghost. You know, ghosts can be good, too," he said, his voice rising as though he really meant it. She started to laugh.

"Now you're an expert on the supernatural. All right," she said. "Let's go back to bed. I'm sorry."

"That's all right." He followed her in, looked out on the walk for a moment and then closed the door. In bed he embraced her. She turned and pressed her head against his chest. He was warm and comforting. She felt secure and protected. She fell asleep dreaming of ships passing each other softly in the night.

They rose early in the morning and had another one of Mrs. O'Shane's fabulous breakfasts. Afterward she and Ron walked along the beach gathering interesting sea shells. Shortly after they returned to Portuguese House, their taxi arrived to take them to the airport. Mrs. O'Shane said goodbye to them on the porch. Jillian lingered behind for some final words while Ron saw to their luggage being loaded into the taxi.

"It was like stepping in and out of a dream," Jillian said. "I just loved it here."

"It won't always be this way," Mrs. O'Shane said. "It's foolish to think that it would, but there is something special about seeing the world with someone you love. I miss that. Some of us are strong enough to go on with only the memories and some of us...are more like my aunt, refusing to let go."

"I can't blame her," Jillian said, looking up at the attic apartment. "In fact, I feel almost as though I know her now, since we spent two nights in her apartment." They were both silent a moment and then Jillian laughed. "You think I'm silly."

"No, I don't. Good luck," Mrs. O'Shane said. They hugged and Jillian got into the taxi. Jillian couldn't help looking back at the house, locking the picture into her memory. Mrs. O'Shane remained in front until they disappeared from sight.

Jillian dozed on and off during the uneventful trip back to New York. The limo was waiting for them at the airport and they started out for her apartment.

Almost as soon as they got onto the expressway, the reality of the city impressed itself upon her. She was back in the real world and that made all that had happened over the weekend seem even more dreamlike.

Ron made no effort to remain with her much longer. They kissed after he dropped her off. She thanked him for a magnificent time, but he seemed to resent that. Maybe it was just their arrival back in the world of work and the contrast between the upbeat activity of the city and the quiet, scenic beauty of the cape, but whatever it was, she sensed that it had an effect on Ron, too. He was shorter with his words, impatient with traffic, unusually nervous and withdrawn. He was tense. For a moment she felt like Cinderella, afraid that her carriage would turn back into a pumpkin before she had returned.

"I'll call you tomorrow night," he said, but he didn't mention the ring. It was almost as if he had forgotten he had given it to her to hold and to consider.

"All right."

She stood in the doorway of the apartment building and watched the limo go off with Ron hidden behind the darkly tinted windows. Suddenly she had a terrible chill; she had been given a premonition.

Illusion

She thought it was stupid and refused to accept the words. She blamed it on her infatuation with the ghost of Mrs. O'Shane's aunt, but the words followed her into the apartment and remained with her as she rode up the elevator. They were still on the tip of her tongue when she opened her apartment door and set her overnight bag on the bed. They repeated themselves as she walked into the living room to check her phone messages.

Finally she took out the ring and put it before her on the living-room table.

"There," she said to the voice whispering within her. "It was real."

Nevertheless she touched the engagement ring to be sure it was really there before her. The feel of it was reassuring and the whispering came to an end.

But for some reason she suspected it would return.

CHAPTER EIGHT

FROM THE MOMENT she woke up Monday morning, Jillian was on an emotional high. It reinforced her belief that the weekend had changed her. Her senses were electric. Everything looked different: the colors in her apartment were sharper and brighter, the furniture looked newer, and when she looked at herself in the mirror, she saw that her eyes sparkled with an alertness she rarely felt. Even the morning news on the radio didn't depress her the way it often did. She felt invulnerable; nothing could burst her bubble.

She had all but made a definite decision to accept Ron's proposal. After she had settled in last night, she didn't call anyone. Instead she sat quietly in her living room and considered Ron's offer of engagement. She and her stuffed Snoopy debated it. Being what Snoopy was and represented, she had to give him the positive viewpoint. She imagined his opening statement.

"You've never been like this with any man before. I've never seen you so radiant, so alive. He must be good for you."

"It's always like that in the beginning. Even Mrs. O'Shane made the point that things wouldn't be as intense," she said.

"So what? You don't want them to be that intense. Who could live that intensely, day in, day out?"

"I don't really know him as well as I should."

"You made love to a man and you don't know him as well as you should?" Snoopy seemed to tilt his head and take on a look of disapproval.

"Making love is one thing; committing your life is another. What would I have to sacrifice?"

"You never got into that."

"I'd have to know that before I accepted."

"You can see he's the type of man who would not cramp your style."

"I don't want to leave my career and New York," Jillian said quickly. She couldn't help feeling as if she were scrambling for excuses.

"You won't have to; you know that. Come on, you're just creating false obstacles. You and Ron will buy a co-op and you'll have the country home as a weekend retreat. He can do it. He wouldn't be proposing if he couldn't."

"I don't know. I want to say yes, but I..."

"You're afraid. Admit it. You're afraid of commitment. Your mother's right about you."

"No, that's not it. Or is it? Oh, Snoopy." The stuffed animal stared at her. "I can't fool you, can I, Snoopy? You know me too well."

She got up and hugged the soft, toy dog.

"It's true," she said. "I am afraid of commitment, but I'm going to overcome it because he's right for me and I'm right for him. Thank you, Snoopy," she said, and kissed him.

Even though she was ninety-nine percent sure that she would say yes to becoming engaged, she didn't put the ring on in the morning. It seemed wrong to do so before speaking to Ron and telling him she would. Until she did so, she locked it in a jewel box and put it at the bottom of a lower dresser drawer. Then she went to the office.

Before she could say good morning, Betty Lincoln greeted her with the news that Nelsen wanted to see her as soon as she arrived. As usual it was impossible to tell whether it was good news or bad from the way Betty spoke. She added her characteristic smirk to the end of the message, just as she did to every message. But even Betty Lincoln couldn't ruin Jillian's attitude. She smiled and thanked her so emphatically that Betty tilted her head and widened her eyes in surprise.

"The Bentons are going to be here at ten-thirty," Nelsen said when she walked into his office. Then he took a good look at her. "Wow, where were you this weekend? Great tan."

"Provincetown," she said as nonchalantly as she could.

"The cape? Very nice, very nice." He nodded as if he were supposed to pass judgment on everything she did with her life and then he sat back. "Anyway, Jerry Thorton will be here in a half hour to go over some of the details before the Bentons arrive. We'll hold all the meetings in my office. Get yourself settled in and come right back. There's going to be a big media blowout on this." She nodded and started away. "And don't be surprised if we hear from Bob Geldorf before the day is out," he added before she left the office. "I got some good feedback this weekend. I'll tell you all about it. I stayed in New York with the peasants," he said, and she laughed.

Everything was happening so fast she realized she would have little time to give much thought to anything else but work. Maybe that was good. At least she could calm down, even though she didn't want to do so. Work was always good for her before; it would be good for her now, she thought.

She had only spoken with the Bentons on the telephone, and just as it was with most people not seen and only heard, they were not what she had expected. Besides, she had to confess that she had assumed a stereotyped image of two people who had suffered and been treated for cancer. She thought they would be pale and thin, their life force making a slow revival. Had she only projected the sounds of weakness in their voices or was it there?

They certainly didn't fit the part. Greg Benton was a strapping six-feet-two-inch man who looked like he had just finished a season with the Giants or the Jets. He was a robust forty-five-year-old with cheeks so pink he looked sunburnt. His long, light brown hair was almost blond. Ellen Benton was round faced with an attractive figure. She was only an inch or two shorter than Greg and five years younger. She had her dark brown hair cut about midway down her neck. The strands were styled and curled at the sides so they dipped under her ears. Jillian thought it was a flattering hairdo that took away from Ellen's chubby cheeks.

They were both dressed in jeans. Ellen wore a pink, short-sleeved cardigan that gave her an even brighter look. Greg wore a dark blue, short-sleeved shirt and draped a light, gray jacket over his shoulders, the sleeves tied once at his chest. Jillian thought they looked collegiate, athletic and vibrant. She wondered if people would disbelieve the tale of their recent illness.

Besides their meeting with her and Nelsen for the first time, this was also their initial meeting with Jerry

Thorton. There was only one great fear on their minds, a fear they verbalized immediately: they didn't want to be exploited to help promote the sale of Pooley shoes. Jillian took the initiative in responding. Since she had been the one to create the marriage, she felt responsible.

"There'll be no endorsements whatsoever on your part. You don't even have to mention the shoes you're wearing. The kind of promotion Pooley will have will all be subtle. We'll be at your news conference to simply explain what Pooley is underwriting and providing and the point will always be made that this is Pooley's contribution to the fight."

"That sounds fair," Greg Benton said. He looked at Ellen and she nodded. Jerry Thorton released the air he was holding in his lungs.

"Just like anything else," Jillian went on, "it's who gets there first. I'm sure that other shoe manufacturers would have liked to have had the opportunity to be associated with you and your fight."

"But they didn't have you managing their promotion," Greg said, and everyone laughed. The tension was broken. With the rest of the meeting, Jillian explained the kind of media exposure she would attempt to provide. The Bentons were eager to do any talk shows and news programs. They had already been offered several things, mostly radio, and one local afternoon television interview.

"You should be on all the morning network shows," Jillian said. "After all, you're directing yourselves to a national problem and your walk is going to take you all over America."

"Exactly," Greg said. "Can you get us that kind of exposure?"

"I'm going to work on it real hard," she said. "I've already contacted someone at *People* magazine and that looks assured." Her tone of determination brought smiles to their faces again. Before the meeting ended, Jerry Thorton offered to take her and the Bentons to lunch. She had other things to do, but when she looked to Nelsen, she saw he wanted her to go.

Afterward she was glad she had because she got to know Ellen Benton a lot better and she was pleased with the woman's character and personality. Jillian quickly recognized Ellen's fortitude. There was a sense of independence and strength that made understandable her successful struggle against serious illness.

"We never permitted ourselves the luxury of self-pity," Ellen explained. "Of course, it was depressing at first, but that was something to quickly overcome."

"Who was..."

"Sick first? I contacted the cancer first and Greg was wonderfully supportive. In the beginning we behaved as though it hadn't really happened. We had all sorts of euphemisms for the treatments and the symptoms. You can't imagine the illusions we created and the world of fantasy we lived in. And then he was diagnosed. Do you know what we did the moment we learned about him?"

"What?" Jillian looked to Jerry Thorton, but he and Greg were into their own conversation at the table.

"We laughed. We were hysterical. It was like a great practical joke. Some of our friends, and this is interesting, thought I had contaminated him."

"Really?"

"Yes, but when someone else in our neighborhood developed a form of leukemia, people started to think environment and the seeds of this began. Then we found out about the toxic wastes and the water table. That changed everything."

"In what sense?" Jillian asked.

"We dropped the euphemisms and the illusions and replaced them with anger and brutal reality, because this wasn't the result of some toss of the dice. This was the result of criminal negligence. What happened was, we developed a common enemy and nothing unites you as much as a common enemy," Ellen said. Her eyes burned with the passion of her anger. Jillian was fascinated. This woman had brushed up against Death, but instead of coming away meek and fearful, she came away strong and determined. "In some ways," Ellen added, "I attribute our remarkable recoveries to that anger. It strengthened us. This wasn't the time to lay down and die."

"Do you mind if I use some of what you've told me when I do the promotion?" Jillian asked.

"Of course not. Use what you have to. We trust you."

Jillian thanked her but wondered if she deserved such trust. She had to admit to herself that when she had first thought of the idea, her priority was to advance her own career. Now that she was involved in this and had met these people, her own career seemed insignificant. In fact, all the problems she had paled beside the struggle Ellen Benton endured.

She was glad she had gotten herself and Pooley Shoes involved in a real cause for a change. There was something more noble about this, certainly something more satisfying than figuring out ways to increase the sales of Carson Makeup or Tingleman's Discount Appliances. She told herself she really would make an all-out effort to get them the best publicity and the most exposure possible.

She was eager to get down to the nitty-gritty work, but when she returned to the office after lunch her excitement wasn't allowed to diminish.

Nelsen was waiting for her with the big news: Bob Geldorf had called. They were going to have dinner at Gracey Mansion with the mayor of New York City.

"YOU WERE TO DINNER at Gracey Mansion," Jillian told Betty over the phone, "what does one wear?"

"Jack Bradley will probably greet you in a tux and sneakers."

"Jack? You're on a first-name basis?"

"He doesn't like to be called mayor or Mr. Mayor. He'll tell you that right away. That's for formal gatherings and press conferences. It's his down-to-earth style that got him elected in the first place. How else can you explain his winning while running only on the Liberal line in New York?"

"That and a media genius named Bob Geldorf."

"Right. Back to what you should wear... Didn't you tell me you had a light blue silk suit?"

"The skirt has a slit up the side, a little higher than mid-calf."

"No problem. Jack will appreciate it. He can be very sexy and charming. You remember he got nearly ninety percent of the women's vote."

"The suit has a one-button jacket and padded shoulders."

"The 'Dynasty' look. How chic."

"I'll wear the pure white blouse with the blue print pattern. This is an opportunity to wear that gold necklace my uncle Phil bought me. Now I'm glad I bought those matching earrings during the sale at Fortunoff's last month."

"Wear your low-heeled white pumps. Bradley's just five eleven and he likes to stand tall next to women."

"Thanks. I knew you'd know what I should do. I had such little notice. Nelsen hit me with it after lunch, and even though he told me to go home early to get ready, I had so much to do on the Pooley Walkathon, I couldn't leave before four."

"I'm sure you'll do all right."

"What's he really like?"

"To be honest," Betty said, "I didn't spend that much time with him. I got sidetracked with Mrs. Bradley, who, much to my misfortune, follows the soaps."

"Oh, God, I hope that doesn't happen to me."

"I sort of doubt it, my dear. This sounds much more like a business dinner with you running center attraction. Speaking of center attractions, what was your weekend like? You haven't said a word about it."

"That's because it still seems like a dream, a beautiful dream. My God," Jillian said, "Ron might be trying to call me. I've got to hang up. I haven't got all that much time before Nelsen comes by to pick me up and I must speak to him."

"You creep."

"I'll make it up to you. Lunch tomor...oh, I can't tomorrow. I'm having lunch with Michael Curtis."

"Page Six of the *Post*. Publicity, publicity."

"It's for a good cause, the Bentons. How about the day after?"

"It's a date. Good luck, honey."

"Thanks."

She hung up quickly and then stared at the phone for a few moments. It was only a little after five. Ron wouldn't expect her to be at her apartment until closer to six. Nelsen was coming by at seven, so there was really time. She didn't have to be so nervous, but with all this happening at once, it was difficult to contain herself. It was best to keep busy. She went to her closet and began to lay out the wardrobe. After that she took a shower with the door partly opened so she could hear the phone ringing. It didn't.

She started on her hair and her makeup, all the while listening for the sound of the phone. She had one fear—he would call just before she had to leave with Nelsen and they wouldn't be able to talk much. Once he heard where she was going, however, he would understand. And he could call her later that evening anyway, she thought.

By the time she was completely dressed, it was six-thirty and still Ron had not called. She went back into her bedroom and took the jewel box out of the bottom drawer. She opened it and took out the ring. When she slid it over her finger, she was amazed at how well it fit. There would be no need for any adjustment. That had to be a good omen.

She held her hand up before her and turned it into the light so the diamond would glitter. She smiled, remembering how Ron had told her the ring would haunt her. He was right. Maybe it had some magical power and that was what caused her to agree. She didn't care. She wanted this; she wanted it more than she ever expected she would, and none of it had anything to do with the pressures her family might place on her. Her decision was completely independent of all that.

In fact, she never thought about her sister or her brother, or her father and mother while she thought about herself and Ron. Wasn't that odd? It was almost as if she and Ron had stepped out of this world when they were together and none of the memories of this world could follow them into their private one.

She nearly jumped when the phone rang. It was a quarter to seven, so she rushed to it.

"Hello."

"Jillian, it's Nelsen. I'm calling from the limo. Will you be ready on time?"

"Yes. I'm ready now."

"Okay. We're on Fiftieth and York. We should be right on the money. You might as well be down at seven."

"All right," she said, and hung up. She looked at the miniature grandfather clock, wishing that she could hold back the second hand somehow. But it ticked on and on.

She went back to the bathroom and studied herself in the mirror again. She fixed some strands of hair, smoothed out her lipstick, adjusted her necklace, and then went out to the living room. For a few moments she just stood there next to the phone. She took her pocketbook off the table and went to the bedroom to put out the lights.

It was five to seven. She had to leave now to be downstairs and waiting when Nelsen arrived. Why had Ron waited so long to call? She shook her head in disappointment. This wasn't the night she wanted to be depressed. She had to be at her best to deal with the people they were about to meet. She was going to have dinner with the mayor, for chrissakes. How could she walk into Gracey Mansion wearing a long face?

She started for the door and then stopped. She had forgotten she was still wearing the ring. She couldn't do that; it would create all sorts of digressions with Nelsen, and besides, she had made up her mind she wasn't going to wear it out in the open until she had talked with Ron.

She walked back into the living room and took off the ring, placing it right beside the telephone and the answering machine. Later, after she returned from what she hoped would be a very successful meeting with the New York executives, she would find Ron's message on the machine and then call him. She was confident that before she went to sleep tonight, she would be Ron Cutler's fiancée. Even the sound of it sent tingles along her spine.

Pushing her disappointment back as she would a bad dream, she left the apartment and took the elevator, arriving in the lobby just as Nelsen's limo pulled up in front of her apartment house. Her timing was perfect.

When she got into the vehicle, she was surprised to find Nelsen so excited. It made her more nervous, but nevertheless she remained confident and optimistic. She was filled with the anticipation that had begun to draw her attention away from her private life.

She looked back only once, thinking about her telephone ringing and ringing until her answering machine clicked on and told the man she loved to leave his name and number.

ACTUALLY NOTHING but having dinner at the mayor of New York's residence would have kept Jillian's mind off Ron Cutler. It didn't occur to her until she and Nelsen were in the limo again and pulling out of the long driveway that she hadn't thought about Ron once the whole time she was there.

How could she? From the moment she arrived and was introduced to Jack Bradley, she was the center of attention. Betty was right about that, too. Mrs. Bradley was in Paris on a shopping spree, so it was only the four of them, with her being the only woman.

Although Betty's exaggerated prediction that Jack Bradley would be in a tuxedo and sneakers when he greeted Jillian wasn't correct, Jillian was surprised by his choice of colors. He wore a bright green sports jacket with beige pants. The tie was only a shade or two lighter green and had thin white stripes running across it. Instead of sneakers, he wore eggshell white loafers with what looked to her to be extra thick heels.

The mayor made her feel comfortable immediately.

"I've been anxious to meet the young woman who has so dazzled my high-priced media people," he said when they were introduced. She wondered where he had gotten his even California tan.

She thought there was something cinematic about Jack Bradley. Maybe it came from having seen him on television all those times, or maybe it came from the fact that the mayor of New York was more of a celebrity than a politician. Bradley was as flamboyant as Ed Koch had been, only Bradley was a very young-looking, handsome man with light brown hair, Paul Newman blue eyes and an impish grin that made women tingle.

Jillian sensed he was confident about his sex appeal and aware of how to use it. Whenever he looked at her, he fixed his gaze intently, making her feel that he was giving her his full attention. No wonder he was so effective at live, hand-to-hand political combat, she thought. He had the ability to make someone he spoke to feel important. The mayor of New York was sincerely interested in what the person had to say. He was really listening.

"You know," he said, after they had dinner and Bob Geldorf once again presented the program Jillian had designed, "I think the thing that attracted me to this promotion campaign the most was the sense of the people you've captured. I pride myself on being the people's candidate, the man who beat the politicians and the machines. It makes sense I would launch such a Big Apple campaign.

"How will you go about casting for the commercials?"

"Casting?" Jillian looked at Geldorf and then at Nelsen, but neither seemed to pick up anything odd in the mayor's question. "You mean, how will I find the people?"

Bradley leaned forward.

"You weren't intending to use actual people, were you?"

"Why, yes," she said. "It's not uncommon in commercials."

"But until you find the right ones... It could be costly, running one screen test after another. Wouldn't it be more efficient to get some good character actors?"

"I don't think so," Jillian said. She saw that Nelsen wanted her to simply agree. Geldorf, on the other hand, looked like he was auditioning her. The mayor waited for her to continue. "No matter how anonymous a face we find in the professional acting world, there will be that slickness that comes from experience before the cameras. I'm looking for sincerity here. People should be able to identify immediately with the people we use."

For a moment the mayor said nothing. Then he smiled.

"I like that," he said. "I think you're right." He sat back. "This young lady sticks to her beliefs, Nelsen. Be careful or I'll steal her away from you and have her working for me."

Nelsen laughed, but Geldorf didn't, and the mayor kept his gaze fixed on Jillian. She thought he was flirting and she wondered if those rumors about his assignations with some Broadway starlets might not be true. Marvin Glade over at Jason, Carson and Rawly once told her it was good for a politician to have some of that in the image projected. It made him more interesting to the population. She didn't want to believe it, but she had to agree that gossip had a way of promoting a client, as long as the gossip wasn't vicious. It certainly didn't matter if it were true. What was that statement attributed to Katherine Hepburn..."I don't care what they write about me as long as it *isn't* true."

By the end of the evening, it was determined that they would go ahead and produce half a dozen spots for the mayor to consider. But just before they left, Geldorf made it clear that he expected they would feature the mayor somehow in every set of spots.

"We can't overlook how the Jersey campaign skyrocketed Kean," he said. Nelsen nodded.

"Of course."

"And the way I see it, it wouldn't be possible to talk about New York City without talking about Jack

Bradley today. He's come to personify what New York is all about. You see that, don't you, Jillian?" Geldorf asked. Once again she felt as though she were being tested.

For a moment she didn't respond. Then she smiled.

"Of course," she said. Geldorf looked pleased. "Is anyone who they say they are?" she asked Nelsen after they got into the limo and started away.

"You can't expect a politician not to look for new and better roles to play. Remember that quote from one of Kurt Vonnegut's books. It went something like, 'Be careful about whom you pretend to be because you are who you pretend to be.' So Jack Bradley sees himself as personifying New York. In his mind he is. If he wants to live that illusion, who's to argue? As long as he doesn't hurt the city," Nelsen added.

Jillian said nothing. Her fantasies about the mansion and having dinner with the mayor of New York were over. Like any fantasy, the reality proved a little disappointing, even though it was still very exciting.

In the end everything was political, everything was driven by base motives. She was determined not to let that happen to the Bentons and their walkathon, but she didn't feel as confident about her possibilities of success as she had before coming to Gracey Mansion for dinner.

It was times like this when you need someone close to talk to, Jillian thought, and then she thought about Ron and looked forward to getting back to her apartment and finding his voice recorded on the answering machine. It was nice to have that right now.

"I thought you were wonderful, charming, and bright," Nelsen said. "I'm proud of you and the way you handled yourself. Geldorf was impressed, too; I could tell."

"Thank you, Nelsen."

"You're going to go far in this business, Jillian. Who knows where it's going to take you?"

"That's just it...who knows? Good night, Nelsen," she said and got out of the limo. She was impatient with the slow elevator and fumbled with her apartment key when she got to the door.

Turning on the light as she entered, she was relieved to see the little light on the answering machine flickering. The numbers told her there were two messages. He probably called twice, she thought, and ran the tape back quickly.

It beeped and her mother came on.

"We haven't heard from you in days. What have you been doing? You know how nervous your father gets when we don't hear from you. Call."

She let the tape continue. It beeped, signaling another call had come in, but there was only silence afterward and then the horrible sound of the phone being hung up.

Ron wouldn't do that, she thought. It was just someone who hated talking to an answering machine. Many of her friends were like that. Sometimes Betty cursed over it. Trish giggled and hung up. Sally Feldman simply groaned. But Ron would surely say something. His calling was too important to both of them for him to simply hang up.

She stared down at the machine incredulously. No other messages; no other calls.

It was almost eleven o'clock. He would have had to call. It made no sense. Something had to be wrong. She had to call him.

Illusion

And then it hit her. He had never given her his phone number. How had it happened that she had not asked? He had always left it that he would call her. Even when he had been staying in New York though, he never told her exactly where he was and how to reach him if she wanted to. Why was that? Was it just because things moved so fast between them? Right now, because she was nervous and disappointed, it was all in a blur.

Well, she knew where he lived. She knew the town was called South Fallsburg and she knew where his stores were located. How hard could it be to reach him? It was late, but still...she had to phone.

She dialed information and gave the operator his name. With the way things were computerized, there was a nearly immediate response.

"We have no listing for a Ron Cutler in South Fallsburg."

"Oh. He lives with his father. The phone must be under his father's name."

"What's his father's name?" the operator asked, and she realized she didn't know that, either.

"I'm not sure. Are there any Cutlers listed?"

"Yes. There's a Phyllis Cutler."

"No, it has to be a man's name."

"Sorry, that's the only Cutler in South Fallsburg. Oh, wait a minute," the operator said. Jillian breathed relief. "There is another Cutler listed, a John Cutler."

"What's the number please?"

"I'm sorry. It's an unlisted number."

"But I must call him. Isn't there any way?" she asked knowing very well that there wasn't.

"Sorry, we are not permitted to give out this number. Was there anything else?"

"No," Jillian said. "There's nothing else," she added angrily and hung up. For a few moments she stood there staring down at the phone. Then she saw the ring beside it. She picked it up and held it before her.

"Why didn't you call?" she asked it. "What's going on? Who are you, Ron Cutler, and what have you done to me?"

The silence that followed remained with her until she went to bed, but she didn't sleep. She lay there staring up into the darkness, thinking.

The image of Ron out on the widow's walk at Portuguese House returned. She thought of him staring into the darkness. It gave her the chills.

Sometime close to two in the morning, emotionally exhausted, Jillian passed into a restless sleep, and even when the sun came through the window and woke her, she felt she was still in the middle of a nightmare.

CHAPTER NINE

JILLIAN SAT IN THE KITCHEN and stared at the telephone, which had become an object to hate. Why should something so inanimate, something so cold and hard hold so much power? She brought her coffee cup to her lips and held it there without sipping. Her appetite this morning was nonexistent; it was even an effort to drink a small glass of orange juice. Now her coffee, which she made the same way she always did, had a bitter taste. Anger and frustration had a way of turning the world inside out. Her apartment was transformed. Yesterday morning everything looked bright and new. Today the walls were dreary; the furniture looked tired and worn, and the sunlight that penetrated the opened blinds only pointed up dust.

She checked the time and then shook her head in disbelief. This was some kind of cruel joke; this wasn't happening. Perhaps he would call her at work, and when he did, he would have a logical and satisfying explanation. It was that thought that motivated her to continue dressing and go to the office. Not that she had the time for or the luxury of self-pity. There was just too much to do. She caught a cab right outside the apartment building. Whenever that happened, she considered it a good omen. Today she was dependent upon omens, she thought. Her life was out of her control. It was in the hands of capricious fate.

When she arrived at the office, Betty Lincoln looked up expectantly, waiting for Jillian to offer the first good morning as usual. She behaved as though it was coming to her, as though it were some unwritten fringe benefit that went along with the job. But this morning, Jillian was in deep thought and had no patience for her. She walked right past her, not even stopping to ask for messages.

"Well, how do you do, yourself," Betty cried. Jillian didn't turn around. She went directly to her office, entering it like a somnambulist. But her sleepwalker's demeanor couldn't continue. She had a phone call almost immediately. Although it wasn't Ron, she couldn't be disappointed. It was a confirmation for an appearance by the Bentons on NBC's "Live at Five." Ten minutes later, the production assistant at "Good Morning America" offered a date for the Bentons, and a reporter she knew at the *Daily News* called to tell her the managing editor had okayed a feature story on the walkathon. It was all starting very well.

When there was a break in the activity, she turned her attention to acquiring the phone numbers of the Cutler's department stores. It was late enough in the morning. Surely Ron would be at one of them. Before she could make her first call, however, Nelsen came to her office to discuss the production company they were going to use for the New York City commercials.

"I've got a list of locations I want you to consider," he said. "And I think I found a way to use Bradley in every spot. For example, before we have the cab driver speak, Bradley steps out of his cab."

"And at the senior citizen club, the mayor is at the bridge table," she said, half-facetiously.

"Yeah. It's like a Hitchcock. He makes cameo appearances everywhere. I love it."

"I'm sure he will, too," Jillian said, disguising her sarcasm well.

"All right. I'll go ahead and contact Tristar. You start to perfect the copy. When are we having the news conference for the Pooley Walkathon?"

"Thursday, twelve o'clock at the Plaza."

"Did you contact CNN. The cable network is acquiring quite a reach."

"Already took care of it," Jillian said. Nelsen nodded and started out. Then he turned to look back at her.

"You all right? You look a little pale this morning."

"Could have slept better," she said.

"Yeah. I know what you mean. Sometimes the excitement gets to you. See you in awhile," he added, and left.

Jillian stared blankly at the door, recalling how Ron had looked when he had stepped back in to ask her for a date that first day. It seemed like ages ago; his image appeared vivid for a moment and then faded. She looked down at the phone lines, noting that three of them were lit up. She waited to be buzzed to receive his call, but nothing happened.

Her stomach was twisting into knots. What was going on? Why would he wait so long to call after spending such a romantic and intense weekend together? And after giving her the ring? Did he think that by his keeping away from her he would get her to assent that much quicker? Was this all part of some male, masterminded plan? Ron's apparent self-enforced silence had left her feeling empty and depressed, but now anger was rushing in like air into a vacuum.

She dialed the first Cutler's department store. It rang for quite a while before a woman picked it up, barely disguising her annoyance at having to answer the phone. What was it, Jillian thought, people never called department stores?

"I would like to speak with Mr. Ron Cutler, please."

"Who?"

"Mr. Ron Cutler."

"You mean, Mr. John Cutler," the woman said in a most pedantic tone.

"No, I—"

"Mr. John Cutler is at our Monticello store," she said, ignoring Jillian.

"I don't want Mr. John Cutler."

"Do you want the number of the Monticello store?"

"I've got that number. There's no Mr. Ron Cutler there?"

"John Cutler is at the Monticello store," the operator repeated and then hung up before Jillian could reply.

"Damn," she said. She looked for the Monticello store's number, but before she could dial it, the producers of CBS's national news called. They intended to give the Bentons a full five minutes on next Wednesday's program. They would interview them, shoot their home location with the nearby toxic waste landfill, and then exhibit the itinerary of their walkathon. Dan Rather had indicated that he wanted to do the story personally. Would she stop by to see him about three o'clock this afternoon?

She almost couldn't respond. Dan Rather, face to face, the day after she met and had dinner with the mayor of New York!

"Of course," she finally said. "I'll be there."

As soon as she hung up, she buzzed Nelsen and told him.

"Doesn't surprise me," he said. He tried to act nonchalant, but she heard the excitement in his voice. "Now try to take all this in stride, Jillian. I don't want you coming in pale tomorrow," he added.

That reminded her of Ron and she went to the second Cutler's store number. She dialed it right after hanging up. The voice that responded this time was male and for some reason, a great deal more calm and polite.

"I'm trying to locate Mr. Ron Cutler," she said. "One of the other stores suggested I call this one."

"You must mean John Cutler. I'll connect you with his office."

"No," Jillian said quickly, but the in-house line was being rung. After a moment, a secretary answered.

"Mr. Cutler's office."

"Is this Mr. Ron Cutler's office?"

"No. This is John Cutler's office."

"Can you tell me how to reach Mr. Ron Cutler?"

"I'm afraid you have the wrong number. This is Cutler's department stores."

"Yes, I know that. I want to speak to Mr. Ron Cutler." The operator was silent. "Can't I reach him through this number?"

"The president of Cutler's department stores is Mr. John Cutler. What is the purpose of this call?"

"The purpose," Jillian said, no longer disguising her frustration, "is to speak with Mr. Cutler's son, Ron. Is that a major problem?"

"May I ask who this is?"

"My name is Jillian Caldwell."

"Are you selling something, Miss Caldwell."

"Jesus Christ. Why the third degree? Can you please inform Mr. Cutler—Mr. Ron Cutler—that I am on the line."

"I don't think this is very funny," the secretary said.

"It's not meant to be funny."

"Then you have the wrong number," she said and hung up. Jillian sat there in disbelief, keeping the receiver pressed against her ear. When the dial tone came on, she lowered the phone to the cradle and sat back.

"What the hell..."

She had barely a moment to give it thought. The lines were lighting up again. It was impossible to give it any more time for now. As difficult as it was for her to do so, she pulled away from her personal problem and continued to work on the publicity campaign for the walkathon. They had started a media bandwagon and it was rolling like nothing she had ever done before ever had.

She wished there were some way she could get out of her lunch date with Michael Curtis, but getting the publicity in the *Post* was important. She told herself she had the interests of the Bentons to think about, not to mention her client, Pooley Shoes. It was just that she wasn't in the mood for Curtis, whom she considered a rather dandified man. Sometimes she thought he literally fed on gossip, his face swelling with each good tidbit, especially a tidbit that would embarrass some prominent person. She knew the angle that attracted him to the Bentons' story was the fact that by conducting the walkathon along a path of toxic waste dumps, they would embarrass state and local governments and politicians of both major parties.

She brought all her fact sheets and promotional copy to the lunch with her, hoping to do the lunch as quickly as possible. To her surprise Michael wasn't as interested in the Bentons as she had hoped he would be. He accepted the information, but right after they ordered their food, he brought up her dinner at Gracey Mansion.

"How did you find out about that so quickly?"

"New York is a smaller town than most people think," he said, looking very contented with himself. She thought he was smug. His thin, feminine lips stretched into the smile that puffed up his cheeks and made his eyes smaller. He was a chubby man to begin with, and had a short, almost stunted body with stubby little fingers. Betty Dancer called him Toulouse-Lautrec.

"Well, nothing's definite yet, so I can't give you any specifics. We're still talking concepts."

"Are you going to continue to deal with the mayor directly?" he asked. She saw the twinkle in his eyes.

"Michael, what are you up to?"

"Just doing my job, Jillian. You know the reputation Jack Bradley has."

"Well you can put your overworked imagination to rest. For me this is purely and solely a business relationship, if even that. Nothing has been confirmed."

He nodded, but she saw his cynical look and sharply felt the difference between promoting through public relations and making a living on the promotion of innuendo and rumor. Never before had she been as disdainful of a gossip columnist. Up until now she thought of them more as harmless amusement, and when she could use them for her own purposes, she did. She wondered if she cheapened herself by doing so. But then she thought they had such a following and they could be so influential. She concluded this was just one of those necessary but difficult parts of the job.

Jillian practically fled from the lunch, not only because she wanted to get away from Curtis, but because she wanted to get back to tracking down Ron. She had only an hour or so before she had to go up to CBS. She called the third and fourth Cutler stores, but the operators there did the same thing the operator at the first store had done—they referred her to the Monticello store and Mr. John Cutler.

Frustrated, she hung up and sat back. How do you locate someone who has an unlisted number and who seems nonexistent? What was going on? Was Ron some kind of silent partner in his father's business? That didn't make any sense, but then again, none of this did.

She tried to direct her attention to the copy for the New York City commercials. There were pages to review and rewrite, but her mind kept wandering and she began to feel the impact of pressure. The clock tormented her. She had to get hold of herself because she was soon going to meet Dan Rather up at CBS. If there was one thing she didn't want to appear as, it was a disorganized, dizzy dame. No, not at this juncture.

A half hour before leaving for CBS, she reviewed the Benton file just as though she were cramming for an exam in college. Her self-confidence returned and she set out for her meeting with Dan Rather reassured. When she was led into his office she was surprised at how down to earth and relaxed he appeared. In a few hours, he would reach millions of people throughout the United States. They would take his words for gospel, and depending on how he emphasized and enunciated each story, they would react accordingly.

It couldn't be that he was unaware of his power and influence, Jillian thought. It was simply a matter of growing comfortable and accustomed to what he did. Perhaps if the nation saw him this way, his influence would diminish. In a way it was damaging to the medium to humanize the television gods. Illusions played a necessary role.

She had a wonderful discussion and left even more excited about the project because Dan Rather exhibited a sincere anger about the pollution of America. Once again she felt she was working on the most significant work of her career.

There were more messages from media people back at the office, but nothing from Ron. The end of her day was taken up with phone calls. She didn't have any time to go back to work on the copy for the New York City ads and left frustrated and pressured. Even though this wasn't the first time she'd had to take work home with her, she was disappointed because she thought she would have done better if she wasn't distracted by Ron's behavior.

Her initial anger began to grow. Something she thought would be good and beautiful was now damaging and ugly. She hardened herself against the romantic memories. Hers had always been a life of logic and order. She was efficient, ambitious and determined. This formula had brought her the success she now enjoyed. If she were making mistakes and working at a level far below her capabilities, it wasn't her fault. She had relaxed her guard and let someone else come deeply into her life. Here she was, ready to make sacrifices and compromise her individuality. She had come to believe that her mother might have been right about her all along—she was too enamored of herself to experience a real relationship with a man.

Now, as far as she could see, it was the man who was too enamored of himself. All the way back to her apartment she developed arguments against him. What he had done was insensitive, if not downright cruel. How could he profess to be in love with her and at the same time put her through such agony? She was determined to break it off, no matter what his excuses were.

But then she couldn't help recalling the warmth and the loving. She saw his laughing face, his smile of adoration, the gleam in his eyes when he held her hand, the way he turned away from the night sky to look at her longingly. Try as she would, she couldn't prevent her body from reliving the ecstasy. It tingled with the memories of their lovemaking in the attic apartment. She could almost feel the warm, ocean spray as the sailboat turned into the wind and he held her tightly against his chest.

Oh, Ron, what are you doing to us? she wondered, and opened the apartment door eagerly, hopeful that his message would be on her machine. Once again, there was a message there, but once again it was only her mother.

"Why haven't you called? Do I have to call you at work? We're beginning to worry."

She was certainly not in the mood to do it, but she realized she had to. Actually she was afraid her mother would hear the tension in her voice. Her mother had great perception when it came to something like that. How Jillian wished she could confide in her, but she knew the moment she mentioned Ron and described what had occurred, her mother would grow hysterical, imagining all sorts of terrible things. Maybe she would be right to do so.

"You sound so tired," her mother said as soon as she called. Jillian went into a description of the Bentons' walkathon and then told her about her dinner with the mayor of New York and her meeting with Dan Rather. For the first time, her mother sounded excited and proud of her. She couldn't wait to tell her friends all about it. "Your father's not home yet, but he'll probably want to call you to hear about it."

"Okay," Jillian said, grateful that her mother hadn't picked up on anything else.

She had no appetite, but she made herself some soup just to have some nourishment, and then she went right to work on the New York City ads. A little after seven her father called and she went back over everything she had told her mother. His words of admiration and tone of pride brought her to tears.

"Maybe I've been wrong about all this," he said. "Maybe my little girl is going to be someone very important after all. Be careful," he said. "We love you."

She couldn't go back to work; she just sat there by the phone, her tears streaming down her face. When Betty Dancer called ten minutes later, Jillian sounded so grateful for it that Betty immediately knew something was terribly wrong.

"I'm calling to tell you I have to cancel our lunch date tomorrow," she said, "but I have a feeling that I'm making a mistake. What is it, Jillian?"

Jillian was surprised at her own eagerness to pour forth the story. She had always considered herself a rather private person, despite the intimate conversations she and her girlfriends often had. There was always something she would hold back, something too intimate to be shared. But now she felt a great need to expose it all. It was as if she were making a confession and needed the relief that would follow. Maybe in her mind she had committed some sin by giving so much of herself so quickly to a man.

When she was finished, Betty was silent for a moment, and then, to confirm it for herself, she asked Jillian to repeat the way Ron had given her the ring. She described the evening and the conversation between her and Ron, holding the ring in her fingers and staring down at it as she did so.

"No call yesterday and no call today, no phone number and no one responded to his name when you called the stores?"

"Exactly. One person who answered practically accused me of some kind of sick joke."

"God, this is weird."

"What do I do now?"

"My imagination is going wild," Betty said. "From some of the things you told me about him and his father... maybe his father did something to keep him from seeing you again... who knows?"

"I don't want to start letting my imagination loose, but I can't help it."

"Yeah, I bet. Well, there's only one thing you can do, honey, besides wait, that is; and that's take a trip upstate. Confront him and the old man, if you have to."

"I'm in the middle of so much at the office. It's the busiest week of my career. Oh, God, I forgot to tell you, I had a meeting with Dan Rather today," she said, and described it. "So now you can understand why I am in such a panic."

"Understand? I don't know how you're still functioning. Why couldn't you fall in love with a ghost two weeks ago?"

"Don't say that. Don't even joke about it. At this point…"

"Jillian, I know this is easy for me to say. I didn't go through what you went through, but you've got to get hold of yourself. There will be an explanation for all this; maybe not one you'll appreciate or accept, but there will be something."

"I hope so."

"What are you going to do?"

"If I don't hear from him by the end of the week…despite the activity at the office, I'll take the Friday off, rent a car, and drive up there. It's only a two hour ride."

"I'd go with you, but I've got to fly to Atlanta for the show."

"I appreciate your thinking of doing it, but this is probably something I should handle myself anyway."

"I'll call you tomorrow night. Men. Maybe some day we'll be able to live without them. Maybe some female scientist will invent a pill that provides us with everything necessary that is male."

Jillian laughed. It felt so good to do so.

"Thanks for your help, Betty," she said.

"What help?"

"Just being there, just caring. Thanks."

"I'll call you as soon as I can tomorrow night," Betty repeated, and said goodbye.

There were no other calls that evening. Jillian successfully kept her mind off Ron by throwing herself into her work on the New York project. She was surprised to discover that it was close to twelve o'clock when she looked up from her papers. Grateful for the physical fatigue, she went to the bathroom and prepared herself for bed.

After the lights were out, she turned over so she could look out her bedroom window. It was a cloudy night; there were no stars visible. Perhaps that was an omen, she thought. The day had begun with omens, so why shouldn't it end with one? She closed her eyes and then opened them quickly when a frightening thought occurred to her.

Wasn't she now like Mrs. O'Shane's tragic aunt, waiting for the return of her lover? Where's my widow's walk? she wondered. Was this why Ron had wanted them to take that apartment in Portuguese House? She recalled telling Betty she didn't want to let her imagination run loose.

"I'd better listen to my own advice," she muttered, and fought her way into the dark valley of sleep.

THERE WAS NO CALL from Ron on Wednesday. She was in and out of the office a few times, once to go with Nelsen to see the people at Tristar, the production company they wanted to use for the New York commercials, and once to escort the Bentons over to *People* magazine. Each time she returned, she looked for his name on her message slips, but it wasn't there.

Illusion

The rest of the afternoon was taken up with the arrangements for the Bentons' news conference on Thursday. Jerry Thorton came to the office for a briefing, bringing with him another executive from Pooley Shoes.

At the end of the day, she left feeling exhausted. Recognizing that her fatigue was mostly mental, she did something she rarely did: she went to a bar alone. There was a place on Sixtieth and Third that she felt safe going to. It had a certain understated look about it that suggested refinement. Jillian imagined it to be the kind of a tavern other single, career women might frequent, and indeed there was another unescorted woman at the bar.

Her name was Lila Thomas. She said she worked for a brokerage house off Wall Street. Jillian estimated her age to be close to forty and recognized an experienced but worn look about her. She wondered if she were possibly looking at herself in a few years.

Lila was friendly enough and eager to talk, but she had such definite and fixed ideas about men, Jillian thought it was no wonder she was unescorted. From the way she spoke, none of them were any good. Jillian wondered why the woman hung out here. It was as though she wanted to confirm her beliefs by tempting a man and then turning him down.

Getting into a conversation with her, listening to the music and watching the tavern fill up with its regulars, Jillian lost count of how many Rob Roys she drank. Just before eight o'clock, Lila left and Jillian started out herself, surprised and frightened by her dizziness and unsteady gait.

She stepped onto the sidewalk and stood beside a closed newsstand, leaning against it to steady herself while she took in the air. It was nearly twenty minutes before she could successfully catch the attention of a taxi driver. After she was safely ensconced within it, she broke into a fit of giggling, thinking about the reactions of her mother and father should they have discovered her swaying on a New York street.

When she got back to her apartment, she went right to the answering machine. This time there were no messages at all.

"Very funny," she said to it. "Very funny joke you're having at my expense."

She went to make herself coffee, thinking she would sober up and have something to eat. Just before ten, Betty called and Jillian described her day.

"You sound skunked," Betty said.

"I've tipped a few."

"Jillian Caldwell. Look, how about lunch tomorrow?"

"Can't. Got the news conference and all that. I'm a busy little beaver," she added, and laughed.

"My advice to you is go to sleep."

"Soon. Soon I shall go out on my widow's walk and stare into the night."

"Huh?"

"Nothing. Just a private joke between me and a ghost. I'll talk to you tomorrow."

"You're beginning to worry me, honey."

"I'm worrying myself. I'll be all right. I'm getting something solid in my stomach. Don't worry."

Afterward she did eat a little, even though the coffee didn't have the sobering effect she expected. Actually she was grateful for her fatigue because she put herself to bed early. Unfortunately, however, she opened her eyes a little after two in the morning and discovered she was wide awake. She had to get out of bed and make herself some hot milk. Then she read for a half an hour before turning out the lights and trying again.

Thursday was the busy and exciting day she anticipated. The entire agency was geared to the Benton walkathon. Jillian had a map of the Bentons' route blown up for the news conference at the Plaza. The Bentons appreciated their opportunity to expand on their journey and describe the polluted sites.

Jerry Thorton spoke about the commitment Pooley Shoes was making. He even introduced the podiatrist they had hired to go along with the Bentons, winking at Jillian as he spoke.

Afterward there was a beautiful luncheon paid for by Pooley Shoes. Many of the media people remained and Jillian found herself making new contacts. Nelsen was satisfied with the way things had gotten launched.

"With this under way," he told her, "we can turn more of our attention to the New York campaign."

"I've got to take tomorrow off, Nelsen," she said. She figured this was a good time to break the news. She didn't want to go into the reasons. Thanks to Nelsen, she didn't have to.

"I was going to suggest it," he said. "I've been watching you closely all week, Jillian. You've been going at quite a pace and you haven't looked good. I know you're tired. I don't want you falling apart on me in the middle of all this. Take a good three day rest. Go see your mother and father."

"That's no rest, believe me," she said. Nelsen laughed.

After the luncheon she went back to the office and checked for messages. Not finding the one she wanted, she completed work on some smaller accounts and then called to arrange for a rented car for the morning. Before she left the office, she went to Marlo Abromowitz, whom she knew was familiar with the area of the Catskills in which Ron's family lived. Marlo gave her directions for the trip.

Armed with determination, Jillian left the office and went directly to her apartment. She wasn't surprised at the absence of any phone message; she expected it by now. She felt that whatever the reasons were for Ron's strange behavior, they were still in effect. She sensed they would be until she confronted him.

Not knowing what her trip would bring or how long it would take her to discover the truth, she packed a small bag. She wrapped the engagement ring in soft paper and put it in a makeup pouch.

Every time she touched or looked at the ring now, she had an eerie sensation. It was as though she had brought something back from another world, something from another dimension. Ron had told her to keep it so it would haunt her. Those words lingered in her mind. She stuffed the pouch into the bottom of her bag and zipped it closed.

Then she called her parents to tell them she was going away for the weekend to visit an old college friend.

"Daddy and I saw the Bentons' news conference on Channel Four," her mother said. "Daddy says he saw you standing off right. Were you off right?"

She wasn't, but she said she was. Her father got on the phone.

"I told your mother. I know my daughter when I see her, even if it's just a passing glance."

"That's right, Daddy," she said.

"What's this about a trip?"

"Just a short one. I need a little change of scenery."

"Sure, you're working too hard. Okay," he said. "Call us when you get back."

"I will."

She was terribly sad again after she hung up. The change in her father's attitude concerning her work didn't have the impact of satisfaction she once believed it would. Of course, some of that had to be blamed on what was going on between her and Ron, but she sensed something else as well. It was as though she were deceiving her parents by presenting them with so much of her instant success at once. Maybe it was because the success, as great as it was, wasn't enough.

She had so wanted things to go well between her and Ron. How could something so wonderful and good go so wrong? She had to discover the answers and until she did, she realized that nothing she accomplished would bring her the satisfaction it should.

BY THE TIME she got her rented car and left the city, it was nine o'clock in the morning. She went over the George Washington Bridge and took Route 80 to New Jersey 17 North, which brought her to the New York Thruway. Following Marlo's directions, she exited the thruway at Harriman and followed New York 17 West until Exit 107 in Sullivan County. From there she followed the signs into the hamlet of South Fallsburg.

The resort season was under way in the Catskills. Although she had never been up here, she had heard that the hustle and bustle in the small hamlets and villages that were surrounded by hotels and bungalow colonies could rival the turmoil of a Manhattan street.

South Fallsburg was small, not much more than one long street with luncheonettes, bar and grills, clothing stores, drugstores, groceries and small department stores on both sides. Most of the buildings were early twentieth century vintage. They were tired, worn structures, box shaped with flat roofs and stucco sides. Here and there she saw evidence of modernization and rehabilitation. She wondered how far Ron's closest store was.

When she reached the middle of the hamlet, she stopped and rolled her window down to attract the attention of a policeman who was standing on the corner. Almost immediately, drivers in cars behind her leaned on their horns. This was no different from driving in New York, she thought.

"Pull over," the policeman commanded, and crossed the street to join her.

"I need some directions," she said. The cop looked no more than a boy in his late teens. He had very light brown hair, freckled skin and bright blue eyes.

"What's the problem?"

"I'm looking for the Cutler residence."

"You mean the department store people?"

"Yes." Her face lit up. At least she was in the right place.

"Well, you won't have trouble finding it. It's the biggest house in this town, a Colonial. You follow Main Street up to Lakeland and take the first right off Lakeland. Go until you come to an intersection and make a left. The road climbs. It's a dead end and the Cutler house is at the top. You can't miss it."

"Thank you," she said, and started to follow his directions. She was very intent on not making a mistake, so she didn't really look at the residences or the scenery as she drove on, but she was vaguely aware of the quiet countryside and the forests filled with full bloomed maple, oak and hemlock.

As soon as she made the left at the intersection, she saw the house ahead. It looked like a Southern mansion with its tall pillars in the front and long, rambling lawns. There were well-trimmed hedges and a beautifully organized flower bed with a fountain in the center.

She slowed down and whistled to herself. Then she turned into the circular driveway and followed it up to the front entrance. She saw where the driveway went off to the right to what looked to be a triple car garage.

After she stopped and turned off the engine, she sat staring at the front of the house. Her heart was beating rapidly because she knew the mystery would soon come to an end. Ron might answer the door himself. What would her first words be? She could almost imagine him smiling and saying something like, "I knew you'd come here. I'm just surprised it took you this long to do it."

If this was all a game to him...

What would she do? Hand the ring back to him and turn around? She would; she should. Playing with someone's emotions like this was no game. She couldn't love a man who was capable of doing such a thing.

On the other hand, maybe he was seriously ill and even though he asked his father to call her, his father didn't do it. Maybe Betty was right—maybe his romance had caused some kind of family feud and he was trying to find a solution.

Sitting here like this and wondering is ridiculous, she thought. Jillian Caldwell, get hold of yourself and get going. Before moving however, she reached over to her overnight bag, unzipped it, and took out the small pouch that contained the ring. She took out the ring and held it tightly in her right hand. Then she opened the car door and stepped out. She had half expected someone would have come to the door by now. Certainly anyone approaching this house would be spotted very quickly. There must be servants. She imagined a house like this probably came with them.

But the curtains on the lower level windows were drawn closed and there was no one peering out. She looked up and saw one window with opened curtains, but there was no one there, either. She saw no one on the grounds. It was so quiet, it looked deserted. Perhaps no one was home. After all, it was early in the day. Ron should be working. All she hoped for then was to meet someone who would tell her how to find him.

She walked to the door and pressed the button that set off the chimes. She could hear the way the sound echoed within and she pictured the huge rooms. A few moments later the door opened and a slim, elderly woman dressed in a blue and white cotton print dress looked out at her. The woman's silver-gray hair was pulled into a tight bun behind her head. The thin, fair skin of her forehead looked stretched against the bone. She appeared to be only about five foot three, even though she stood in shoes with inch heels.

Jillian thought she saw some resemblance to Ron. The woman had the same shape jawbone and similar color eyes. There was also something familiar about the way she carried herself. Perhaps it was the Cutler confidence, Jillian mused.

"Yes?"

"I'm—I'm Jillian Caldwell." She waited for some signs of name recognition, but there was none.

"What is it you want?"

"I must see Ron," she said, practically spitting the words at her. The old lady blinked rapidly and stepped back as though Jillian actually had spit. She brought her right hand to her throat as she widened her eyes.

"Who?"

"Ron. This is where he lives, isn't it? Please, it's very important."

"Is this some kind of joke?"

"What?"

"Because if it is, you're damn lucky my brother isn't at home." She started to close the door.

"Wait. Please. It's not a joke. Look," Jillian said, holding out her opened hand. The ring caught the sunlight and glittered. The woman held the door in place and stared. "It was his mother's...we're supposed to get engaged. I mean, I didn't say yes yet, but..."

"His mother's?" The old lady opened the door wider and stepped forward. She plucked the ring from Jillian's palm and studied it a moment. "This is not his mother's ring. His mother's ring is one of a kind and somewhat larger." She dropped the ring back into Jillian's palm and started to close the door again.

"But we've been seeing each other and last weekend we went to the cape. That's where he gave me the ring—"

"Who gave you the ring? What are you talking about?"

"Ron. This is the Cutler residence, isn't it?" Jillian thought for a moment. Could there be another house, even larger than this one? The policeman said it was a dead end and she thought she had gone as far as she could.

"You say Ron Cutler gave you that ring on the cape last weekend?"

"That's right. And I haven't heard from him since. I must see him; I must know what's going on. Is he here? Where can I find him?" she asked quickly. Perhaps if she got more demanding, she would get some results, she thought. "I've just driven up from New York and..."

The woman's face softened under the shadow of Jillian's intensity. Her eyes became smaller and then she stepped forward.

"But you can't mean Ron Cutler, my dear."

"Why not? Why is it impossible to get in touch with him? I called all the stores and..."

"Because Ron Cutler was my nephew and he's dead. He's been dead for more than five years."

CHAPTER TEN

JILLIAN'S FIRST THOUGHT was she had been involved with an imposter, albeit a very charming, handsome and intelligent imposter. She wasn't one to believe in ghosts, and anyway, Ron Cutler's spinster aunt, Emma Cutler said the engagement ring had not belonged to her sister-in-law. Apparently the only connection was the use of the Cutler name.

The blood had drained so quickly from Jillian's face when Emma Cutler told her about Ron that she had to take hold of the doorjamb to keep from losing her balance. The old lady became frightened.

"Oh, come in, come in," she said. "I'll get you a glass of water." She started to help her, but Jillian said she could manage. She took a deep breath and stepped into the large house.

The vestibule had a white marble floor and two rectangular full-length mirrors in oak frames on both sides. There was a closet to the right side of the mirror. The walls were done in an eggshell white paper with specks of sea blue, and they looked as if they had been papered only yesterday.

Without going much farther, Jillian sensed that the house had the air of a mausoleum about it. It looked untouched, uninhabited by living beings. The walls, the carpets, the fixtures were all immaculate, and it was so quiet that the soft sound of their footsteps on the rugs seemed enormous. Usually houses and apartments had their own identifiable scents reflecting the perfumes, colognes, detergents, foods of the inhabitants; but the air in this house carried none of these familiar odors. It was more like being in a public building.

Because all the windows downstairs were covered with shades and curtains, the warm daylight was left behind the closed front door. It made the house a home of shadows and gloom. She continued to hesitate, reluctant to go into it much farther.

"This way, my dear," Emma insisted.

Jillian moved forward, following the old woman to the sitting room on the right. It had a plush, cream-colored carpet and French Provincial furniture, consisting of a love seat, two wing chairs, a couch, a long, dark pinewood coffee table and two small side tables. There was a dark pinewood bookcase on the left wall, filled with volumes, but the room looked like it was rarely used. The light within it came from a single, standing lamp beside the love seat.

"Sit on the couch. It's the most comfortable piece," Emma said. "I'll be right back with your water, or would you like something stronger?"

"No, water's fine. Thank you."

Jillian went to the couch and sat in the left corner. It was softer than it appeared. She leaned back and closed her eyes. Her pulse had begun to normalize, but she still had a cold, clammy feeling.

I should have expected something like this, she thought. I did expect it. In my heart I knew something was wrong; something was strange. I sensed my instincts were true the moment this woman opened the front door. It was as if it all came rushing out to me.

Illusion

She sat up when she realized she still had the engagement ring cupped tightly in her hand. When she opened her hand and looked at the ring this time, it took on an ominous appearance, as though it were a bewitched piece of jewelry. She felt endangered, but she didn't know what to do. Should she simply throw it away? Maybe it was a meaningless piece of glass. Why would an imposter give her something valuable anyway? she wondered.

Why did he do it? All this fabrication and all the money he spent, for what? Who was he? What was this about? It would drive her mad.

She sat up when Emma Cutler reappeared with a tumbler of cold water and ice.

"Thank you," Jillian said. She took a long sip and sat back, enjoying the feeling of cool refreshment. It did help and color returned to her face. Emma Cutler stood by, staring down at her. "I don't know what to say," Jillian began. "I've been having a romance with a man in his thirties who came to my agency to develop a promotional package for his department stores. We started to see each other socially. It all happened so fast. I'm in public relations," she added quickly, sensing that she was babbling.

Emma shook her head sympathetically and sat in one of the wing chairs.

"And he told you he was Ron Cutler?"

"That's right. The work was to be done for the Cutler department stores. He seemed so sincere. I'm not the only one who was fooled," she added, as if to justify everything.

"I wish we could find this man," Emma said. Her face tightened even more and her eyes became hard and cold. "I'd like to see him arrested. It's a cruel hoax. I wonder if it's anyone from this town."

"He did seem to know a great deal about the area and the stores," Jillian said.

"Do you have a picture of him?"

"No." Jillian thought for a moment. "I know that seems strange..."

"He gave you an engagement ring and you don't have a picture of him?"

"As I said, things happened pretty fast between us, but now that I think about it...there were a few chances to take pictures, especially at the cape, but he didn't bring a camera and I didn't and...oh, what's the difference? Obviously he didn't want me to have a picture." She took another drink of the water and then looked down at the ring. "I don't even know if this is real now. It's probably a good imitation."

"Let me see it again," Emma said. She rose from her chair and came to Jillian to pluck the ring from her palm. She held it in the light for a moment and nodded. "I know jewelry," she said, "and this is real."

"I don't understand. Why would he give me a real diamond if... Did he think he could carry it on forever?"

"Or long enough to get married, perhaps. My nephew was what people would call an ideal marriage prospect. He was a bright, handsome, strapping young man destined to inherit a fortune. He didn't want for female companionship. I can't blame anyone for choosing him as the person to imitate. It's just a cruel thing to do. My brother has never stopped mourning his death. Ron was his only child."

"I understand," Jillian said. Emma gave the ring back to her. She looked at it again and then closed her fingers tightly around it as if to block its effect. "Well, thank you for the water." She stood up and Emma took the glass. "There's no sense in burdening you with this any further."

"You should probably go to the police," Emma said. Jillian nodded.

She started toward the doorway when a photograph on the lower shelf of the bookcase caught her eye. In it a man and a teenage boy were standing in the front of this house. Emma saw where Jillian's attention had gone.

"That's my brother and Ron when Ron was in high school."

"May I look?"

"Of course."

Jillian went to the bookcase and looked at the photograph. Her heart began to beat rapidly again, but she contained herself. Keeping her voice as calm as possible, she turned back to Emma Cutler.

"Do you have a more recent photograph of Ron?"

"There's a rather large photograph in a frame on the wall in my brother's den," she said. She didn't move, however.

"Please let me see it."

"I will, but you must leave right after that. To be honest, this is beginning to disturb me."

"I appreciate that. Thank you."

Emma led her from the sitting room, down the corridor, past the long dining room, toward the rear of the house. The walls were covered with replicas of fine artwork, mostly eighteenth and nineteenth century English—Hogarth's *Shrimp Girl*, Gainsborough's *The Honorable Mrs. Graham*, replicas of the pre-Raphaelites such as Ford Madox Brown, Dante Gabriel Rossetti, and William Hunt. Jillian's art appreciation course came quickly to mind. She wondered who did the purchasing of the art, because she noted that there was nothing after the nineteenth century.

They stopped at the door of the den. Once again Jillian felt she was about to enter a tomb. The door was closed and when Emma Cutler opened it the room within was very dark because the curtains were drawn.

The sight of it gave Jillian a chill. She embraced herself. Now that she had gotten the old lady to show her the room, she was hesitant about entering it. She felt as though she would be violating some sacred place. The thought made her consider turning and running out of the house.

Emma stepped into the room and flipped the wall switch that turned on the ceiling fixture. Looking through the doorway, Jillian could see that the light revealed shiny walnut panelled walls, more bookcases, a black leather couch, a desk so neatly organized it looked unused, and a half dozen shelves covered with family mementos. Emma Cutler turned around, surprised at Jillian's hesitation.

"You can come in," Emma said. To Jillian it did sound as if the old lady was granting a permission that was rarely extended.

"Thank you," she whispered, stepping through the doorway. She looked down at the floor and then to the left. Gradually she lifted her gaze and panned the room, turning from the desk and looking up.

There, in a rich, oak frame high on the wall so it would dominate the room, was a rather large blowup of a portrait photograph of Ron Cutler.

Jillian stared up at it.

"There he is," Emma said, shaking her head slowly. "So handsome with so much to live for." She turned and looked at Jillian, who had stepped back. "What is it?"

"That...is the man..."

"Man?"

"With whom I have fallen in love," she whispered.

IT WAS IMPOSSIBLE to remain in that house any longer. Jillian could almost hear the thoughts going through Emma Cutler's mind after she had made her comment about the large photograph: this woman is part of some scam; they're out to take my brother's money. She stepped back, her eyes wide, her face filled with both fear and fury.

"I want you out of here right now or I will call the police. I mean it."

"I'm sorry," Jillian said. "I know it's hard to believe, but I'm telling you the truth."

She didn't add to that. She turned and walked to the front door, moving in a daze, her legs numb. She had to look down to be sure she was touching the floor. Her body had become numb; she envisioned herself stepping out of it and leaving it behind in the house.

She reached for the doorknob. She didn't want to turn around, but Emma Cutler was right behind her.

"Don't come back here," she said in a firm voice. Jillian looked into her eyes and saw there was no longer any compassion; there was only fear. "I'm warning you."

"I'm sorry," Jillian repeated. She bit her lower lip and rushed from the doorway. It wasn't until she was in her car and had closed the door behind her that she took a breath. Emma Cutler held the front door of the house opened slightly and watched her until Jillian started the car and began to drive down the circular driveway. Looking into her rearview mirror, she saw the old lady close the door completely.

Less than a half mile from the house, Jillian pulled over to the side of the road. She could no longer contain her tears. She lowered her head to the steering wheel and sobbed uncontrollably. She didn't stop until a man in another vehicle pulled up alongside and beeped his horn.

"Are you all right?" he shouted through his opened window.

She nodded quickly and began to wipe her face. He stared at her for a moment, shrugged, and then pulled away.

Jillian started away again, not happy with the prospect of heading right back to New York. She felt she was caught up in a nightmare. That rich but gloomy house, the terrified aunt, that haunting portrait of Ron—all of it came back at her in undulating images, tormenting her. Now, every memory, especially the soft, beautiful ones, was painful. Whom had she been with? What did it all mean?

At this moment she was so weak she didn't think she could make the drive home. When a roadside diner appeared just ahead on her right, she decided to stop and get a cup of coffee. She had to pause; she had to get a hold of herself.

The diner was still busy with the remnants of its lunch crowd, but Jillian found a corner booth away from the din. The waitress who handed her the menu looked to be in her mid-forties or early fifties. Her hair was cut very short, but shaped into what used to be considered a ducktail style. Her light blue uniform clung tightly to her chubby form. The skirt was nearly a mini. Some of the men at the counter were joking back and forth with her, so that while she served tables, she directed remarks to them behind her back.

"I think I'll just start with hot coffee," Jillian said. She said it so softly, the waitress looked at her curiously.

"Sure honey. Be right back."

Jillian sat back in the booth and closed her eyes, but as soon as she did so, the image of Ron appeared, a wide smile on his face. Without realizing it, she had brought her hands to her cheeks.

"Are you all right, honey?" the waitress asked as she placed the coffee on the table.

"What? Oh, yes, yes. Thank you."

"You look pale, like you seen a ghost."

"I think maybe I have."

"Huh?"

Jillian leaned forward, considering the waitress more closely.

"How long have you lived here?"

"Me?"

One of the men sitting by the counter on a seat close to them heard her question.

"She's one of the original pioneers," he said. He and the short-order cook laughed.

"Shut up, Louie." She turned back to Jillian. "I've been here all my life. Stuck in the mud." She turned toward the man at the counter. "Just like some other people."

"Did you know a man named Ron Cutler?"

"Ron Cutler? Sure, honey. Everyone knew Ron."

"What...happened to him?"

"He was killed in a terrible car accident."

"'Bout five years ago," the man at the counter interjected.

"Mind your own business, Louie. Biggest busybody in town," the waitress said, and gestured toward the short man with curly hair. "Every town has one like him; we got a whole tribe."

"A car accident?" Jillian said, ignoring the digression.

"Drunken driver. Head on, just outside of Monticello. One of the biggest funerals ever. You can imagine. He was a very popular guy and probably the most eligible and desired bachelor. A dream boat in high school...quarterback on the football team, president of the student government... That was one younger man I wouldn't have minded being with."

"She's still robbing the cradle." The short man's heavy cheeks rippled with his subdued laugh.

"Stuff it, Louie." She turned back to Jillian. "I used to envy that family, just like everyone else around here," she said. "Now all the old man has is his money and his spinster sister. Shows you, huh?"

"Shows you?"

"Never wish you was someone else. You never know what you got until you give it up."

"Yes," Jillian said, a dreamy, far-off look coming on her face.

"Why d'you want to know about Ron?"

"What? Oh, I was just curious. I had heard about him, but I didn't know he was...he was dead."

"Oh, yeah, he's dead. What a shame. Think you wanna eat something?" Some other customers had come into the diner and she eyed them ambitiously.

"Oh. Just some toast with some jelly."

"Toast and jelly. Thought you looked sick. Coming right up."

"What are you, a doctor?" Louie asked as the waitress started away.

"Up yours, Louie," she said.

Louie laughed again and stared at Jillian for a moment, but when she looked back at him, he spun around on the counter stool and got involved in conversation with the short-order cook.

Jillian looked out the window. Traffic was light on the quiet country road. The relative stillness reinforced the feeling that she was lost in a dream, floating through some subconscious world in which ordinary things look novel. Fully bloomed trees looked exaggerated by their richly green leaves. Ordinary robins and sparrows flitting from branch to branch seemed hysterical to Jillian. Nature, almost in sympathy with her, had become confused and disoriented.

The weakness she had experienced when she'd first gotten out of the car to enter the diner really hadn't dissipated. But now, as she reviewed what the waitress had told her, her feelings began to change. She had become intoxicated from the shocking revelations. She couldn't help it; she became giddy.

A smile broke out over her face as would a rash. She heard herself giggle. It came just that way; someone else was within her, taking over, making her feel like an observer of herself. She even imagined sitting across the table, having a conversation with herself. Were her answers out loud?

"So you thought you were in love with a man who was in love with you? Romance has never been your strong point, Jillian Caldwell."

"How can you blame me for this?"

"You were so infatuated with him that you failed to see."

"See what? That he's been dead for five years?"

Dead for five years, she thought. I fell in love with a man who has been dead for five years. Her giggle got louder, longer. Louie turned around and stared again, a half smile on his face.

"You say somethin', miss?"

"I don't know. Did I?" She laughed.

"Huh?"

"Are you alive? Are you real?"

"What?" The short man's smile widened with astonishment. He looked about, as if in desperate need of assistance.

Jillian got up and quickly threw a few dollars on the table just as the waitress came around the counter, bringing her toast and jelly.

"Your toast," she said. Jillian turned and smiled at her.

"Give it to her," she responded, gesturing toward the booth she had been at. The waitress looked.

"What?" She turned to Louie, who shrugged. "Say, what?" the waitress asked as Jillian headed for the doorway. But Jillian didn't hear her. The background, where she had been, whom she had spoken to, faded away quickly. Her attention was focused intensely on where she was going and what she was doing. She kept her vision narrowed down to the car, her car keys, starting the engine, backing out, and heading down the road again. It was as if she had never stopped at the diner at all.

Illusion

But of course she had and of course the conversation with the waitress began to replay itself as she drove on and calmed down.

How could all this be true? That portrait photograph was a photograph of Ron and she had been with him and had kissed him and held him to her and been held by him. They had made most passionate love. He was not an illusion or a dream; he was real and the memories were vivid, memories of actual events. What did she have to do to confirm it—go back to the office and have Betty Lincoln testify that the man had come to the firm? Go back to that little restaurant in New York and have the people tell her that they knew Ron Cutler? Go up to Provincetown and see Mrs. O'Shane? Should she gather them all together and bring them all back to Emma Cutler and say, "See, I was telling you the truth. This isn't some scam. Your nephew is not dead, or at least...at least what? At least a ghost?"

Dear God, what was she to believe? She brought her car to a stop again, only this time she tried to be reasonable, logical. There had to be a way to make some sense out of all this. She wouldn't return to New York until she had. She couldn't return. What would she return to—everlasting confusion? She didn't know even how to begin to explain things to her friends.

But what more could she do? As she reviewed her conversation with Emma Cutler, it occurred to her that there was only one person to see, one person with whom she should speak.

She turned the car around and headed back into the hamlet of South Fallsburg. Following the signs on Route 42, she continued on toward Monticello, still feeling as though she were moving in a dream, but at least more aware of her purpose. A large billboard on the highway just before the village of Monticello announced the impending appearance of Cutler's department store. It came up on her left. She pulled into a spot in the parking lot and got out of the car.

For a moment she just stood there looking up at the large sign identifying the store: Cutler's. She recalled her early conversations with Ron, their discussions about the nature of the stores and how best to promote them. His descriptions of the establishment were accurate. From what she had seen so far from riding through the area, this store was the largest building constructed. It was impressive in this setting, even though it would be nothing unusual set in the New Jersey shopping areas or the malls on Long Island.

Inside, the store was neat, clean and well organized. The old tiled floors looked recently scrubbed. Although the walls were obviously not recently painted, they were still a bright beige. The store didn't have a modern look, but there was a strong attempt at coordination of counters, racks, and display cases. It wasn't crowded at this hour, but she could see that there would be sufficient sales personnel when it would be. Store employees were everywhere—straightening out products and displays disrupted by customers, cleaning display cases and restocking shelves.

She looked up and saw the managerial offices were located on the second floor. As she moved down the aisle toward the stairway, salespeople smiled and greeted here cordially. She did sense the closeness and personality Ron had described. There wasn't that hustle and bustle characteristic of the big, urban stores. What was that concept Ron had mentioned—a big town store with a small town attitude. There was no question in her mind: the man she had met knew these stores. She sensed he even knew them intimately.

The second level of the store was only a narrow balcony with a few managerial offices and business offices. She walked on until she came to the door displaying John Cutler's name and his title. Then she paused to take a deep breath.

How do I look? she wondered. I didn't even check myself in the car's rearview mirror. She had been crying; her hair was probably disheveled. This man will probably think he's talking to a lunatic. She looked about frantically and saw a rest room at the end of the balcony corridor. Hurrying to it, she went inside and organized herself in front of the mirror over the sink. But when she studied the face reflected in the mirror, she couldn't get away from the impression she was looking at a terribly distraught individual.

Well, what of it? she thought. I am terribly distraught. He'll have to understand and appreciate that.

Then she thought, what if Emma Cutler had already called her brother and warned him about her, describing her as part of some scam? He might call the police before she had a chance to explain any of it. This whole thing could be a disaster. Was it wise to go on?

She continued staring at herself in the mirror as though the answer to her question would appear on her image in the glass. You'll have to take the chance, she told herself. There's nothing else left to do, but go home and try to forget Ron Cutler...bury the ring at the bottom of some drawer and drive the memories away. She could hear Betty Dancer's advice, "Chalk it up to experience, honey. You're not the first woman to be taken by a man, nor will you be the last."

Maybe Betty could live with that, but I can't, Jillian thought, turning abruptly from the mirror. She would do it—she would confront John Cutler, Ron's father, and she would tell him all of it, as quickly and as honestly as she could. She would spare no details and she would get to the truth, no matter how painful it might be for either or for both of them.

CHAPTER ELEVEN

"No, I DON'T have an appointment," Jillian said, "but I must see Mr. Cutler. It's very important." She fought to keep her voice under control because she recognized that she was on the borderline of hysteria.

John Cutler's secretary stared up at Jillian. The secretary, a woman easily in her early fifties, pulled in the corner of her mouth so tightly it twisted her nose and distorted her face. A face of rubber, Jillian thought. There was no one else in the small outer office, an office that consisted of the secretary's desk, a small adjoining table for a personal computer, and a black, imitation leather couch. There was a small table in front of the couch, but there was nothing on the table.

"Well, what is this in reference to?" the secretary asked, looking down at the papers she had been reading. When Jillian didn't respond immediately, she looked up. "What is the nature of your business?" the secretary asked, speaking more slowly and more deliberately. Her eyes flashed her impatience, but there was no retreat in Jillian's voice.

"It's personal."

"Is it in regard to a job?"

"I said it's personal," Jillian repeated. She glared at her, eyes bright with fury. She had seen and dealt with secretaries who were good at insulating their bosses, but there was something very annoying about this woman. Obviously she was accustomed to a great deal of power. Jillian imagined she made many decisions for John Cutler, perhaps some without his knowledge. She knew the type—they would just assume more and more authority as time went by.

"Does Mr. Cutler know you?"

"Jesus Christ," Jillian said. She said it so sharply the secretary actually backed away from her desk. "I'm not an assassin and that's not the president of the United States. I told you it's urgent I see Mr. Cutler and I told you it's personal. Now either you announce me or I'll walk in unannounced."

"This better be important," the secretary said, but she was intimidated. She buzzed the inner office and a rather small, slight voice responded.

"Yes, Lucy?"

"There's a Jillian Caldwell insisting to see you. She says it's urgent and she says it's personal."

"Jillian Caldwell?"

"That's correct, Mr. Cutler."

"I don't recall...all right, let her come in."

"Go on in," the secretary said. She pressed her lips together so hard it whitened the area around her mouth.

"Thank you." Jillian took a deep breath and opened the door to John Cutler's office.

For the first few moments she looked at everything but John Cutler. The room took her breath away. John Cutler had surrounded himself—no, Jillian thought, it would be more accurate to describe it as buried himself—in memorabilia of his son Ron.

To the left were three shelves upon which were stacked all sorts of trophies...for baseball, for basketball, for track, even for ring toss. Beside the shelves and on every wall in the office, there were pictures of Ron in various uniforms at various ages of his life. There were a number of pictures of Ron and his parents, and two large pictures of Ron donning his high school graduation cap and gown. On the right wall was Ron's college diploma, a variety of letters of commendation and some ribbons awarded for first place in various project contests.

On Jillian's immediate right was a picture of Ron and his father at the construction site for one of the other Cutler department stores. Ron was holding a shovel and both he and his father wore construction helmets.

She couldn't help her reaction. So many of the things she saw had the effect of a small blow. She brought her hand to her mouth and gasped. Then she looked straight ahead at the surprised elderly man seated behind the large oak desk. He was dressed in a double-breasted dark blue suit and tie. His thin, gray hair was neatly trimmed and brushed back. Jillian could see the strong resemblance between him and Ron. There was no doubt in her mind that she was standing before his father.

"Do I know you?" he asked.

She shook her head. It took her a few moments to risk trying to speak.

"No. I'm a friend...girlfriend of your son's."

"Oh. Come in, come in. Have a seat, Miss..."

"Caldwell, Jillian Caldwell."

"Jillian. Take a seat. Where did you know Ron? In college?"

"No, sir," she said. She saw that he was preparing himself for some warm reminiscences of his son. Jillian sat down, afraid that if she tried to stand again, she might not have the strength to do so. It was difficult to take her eyes from the photographs and awards, but she did so. The old man looked patient and gentle, but also exhausted by the weight of his grief, a weight she sensed he still carried at nearly full intensity.

"You say, not college?"

"That's right."

"Well, then," he said, a tense smile on his face, "where did you meet my son?"

"In New York City."

"Oh?"

"Yes." Once Jillian began, she felt the need to continue without stopping. "I'm in advertising. I work for Nelsen Grant Associates, a public relations firm. We have a number of department store accounts. Your son came in to see us because he was interested in expanding your stores, developing other outlets in places like New Jersey. At least that was what he thought about initially. We met because I was assigned to the project, but we began talking less and less about business and more and more about...about each other. I fell in love with your son, Mr. Cutler, and I believed—I thought, your son fell in love with me."

John Cutler didn't respond for a moment. His expression hardened slowly and then he sat back.

"Why have you come to me with this story now, Miss Caldwell? My son's been dead for five years."

"Because I was with your son last weekend, Mr. Cutler, and—" she said opening her right hand "—it was then that he gave me this."

John Cutler's eyes widened. He sat forward and looked over the desk at the ring in Jillian's hand. Then he looked up at her to see if she was serious.

"Is this some kind of a joke?"

"No, Mr. Cutler, but I'm beginning to wish that's all it was."

The elderly man studied her again. Jillian felt sure that he was at least what Ron had said—a man in his seventies, albeit a physically strong seventies. Now though, as he contemplated her, the wrinkles in his forehead deepened and the lines around the corners of his eyes and his mouth lengthened. It was as though he could age at will. But the bright rich blue in his eyes remained sharp, honed into a perceptive vision by the intensity of his concentration. She felt under glass. Surely this was and has continued to be one of John Cutler's strengths—the ability to see quickly and clearly and get himself right to the heart of the matter. A man in business had to have efficient eyesight. He's not a man easily lied to, Jillian thought.

"I'm afraid I don't understand," he said. Although he said it softly, there was a clearly underlying ominous note. He would not be trifled with when it came to any references to his son.

"I don't really know how to begin except to begin at the beginning," she said, feeling as though she were tripping over her own words. She was thrown back to the few times in her life when as a teenager she had been sent to the school principal to be reprimanded for cutting up in class.

"Then I suggest you do just that." John Cutler sat back, folded his left arm across his chest, and pressed the closed fist of his right hand against his face, propping the right arm against his left. Jillian thought he was all eyes.

"Well, as I said, Ron came to us for promotional work. Well, actually, to see if our firm could do what he wanted. We began to see each other socially, a relationship developed, and last week he asked me to marry him. I didn't give him an answer immediately, and when I stopped hearing from him, I tried to contact him and failed. I then decided to drive up here and find him. I went to your house and your sister..."

"You saw Emma?"

"Yes. She was kind enough to let me in and to talk to me. She showed me his portrait and then..."

"She let you in my house?"

"Yes, but..."

"Who the hell are you?"

"I told you, Mr. Cutler. Please, hear me out." Jillian's face began to crumple. She felt her cheeks tremble and her eyes water. Her lips vibrated with the tremors. "At first I thought he might have been an imposter, someone posing as your son to... to impress me or, I don't know what... but then, when I saw the portrait photograph..."

"What about it?"

"It was the same man."

"How can that be? What is this? Are you going to ask me for money soon?"

"No, sir. I have no intention of doing that. Believe me. And I can appreciate..." Jillian looked around the room. "Appreciate what you've gone through. I wouldn't have come in here if I could think of any other way to get at the truth."

"To get at the truth? What truth? Miss Caldwell, five years ago, I stood by an opened grave and watched them lower my boy's body into the earth. I didn't leave until the last shovelful of dirt covered the coffin. I know where he is because I'm down there with him. Now you come in here and—"

Jillian could hold back no longer. The tears broke out with an intensity she had rarely experienced. She pressed her hands against her face to hold back the outburst. Her body shook. She looked up at the shocked John Cutler and then got herself up from the chair. Before he could say another word, she ran from the office.

The secretary looked up with surprise as she ran by her and out to the second floor balcony. For a moment she was too confused to remember how to get downstairs. She went toward the rest room and stopped. Then she hurried to her right and bounded down the flight of steps, intending to run all the way to the front doors of the department store. She was halfway across the floor when a security guard stopped her.

"Please, I just have to get out," she said. He stood before her, holding her back by seizing both her shoulders.

"Mr. Cutler called down," he said. "He wants you back upstairs."

"What?" The guard looked behind her and upward. Jillian turned toward the balcony and looked up. John Cutler was standing by the railing, looking down at her. Jillian searched her pocketbook for a handkerchief and dabbed it over her face. The security guard remained right beside her.

"It's all right," she said. She took a deep breath and forced a smile. "I'm going back up."

She straightened her posture and started back upstairs, sensing that she had somehow broken through the wall of confusion.

"THERE'S OBVIOUSLY BEEN some terrible mistake, whether deliberate or not," John Cutler said after Jillian had reentered his office and sat down. Cutler's secretary stood by the doorway and glared in as though she expected to go to her boss's aid at any moment. Jillian said nothing. She stared down at the floor. Cutler looked at his secretary. "It's all right, Lucy. You can close the door."

"I'll be right outside if you need me, Mr. Cutler," she said, stating the obvious.

As soon as the secretary left, Jillian looked up at the elderly man who stood beside her. There was a softness in his face now that was encouraging. He stood by the corner of the desk, the fingertips of his left hand just touching the surface. His thoughtful expression bore a strong resemblance to Ron's. He was as tall as Ron. Age, even grief, hadn't bent him over. He had the straight, strong posture that radiated confidence. She recalled the first time she had seen Ron and her impression that he was the executive type.

"I know how bizarre all this must sound to you, Mr. Cutler, but can you imagine how it is with me? I thought I was going to marry your son."

"What can I say? You believe me when I tell you my son is dead, don't you, Miss Caldwell?"

"Yes, of course."

"Then what can I say?" he repeated. "This is either a terrible confusion or a sick joke. What else could it be?"

"I know, but the man who came to me, who... courted me," she said, thinking that was a term John Cutler would appreciate, "looked exactly like..." She turned toward the photographs. "Exactly like your son. I have no picture of him," she added quickly, "but there's no mistake about it. And look at how much he knew about you and your business."

John Cutler's face whitened some. He nodded thoughtfully and went back around his desk to his chair.

"Did your wife die of cancer a few years ago, Mr. Cutler?"

"Yes."

"Would Ron be about thirty now?"

"Last February seventh."

"Did he go to Harvard Business College?"

"Yes, he did."

"You're seventy-five years old, aren't you, Mr. Cutler?" The elderly man nodded. Jillian stopped as though she had offered irrefutable evidence, but John Cutler looked unimpressed.

"Do your salespeople keep little books on their customers so that they can contact them personally whenever there are sales or items for sale that might interest them?" she asked, unable to control the excitement that came from remembering the details.

"It's true, they do that, Miss Caldwell." John Cutler stared at her a moment and then leaned forward, folding his hands on the desk. "But everything you asked me is really only common knowledge," he said. "There's nothing intimate about it."

"But why would someone go through all the trouble of accumulating these details?"

"I don't know. Maybe the man looked a lot like Ron and so he tried to take advantage by using Ron's identity. The world is full of impostors of one kind or another," John Cutler said, but he looked deeply thoughtful about it. Jillian sensed there could be something more.

"He wasn't like an imposter though; he was so sincere."

"Forgive me for saying so, but a woman in love is quite vulnerable, especially to phonies."

"But if he was pretending to be your son, he's been doing it for some time. People knew him. People we met while I was with him knew him as Ron Cutler. I can give you the name of the tourist house owner in Provincetown, Cape Cod, for example." She paused, her voice rising with excitement.

"It wouldn't matter. What would it prove? That someone who looks like my son is using his name and his reputation? This is sick, so very sick. I'm afraid you've been victimized, along with the others."

"You've never been confronted by anything like this before? No one has ever told you stories about someone using Ron's name, someone who looks just like him?"

"Of course not. Do you think I would tolerate such a thing if I had heard of it?"

Jillian sat back, feeling frustrated and defeated.

"No, I suppose not."

"I feel sorry for you," Cutler said, but his face took on a far-off, dazed look. Jillian thought for a moment and then sat forward.

"Why did you have only one child, Mr. Cutler?" she asked.

"What's that?"

"Only one child and so late in life, too. Why was that?"

"Why does that matter?" he asked, his voice taking on a note of annoyance.

"To tell you the truth, I don't know anymore what matters and what doesn't. For the last few weeks, I have been with a man who was warm and sensitive and charming. He filled my life with excitement and hope and when he talked about you and this world up here, he did so with the utmost admiration. I believed in him and I saw that other people who met him were taken with him as well. He was an exceptional man, full of personality and intelligence, a very strong man."

"That was my son," John Cutler said, his voice cracking.

"I don't know why, Mr. Cutler; I don't believe in ghosts, but I believe the man I met was the man in these pictures."

"My God." John Cutler shook his head.

"He was your only child?"

"Yes."

"Why did you have him so late in life?" she repeated. He sat back without responding for a moment. "If there is something you know, something, anything, no matter how insignificant it might seem, that would help me to understand what has happened to me..."

"My wife was unable to have children."

"Ron was adopted?"

"No," he said quickly. "Ron was my son." He turned toward the pictures on his left. "The resemblances are too obvious, are they not?"

"Yes, they are, but..."

"You have to understand, Miss Caldwell, this was before the scientific miracles of transplants and artificial insemination..."

"Yes," Jillian said, holding her breath. She understood he was justifying something, but what?

"My boy was exceptional; he was a great young man," John Cutler said, staring at the photographs to his left.

Jillian looked toward the pictures that he seemed mesmerized by now, and then she began to speak, the words simply flowing from her as though they had been memorized. "He could be poetic in a manly way. When he was near you, you could feel his strength. There was a sense of security because he was so confident and self-assured. He had such a wit, but he didn't make jokes at someone else's expense. There was a gentleness, a sensitivity to him. Sometimes you could feel a great sadness in him. One of his favorite poems was Dover Beach by Matthew Arnold."

"My God," John Cutler said. "How do you know all this?"

"I can't say for sure, Mr. Cutler, not yet, not until I know for myself. Please, tell me what you can about Ron's past."

He nodded. Her heart began to beat quickly; she realized she had convinced him.

"What I'm about to tell you is a very personal secret. There are only a handful of people who know, but somehow, for some reason, I don't mind telling you. Maybe, because of what you've been through, you have a right to know. What difference does it make now anyway?" he said. "My wife's dead; my son's dead; the need for secrecy died with them."

"I will appreciate whatever you tell me, Mr. Cutler."

"Yes," he said, his voice tired. He closed and then opened his eyes as if it took great effort to do something so simple. "My wife and I decided that we wanted a child, but we didn't want to adopt. We wanted the child to be a Cutler. Call it family pride, whatever. Anyway, there was this woman... who she is, doesn't matter now, I guess. To make a long story short, Miss Caldwell, she had my baby. Nearly four months before the baby was to be born, my wife went off and when she returned, she had Ron with her.

"She never once thought of him as anything less than her own child," he added quickly. "She even got to believe in the story of the labor and delivery herself. I'm sure you can understand that need... the need to feel he was hers, the need to have gone through the birth. It was an illusion we both learned to accept as reality."

He paused and sat back. He looked lighter, more relaxed. It was as though the disclosure of the revelations had brought him deep relief. Then his face quivered and he took on a look of deep sadness.

"I used to believe we had cheated fate, defeated it in some way, and then... Ron was killed and fate took its revenge." He shook his head. Tears had come into his eyes. Jillian didn't move. She sat so still, afraid that the slightest sound, the slightest movement, would destroy the magic of the moment. Finally he looked up at her as though he had just realized she was sitting there. "That's the whole story. I'm afraid it does nothing to help you."

"Thank you for telling me all this," she said softly. He shrugged.

"It just seemed the time to do it."

"I don't believe, though, that it offers me no hope," Jillian said. She continued to speak quietly, feeling as though she were tiptoeing over thin ice. "There is something left for me to do."

"What do you mean?"

"I need one more thing from you. As you said, it can't matter anymore, except it might matter to me."

"What is that?" His eyes widened with interest.

"I need to know the woman's name and where I can find her."

"I don't know about that," he said. "Anyway I don't even know if she is still where she was thirty years ago. We had no contact at all afterward. It was part of our arrangement. You can understand why, I'm sure."

"Of course. I won't make any trouble. I promise. What trouble could I make anyway?"

"But what good can it possibly do for you to meet her?"

"I'm not sure, Mr. Cutler. I must get to the bottom of all this." She looked at one of the pictures again, the one with Ron and his father at a construction site. "Whatever has happened, it has tied me in a deep way to your son."

"This is ghoulish. If Emma even knew what I had told you..."

"Oh, I won't say anything to her," Jillian said quickly. Her enthusiasms brought a smile to the old man's face. He studied her for a moment.

"You say you're in advertising, huh?"

"Yes, sir." She was more comfortable talking about her career. "I haven't been in it all that long, but I was just made a vice president in my firm."

"That so? What was the firm called again?"

"Nelsen Grant Associates. It's a very progressive and energetic firm. For example, we're doing the Benton walkathon. It's a walk across America. The Bentons—"

"I heard about that. I saw something about it on television. That's your project?"

"Yes, sir. I brought Pooley Shoes in on it."

"Good cause. Good business move, too," he added. John Cutler paused to scrutinize Jillian again.

"Somehow I think you're the kind of woman my son would have married, Miss Caldwell. He wasn't one to go for the clinging-vine type. He liked a woman with grit. Not that he would have gone for some of these woman's liberation fanatics," he added quickly, his eyebrows dipping. "He still liked feeling in charge," Cutler said, a memory replaying over his face.

"I know, sir."

"You make me feel as if you do." He looked down for a moment. "Her name was Gloria Simon," he said quietly. "She lived in Oneonta. It's a small city in a more rural area a little over two hours from here, but as I said, that was thirty years ago and I have had no contact with her since. She had had another child out of wedlock and she needed money. She was a strong, healthy woman."

"How old was she?"

"About twenty-two. No real job at the time. I have no idea what she got into since."

"Was there an address, a phone number?"

"I never forgot the address...73 Maplewood Avenue, although I was there only three times. She took these fertility pills..." A redness came to his face. "Never worked for my wife. Ironic, isn't it?"

"Yes, it is."

"I wouldn't want you to disturb her," he said firmly. "Who knows how she feels about it all now? She might have gotten married and started a whole new life, not revealing any of it to her husband. It wouldn't be fair to hurt her. She lived up to her part of the bargain."

"I can understand that. I'll be discreet."

"What could you possibly want with her?"

"I don't know. I don't even know if I'll approach her."

He thought for a moment.

"On the other hand, if I believed for one moment that she had something to do with an imposter..."

"That's a possibility, I suppose," Jillian said, the reality of such an event occurring to her. What would she do if it were true? The ramifications seemed enormous at this moment.

"I want you to promise me that if you do discover who is impersonating my son, you will call me immediately and not try to do anything about it yourself. You owe me that much."

"I will."

"Fine." He sat back, seemingly satisfied. John Cutler turned his chair so he faced the window.

"Thank you," Jillian said, and stood up. "I'm sorry for the grief I rekindled."

"You didn't rekindle anything, Miss Caldwell. It's been burning brightly on its own power for five years," he said without turning back to her.

Jillian nodded. She said goodbye and left the office. Cutler's secretary looked up from her desk quickly, her eyes flaming with indignation.

"I don't know who you are, miss, but if you did anything to disturb Mr. Cutler..."

"Believe me, honey," Jillian said, "whatever I could do to disturb Mr. Cutler would be nothing compared to what you could do."

Cutler's secretary gasped and Jillian smiled. She felt more like herself. The weakness, the confusion, all the dizziness was gone. She had moved through the eye of the storm and she now believed she would find a way to come face to face with Ron Cutler again, be he dead or not.

CHAPTER TWELVE

BEFORE SHE LEFT Cutler's department store, Jillian got directions to Oneonta. It wasn't until she was a good half hour on the road again that she began to question exactly what it was she was doing. Suppose she was able to locate this woman, Gloria Simon, she thought; what did she hope to gain from her? Now that she was actually on her way, she realized John Cutler had a good point when he asked that question; and of course, she was determined not to cause him any further grief.

She didn't mind the ride. It was, as John Cutler had described, a very scenic rural area. The directions took her down a long mountainside, past a large reservoir and through some beautiful farm country with long flat corn fields. Everything looked clean and fresh. There were endless picture postcard vistas, framed by the light Blue Ridge mountains on the horizon.

She was glad about going in this direction because the scenery had a calming effect. It was easy to sit back and digress, to think about the majesty of nature and the richness of life away from the turmoil of the business world.

Although the roads were in good condition, she couldn't drive quickly over them because they wound sharply around hills and rolled through small hamlets where the people who sat by storefronts or on porches looked relaxed and content, nourished by the warm summer sun and the clear air. She sensed from the way they looked at her that her passing by was the highlight of the day. She waved at some people and some waved back; some simply nodded or smiled.

Onward she drove, drawn by the hope that somehow some piece of information would lead her to an understanding of what had happened to her and what was happening. Whenever she got the urge to turn around and go back to New York City, she felt the frustration that would come by being defeated by the mystery. It turned her confusion and indecision into anger. There were too many things inside her that wouldn't permit a surrender.

Oneonta came up quickly because she had lost her sense of time. It was as John Cutler had described: a small city. Actually, hardly a city, Jillian thought as she drove into the downtown area. There wasn't the traffic, the hustle and bustle, the urban look that characterized American cities today. Its movement reflected the even tempered and complacent world that surrounded it. Even the patrolman on the corner looked and sounded more like a citizen volunteer than a hardened, professional city traffic officer. He pushed his cap back and scratched his temple after she asked for Maplewood Avenue. Then he nodded.

"You know what Maplewood Avenue is," he said, as though she had lived here all her life and they were discussing the changes in the city, "it's one of those dead-end streets with those houses that are supposed to be cleared for that apartment complex. If it ever gets off the ground," he added.

"Would you know a Gloria Simon?" she asked, encouraged by his down-to-earth demeanor. He looked as if he would know just about every resident.

"Gloria Simon? No, ma'am, can't say as I do. Does she have a business of some kind?"

"I'm not sure."

"Well, Maplewood is off of Parker. You can see the back end of Hartwick College from there."

"I see, and Parker?"

"Just make the third left and turn right at the first intersection."

"Thank you," she said, and followed his directions. Maplewood was hardly a street. It was more like something unfinished. The pavement just ended and became dirt road. There were half a dozen houses on both sides, as dilapidated and run-down as the patrolman had suggested. It was difficult to read any numbers, or even understand why there was a need for numbers so large, but she pulled up in front of what she assumed to be 73 Maplewood Avenue.

It was a small two-story building with a box porch that leaned to the right. The sidewalk leading up to the front steps was all cracked and pithy. One of the windows in the front of the house was boarded up, yet there were curtains hanging over the other windows. The dark brown siding was peeled in spots and she could see where the gutter pipes under the roof collapsed. On the right side, one was just hanging. However, what there was of lawn had been recently cut.

Jillian turned off her car engine and stared at the house. Did she simply want to walk up to it and knock on the door? What if Gloria Simon answered? Would she come right out and ask her questions about Ron Cutler? Would the woman tolerate any questions?

The fact that the house looked both deserted and lived in at the same time seemed to fit in with everything else. All else was a paradox, why not this? Jillian wondered. It being a paradox, though, encouraged her. It seemed to fit into the schematic of suspense. Anyway, she had come this far; there wasn't any point in simply sitting in the car and staring at the house in which Ron Cutler's biological mother lived.

She got out and walked slowly up the weather damaged sidewalk to the degenerating building. The wooden steps creaked ominously when she began to climb them. The railing shook. It was as if the entire house were coming alive at her touch, vibrating, straining, even moaning at being violated. She got the feeling she was moving over into a surrealistic world. Shadows darkened; the sounds of the downtown portion of the city died away. She felt a chilling breeze wrap around the building and embrace her.

There was a partially opened screen door that looked like it would never close completely because the jamb and hinges were warped. She pushed it as far to the right as she could and knocked softly on the dark windowpane of the peeling oak front door. Her tapping was absorbed within and gone almost as soon as she had done it. She tapped again, this time harder, firmer, striking the wooden portion of the door.

Now she heard the definite sounds of footsteps, but they came from behind her and not from within the house. Before she turned around completely, she heard a man ask, "What do you want?"

"Oh."

Jillian stared down at a rather disheveled, elderly man dressed in a pair of torn jeans, ripped sneakers, and a red flannel shirt with its sleeves rolled up roughly to his elbows. His long, thin arms were covered by dark gray hair. He was almost completely bald, but over the top of his skull were large, black birthmarks that looked more like welts and bruises. His cheeks were sunken but his nearly toothless mouth pressed his lips out like the lips of a fish. Indeed his bulging eyes reminded Jillian of fish eyes. She didn't feel threatened by him, however, because he looked fragile and tiny, reminding her of pictures of Vietnamese refugees.

"I'm looking for Gloria Simon," she said. "Isn't this where she lives?"

"Gloria Simon don't live there. Luba Porter lives there, only she don't come to the door when she's alone."

"Luba Porter?" Jillian looked back at the front entrance and then turned to the old man. "Is this 73 Maplewood?"

"Yep. The number used to be just right of the door there. Fell off years ago, but her son don't bother to put it back. What for? Nobody comes to see her, but him," he said quickly, as though it was important he answered his own questions before she could.

"I see," Jillian said. She started down the steps slowly. The old man remained where he was, staring at her. He had his hands sunk deeply into his pockets, pushing the loosely fitting pants down below his hips. She imagined the clothing might really be his, but age was shrinking him. "Do you live on this street?"

"Right over there," he said, gesturing with his head. "You're not part of that group trying to get us condemned, are you?"

"Oh, no," Jillian said. "I'm from New York City," she added, not knowing why she did. That didn't prove anything.

"I lived in that house all my life. My wife died in it and I'm going to die in it," he said defiantly. He lifted his curly eyebrows for emphasis. The thin white hairs that spun out of them looked more like thin wire.

"I understand. All your life? Then, you must've known Gloria Simon, right? At one time she lived in this house."

"Yeah, I knew her."

"It's very important that I locate her. Do you have any idea where she is now? Did she get married and move away? Is she still in Oneonta?"

"Whoa. Slow down."

Jillian smiled.

"I'm sorry. It's just that I've come a long way." The old man didn't smile. He continued to study her, obviously deciding whether or not to be cooperative. "Please, I don't mean to do anyone any harm. I just have to find her. I have nothing to do with any housing projects, believe me."

"Her name ain't Simon no more. She got married a good twenty-five years ago."

"Really?"

"It's Kane."

"Kane?" Jillian had seen some billboards with that name on the way into the city. "Does she have anything to do with Kane Construction?"

"She is Kane Construction," the old man said. "Her and her sons. Her husband died a few years ago—heart attack."

"I see. Where is their office?"

"End of Broadway, you make a right onto Burton Hollow. You can't miss it."

"I really appreciate this," Jillian said. For a moment she thought maybe he expected to be paid for the information. He looked like he needed it, but before she could even attempt it, he started away. "Thanks again," she called. He didn't turn around. He just waved and muttered.

"As long as you're not one of them," he said. She smiled and got back into the car.

Following his directions, she came to a large, flat-roofed brick building with two big picture windows over which was written, Kane Construction Company. To the right of the building was a large lot in which there were piles of lumber, metal forms, scaffolding, and a half dozen pickup trucks, all bearing the name Kane Construction across their doors.

Jillian parked just before the entrance way to the largest lot and turned off the engine. She looked into the rearview mirror to straighten her hair and then reached for her pocketbook. Just before she opened the door, however, another Kane Construction pickup truck pulled into the lot before her. She heard some of the men on the lot shout greetings, making jokes about it being "about time they got here." And then she saw the men get out of the truck and start for the Kane Construction office building.

A small sound got caught at the bottom of her throat. She thought she could actually choke to death on it, but she couldn't swallow. Her heart felt as if it had stopped and then began to pump so rapidly it made her dizzy. She brought her hand to her face and pressed her palm against her right cheek. Her skin was on fire.

Both the men who got out of the pickup truck wore construction clothing, but the tall, dark man who led the way was unmistakably Ron Cutler.

As she watched him walk, she heard the words replayed:

"An only child."

"Killed in a car accident five years ago."

"Drunken driver. Head on...one of the biggest funerals ever."

"I stood by an opened grave and watched them lower my boy's body into the earth. I didn't leave until the last shovelful of dirt covered the coffin. I know where he is because I'm down there with him."

Her imagination went wild. Could the wrong man be buried in that grave?

Could Ron, when he found out the truth about his birth, have resented what had been done, and have gone back to his biological mother, punishing his father by having him believe he had been killed? Maybe he was living a schizophrenic existence.

Who was really in the car? Had the body been burned so badly that immediate recognition was impossible, but no one had bothered to confirm because the dead man carried Ron's identification?

He wasn't a ghost, but there was no question that the man who was walking into that office was the man with whom she had fallen in love. And he was the man in the pictures in John Cutler's office!

Why did he do all this?

She wanted to get out of the car and walk right into the office to confront him, but the shock of seeing him moving so nonchalantly and joking with other men stopped her. She was intimidated by his actual existence. She had almost come to believe that all that had happened, had happened between her and a ghost. Now it was certain that there were other, perhaps even logical and understandable explanations. She had hoped for that, but she wondered if she could deal with them.

She decided to watch from a distance and observe for a while. She wanted to ease into the rest of this, now that she had made the great discovery.

Another idea occurred: was this man an imposter, maybe through plastic surgery duplicating Ron Cutler's image? Could it be as John Cutler had suggested, a clever scam? But if that was so, what role did she play in all this? Why did they use her? Perhaps as a test of sorts. If he could succeed in convincing a New York publicity executive of his validity, then...then what? Whatever the reasons, she was both frightened and infuriated by it all.

She started her car and drove away from the construction company site. Then she turned in a driveway and came back to park across the street from the office where she could sit and watch with less chance of being discovered.

What was she watching for? She didn't have long to wait and wonder. Ron and the other man came out of the office and went back to their truck in the lot. A few moments later he pulled out and made the right turn, riding right past her. She covered her face, but looked at him through her fingers as he went by. For a moment they were so close to one another that it sent chills through her body.

She watched as the truck went down to the corner and turned left to disappear. A few moments later she got out of the car, took a deep breath to steady herself, and then walked across the street to the Kane

Construction Company. Now she had a reason to have that conversation with Gloria Simon Kane, the surrogate John Cutler had chosen thirty years ago. After only her short but revealing visit with him, she found she liked John Cutler and was sincerely sympathetic about what had happened to him. Perhaps she would have the opportunity to do something for both herself and for him after all.

ONCE, JILLIAN and her uncle Phil had had a conversation about the family and the strength and determination she'd inherited. She couldn't remember exactly why they ended up by themselves talking for what turned out to be a good part of the afternoon, but they were there on the patio one summer day. She had been with her first firm for nearly six months and she was very excited about the future. Her parents had already indicated some unhappiness about her living alone in New York.

"Actually, you don't surprise me," Uncle Phil said, "and I'm a little surprised your mother is such a wimp." Jillian laughed.

"Maybe it's just an act. I'm sure you know there are women who pretend to be something they're not. It's their way of handling their men."

"Listen to you. Full of experience, huh?" he said, pretending to be impressed.

"Only my share. Nothing compared to you, of course."

Uncle Phil liked that. His eyes lit up and he shook his head in admiration.

"See," he said, "I'm right."

"About what?"

"You and your heritage. Your mother forgets that your grandparents were tough hombres. We come from a hardy stock, Jillian. You know, your maternal grandmother came over here from Europe at the age of eighteen to marry a man she had never met. Traveled all by herself. Tough woman."

"I don't remember her well."

"Too bad. You remind me of her sometimes. She'd get this look in her eyes. You could just feel the determination. Her spine would harden and she would go forward, full speed ahead. If she believed she was right, that is. I think you got that same steel in your veins when you need it," he said, his expression turning serious. "I don't worry about you, Jillian. I don't worry about you at all."

It wasn't just a coincidence that she recalled that conversation with Uncle Phil as she crossed the street to enter the offices of the construction company. There were other times in the past, times at work especially, when she had to reach back for a strength she wasn't quite sure she had.

In a box in her closet back in her apartment, she had a picture of her grandmother. She had looked at it many times after her conversation with Uncle Phil, each time reinforcing the impression that she and her grandmother looked a great deal alike. At this moment she envisioned her and those eyes that had peered into the foggy Atlantic when she crossed the ocean at eighteen to start a new life. The image gave Jillian the strength to meet his challenge, whatever it might turn out to be.

"I want to speak with Mrs. Kane," she said to the young woman who came out to greet her as soon as Jillian walked through the door. The woman carried some paperwork she had been doing on an adding machine. Her glasses were on a chain draped around her neck. She lifted them and put them on quickly, as though it were improper to permit a customer to catch her with them resting on her bosom.

"She went home about an hour ago, but Michael's here."

"Michael?"

"Her son."

"How old is he?"

"Pardon me?" The young woman smiled. "Did you say, how old?"

"Yes."

"He's thirty-five."

Jillian remembered John Cutler saying the woman had had a child out of wedlock.

"Can you tell me how to get to Mrs. Kane's house? This is a personal matter," she added in a softer tone. "It has nothing to do with the business."

"Oh. Well, you continue on down Burton Hollow until you come to Wildwood Drive. It's the third house on the right, a gingerbread house. You can't miss it; it's the only one on the street," she added, a tone of pride in her voice.

"Thank you."

"Any problems, Terri?" a stout young man asked. Dressed in a short-sleeved shirt and dark blue slacks, he looked about five-seven and twenty pounds overweight. His reddish-brown hair was showing signs of early baldness. Jillian saw a slight resemblance to Ron in his face, but the absence of the Cutler characteristics left him rather bland and ordinary. He had dull brown eyes, a soft, feminine mouth, a round jaw, and a pale complexion spotted here and there with rust-colored blotches.

"No, Michael. This woman was looking for Gloria."

"Oh? Can I help you?"

"I think not," Jillian said. "Thank you so much anyway." She started out, aware that they were both watching her, their curiosity piqued.

It took her only five minutes to find the gingerbread house. It was located on what was obviously a block of well-to-do residences. All the houses, like the gingerbread owned by the Kanes, had well-manicured lawns and hedges. Significant money had been spent on landscaping. Expensive cars were parked in the driveways.

She got out quickly and walked right up to the front door. The chimes played the first phrase of "As Time Goes By," the theme song from the film *Casablanca*.

She took a deep breath as the door opened and Gloria Simon Kane looked out at her.

"I'm looking for Mrs. Gloria Kane," Jillian said. She said it for lack of any other way to begin. It was obvious to her the moment she set eyes on this woman that she was the former Gloria Simon, mother of Ron Cutler. Ron not only had the same blue tint in his eyes, but he had her intense gaze, as well. It was the look that had made her feel vulnerable and naked—inquisitive, penetrating and unrelenting.

Ron also had her shape face—the high cheek bones, the sharply drawn jaw and Roman nose. Apparently what she had thought were Cutler characteristics were also Simon characteristics. Ron's brother took after Gloria's first lover more than he did her, Jillian thought. Ron, on the other hand, combined the best of Gloria Simon and John Cutler.

Gloria Kane was a tall woman, standing at least an inch or so taller than Jillian. Although her hips had thickened with age, she still maintained a handsome womanly figure—high bosom, soft shoulders, and a graceful neck. Gray streaks ran through her very light brown hair, which she wore straight and short, cut just below her ears.

"I'm Gloria Kane. What can I do for you?"

"I'm Jillian Caldwell. Does the name mean anything to you?"

"Caldwell?" She thought for a moment and while she did, Jillian concentrated on her eyes. Her initial response was she didn't think there was any deception behind them. "I'm sorry, I don't remember...oh, are you related to Tommy Callwell?"

"No, it's Caldwell," Jillian said, stressing the "d."

"Well, what's this about?"

"It's about Ron."

"Ron?"

Jillian caught the quick blinking, the tightening around the corners of Gloria Kane's mouth, and the stiffening in her posture.

"Ron Cutler," she said, "your son."

For a moment Gloria Kane did not respond.

"I don't know what you're talking about. My name is Kane," she said. "You've made some kind of mistake." She started to close the door.

"I know who you are," Jillian said quickly. She didn't put her foot in the door, but she did step forward in an intimidating manner. "I know all of it. Almost all of it, that is. That's why I'm here. I was with John Cutler today. May I come in?"

Jillian surprised herself with her aggressiveness, but it had its effect. After a short beat, Gloria Kane stepped back to let her enter. She closed the door behind her but she didn't lead Jillian farther into the house. They remained in the short entranceway, the ostentatious and oversized wall mirror capturing both of them in a dramatic posture. Jillian felt she had stepped into some movie and was now watching it played before her.

"Why, after all these years, did he decide to tell someone?" Gloria Kane asked. "Secrecy was so important to him and to her," she added, her mouth curling up in the left corner. "They couldn't wait to get away from me. Why?" she repeated, her annoyance building.

"Because of this," Jillian said, and once again displayed the engagement ring Ron had given her.

Gloria Kane looked at it for a moment and then reached down to take it from Jillian's right palm. She turned the ring about as slowly as would an appraiser and then looked at Jillian.

"Where did you get this?"

"Ron gave it to me. In Provincetown last weekend. We saw a great deal of each other during the last few weeks. I admit it was a fast romance, but I believed it was a sincere one. I don't know what his purpose was, but when Ron didn't call me all week after we had returned from the cape and..."

"Ron?"

"Yes, Ron."

"You mean you believed you've been seeing John Cutler's son, Ron?"

"And your son," Jillian added, determined not to lose the advantage she now felt she was building. Gloria Kane's voice had lowered into a loud whisper.

"But...but he's dead," she said. "He's been dead for—"

"Five years, I know." Jillian smirked to indicate her skepticism. Gloria Kane stared at her until an understanding took hold.

"My God," Gloria said. She looked at the ring again as if to confirm its actual presence in her fingers. "This was my mother's ring."

"What does that mean? Why did Ron have your mother's ring?"

"Ron didn't have it. Ron didn't give it to you," Mrs. Kane said, still staring down at it.

"Look, Mrs. Kane. A little while ago, I was parked outside of your offices and a truck pulled up. I saw Ron get out of it. There's no sense in your pretending. What I want to know is—"

"That wasn't Ron Cutler," she said. "That was my son...Paul."

"What?" Jillian almost laughed aloud at this woman's attempt to cover up. Did she think that after developing a romance with Ron Cutler, a romance intense enough to culminate in a proposal of marriage, she would be mistaken about the identification?

"You didn't see Ron Cutler," Mrs. Kane repeated. "You saw Paul Kane."

"Listen, Mrs. Kane, the resemblance was unmistakable, and as you can see, our relationship was rather intense. I think I would recognize him again. Besides, only today, I saw all those pictures Mr. Cutler has of his son. If I ever needed the image of Ron's face to be reinforced, it couldn't have been better done."

"You don't understand," Gloria Kane said. "I didn't say the resemblance wasn't there, but Ron didn't give you this ring. Paul did." Before Jillian could reply, Gloria Kane added, "He's Ron's twin brother, God forgive us. God forgive me," she said, and turned away.

For a moment Jillian couldn't speak. Then she thought, this was all part of their scam, their way of escaping. "That's impossible. You don't expect me to believe that. Ron Cutler was an only child. John Cutler told me so himself. Why would he lie about the existence of his own son? I want you to know I intend to go back to Mr. Cutler because..."

"He didn't lie; he doesn't know," Gloria said in a loud, harsh whisper that sent a chill through Jillian. Mrs. Kane turned around. "He never knew."

"That he had another son? That he had twins?"

"That's right." Gloria Kane sighed and lowered her shoulders. She looked fatigued, defeated.

"But how could...why would such a thing have happened?"

Gloria Kane studied Jillian for a moment and then nodded as though confirming her own thoughts.

"Come on in," she said, "and I'll do my best to explain." Jillian watched her walk into the living room. Then she followed, realizing she had finally arrived at the threshold of the answer.

She almost wished Ron Cutler had really been a ghost.

CHAPTER THIRTEEN

"TELL ME WHO YOU ARE and how you came to meet my son," Gloria Kane said. She had indicated that Jillian sit in one of the twin blue and white patterned Queen Anne chairs. Although the chairs were side by side with a small glass table between them, she turned hers so that they would face one another and be close as they spoke.

The sitting room was small, but comfortable and tastefully done. The walls were covered with a soft-looking, cream-colored linen wallpaper. On the right wall was a realistic watercolor of the White Cliffs of Dover. Jillian immediately thought of Ron's reference to the Matthew Arnold poem, "Dover Beach." Directly across from them was a dark pine hutch. Within its glass doors she could see a collection of Norman Rockwell figures. Below and to the right of the hutch was a dark blue, camelback couch. What attracted her attention, though, was the small table at the right arm of the couch, because on it were pamphlets and books all about New York City.

"Ron..." She stopped as if she had just uttered a profanity.

"Go on, I'll understand," Gloria Kane said. She clasped her hands together and rested them on her left leg as she leaned over to listen.

"It's just that I don't know him as Paul." Jillian couldn't contain the note of sarcasm, but Gloria Kane seemed unaffected by it.

"Of course."

"He came to our publicity agency," she began, and described how she had come to know her son and how their relationship developed. Throughout it all, Gloria Kane listened with a pained expression. It gave Jillian the creeps. It was as if she were talking to a mother who had always suspected her son was a psychopath. She looked particularly disturbed when Jillian described the trip to the cape and the fact that Paul Kane had been there in the guise of Ron Cutler a few times before.

"And so you can sympathize with my need to understand," Jillian concluded. Gloria Kane said nothing. She sat staring at Jillian as if she were deciding whether or not to accept what she had told her and go on. Finally she nodded.

"Can I get you something? A drink, perhaps?"

"Not yet. Please, tell me how all this came about and what it is that is happening."

Gloria Kane sat back and closed her eyes. Her eyes were still closed when she began, perhaps, Jillian thought, to make it easier for her to do so.

"My doctor suspected that I might have twins, but he didn't confirm it until I was in the sixth month. This was thirty years ago, you know. I suppose they would know pretty quickly today. Anyway, part of my agreement with John Cutler was that I would take the fertility pills. Not that I had had any difficulty getting pregnant the first time, you understand," Gloria said. "I think it was his wife's idea so that our—what should I call them, meetings?—so that there wouldn't be that many. Later I found out it was lucky I didn't have triplets or quadruplets."

"But why did you keep the fact you were having twins a secret?"

"Our agreement had been for one child."

"I get the feeling he would have gladly paid you double."

"Oh, no question about it," Gloria said. She thought for a moment and then stood up. She went to the window behind her and peered through the curtains. Jillian's impatience created butterflies in her stomach. She had all she could do to keep from shouting. "I was starting to feel sorry for myself along about the sixth month, not only because I was going through the pregnancy that would produce children I would never see, but also because of the amount of money I had agreed to accept for this...this sale of my body," Gloria said, still looking out. She turned to look at Jillian. "I see from the expression on your face that you don't believe me. Why, because you know I had a child out of wedlock first? You think that meant I could never have self-pride or care about the children I would bear?" she asked quickly. Her face reddened with indignation.

"I don't want to judge you, Mrs. Kane. I only want to understand what happened."

Gloria Kane's face softened. She walked back to the chair and sat down.

"What happened was, I got greedy," she said. She shook her head and smiled. "Or at least, I thought I did. My plan was simple. I intended to wait a year or so and then tell him, but demand three times the amount we had agreed upon. In a sense I was going to blackmail him."

"Why didn't you go through with it?"

Gloria Kane's smile widened.

"Something unexpected happened... I fell in love with my own child; I didn't want to give him up... ever. I often had nightmares about giving up Ron. John Cutler never knew it, but I visited South Fallsburg from time to time and spied on the Cutlers. When Ron was doing things in high school, playing football, starring in school plays... whatever his activities, I went to them, sufficiently disguised, and watched him. Many times I was there, but neither John Cutler nor his wife were. At least he had someone, even though he never knew it. I felt a mother's pride, but I also felt so guilty for feeling it. It got to be terrible, mental torture, but I couldn't stop going."

"Even after you got married?"

"Yes, but my husband never knew what I was doing or what I had done. He did not know about Ron. Although, I really don't think it would have changed things between us. I was very lucky. I met and married a man who worshiped me, and as you can see, gave me and my boys a great deal. It was because of him that I developed pride in myself, went to the state college here, got a degree in business education, and eventually became heavily involved in the business. I'm glad I did because we lost him at a rather young age."

Jillian said nothing for a moment. In a way she couldn't quite understand, she found herself admiring this woman. Gloria Kane, from what she had told her so far, had significantly turned her life around. Perhaps there were women with grit in her heritage, as well.

"But what about your son? I mean, the twin you kept?"

"What about him?"

"Did he know he had a brother?"

"Not for a long time, not until he was in his mid-twenties."

"How did he find out? Did you tell him?"

"Not right away. He was working on a job in Downsville and the man who had contracted with us told him that he bore a remarkable resemblance to Ron Cutler. The man had had dealings with the Cutlers. Naturally it caught Paul's interest, and one day, without my knowing it, when he was near South Fallsburg, he went to see for himself. I'll never forget that day, the day he returned and came to me."

"Did they meet?"

"No. He just saw him from a distance, but it was enough for him to realize he was looking at his identical twin. After that and after he had learned the truth, he became obsessed with him. I thought it would end after Ron's death, but it only intensified." She paused and looked away. "I suppose it was my fault that all this has happened to you. I should have gotten some professional assistance. But I did begin to think that it was easing up," she said, turning back. "He seemed to be more himself, especially during the last year or so."

"I don't understand. What do you mean by obsessed?"

Gloria Kane looked at her watch.

"We still have time," she said. "He won't be coming home for at least another hour." She stood up. "Follow me and I'll show you."

Jillian walked out of the room with her and down the corridor to the short stairway that would take them upstairs.

"He doesn't know that I discovered all of it," Gloria said. "I couldn't confront him. I couldn't show him that I had been spying on him. Actually," she said, turning on the bottom step, "I was afraid. It had gotten that bad. I suppose what I've been doing this last year is ignore it. Guilt can do that to you: force you to ignore reality."

Jillian said nothing. She was beginning to grow frightened herself. What was it Gloria Kane wanted to show her? The woman sensed Jillian's anxiety. She reached out to touch her shoulder reassuringly.

"You'll see what I mean in a few moments," she said, and continued up the stairway, moving like one hypnotized and drawn forward by the magic of the unraveling mystery.

"THIS IS PAUL'S ROOM," Gloria Kane said. Jillian stood beside her and looked through the opened doorway. Although it was distinctly a man's room because of the colors, the pictures of cars and hunting scenes, and the gun rack above the bed's headboard, Jillian did not sense Ron Cutler. There were things rural and earthy about the man who lived in this room.

"I don't know what Ron's room would have been like," Jillian said softly, "but..."

"This wouldn't have been like it. I know. Come," Gloria said, and continued down the hallway to a closed door. "I use to keep this as a guest room, but since Michael got married and moved out, I use his room for that purpose. Now it's a bedroom for a ghost."

"Ghost?"

Gloria opened the door and stepped in, Jillian following slowly. This room was different. There were shelves of books on the right wall. Filling out the remainder of the wall space to the right were three abstract paintings. She recognized a Kandinsky and a Mondrian. To the right of the queen-size bed was a small desk. On it were stacks of business magazines, copies of the *Wall Street Journal*, and a small personal computer. She saw that the software beside it had to do with business management.

Gloria Kane went right to the wall closet and slid the doors open. Then she stepped back as though she were displaying the jewels of King Tut. Jillian stepped forward, recognizing the aroma of Ron's cologne. She touched the suit jackets, shirts and slacks.

"Well?" Gloria asked.

"It's his stuff," Jillian said. Tears had come into her eyes. Her throat threatened to close. She swallowed and stepped back. "What is he doing?"

Gloria closed the closet without replying. She, too, looked close to tears. She went to the desk and opened the top drawer to take out a stack of newspaper clippings. Still, without commenting, she handed them to Jillian.

There were stories about Ron Cutler in high school, articles about the teams he was on and the activities he was in. There were stories about the Cutler stores, their expansions and development. Every reference to Ron was underlined. And there were the stories of his fatal accident. She looked at the pictures of the car and the pictures of Ron as a young man and a picture of him that was taken relatively close to the time of his death. The obituary was there, as well.

"He has this, too," Gloria said, handing Jillian a copy of Ron Cutler's high school yearbook. "In fact, he has gotten and has been getting his hands on everything he can that has anything to do with Ron."

"How long has he been doing this? Ever since he found out he had a twin brother?"

"Mainly since the accident."

"I can understand the curiosity about his brother; that's only natural, but—" She looked about the room. "It's almost as if he's..."

"Possessed by him?" Jillian nodded. "I use to think that, too, but it's more serious than that."

"Pardon?"

"If he was possessed, if such a thing could be, I'd go get an exorcist somewhere and free him of it," Gloria said, and smirked. "What I should have done, as I said before, is get him to a psychiatrist; but he did all this subtly at first, and slowly. It just built into something."

"Into what?" Jillian asked, lifting her hands in frustration. "What's Paul trying to do?"

Gloria took the clippings and the yearbook and put all of it back into the drawer. Then she closed it quietly and stood looking down for a long moment.

"I didn't get married until Paul was a little more than five years old. Michael was ten. In the beginning," she went on, walking to the bed and sitting on it, "my husband had only a small construction business. By the time Michael graduated from high school, we had built a respectable company. Paul was always a strong boy. He could have been an athlete like his twin brother, but right from the moment he could, he went to work alongside Robert, my husband. He had no time for after-school activities. He liked working with his hands; he liked mechanical things. He was never what you would call a great student in school, but he did fair. He could do better, but he just wasn't interested in schoolwork."

Jillian stood with her arms folded, listening. She could tell from the way Gloria paused that telling all this was difficult emotionally for her. In fact, Jillian thought, the woman might not have gone through it all this completely and chronologically before.

"He never won awards; he never got his name in the paper; his stepfather was building up a small business slowly, although not anywhere as dramatically as Cutler's. And Paul never went to college. At least, not until relatively recently. Suddenly that became important to him."

"College?"

"Suddenly he wanted to take classes in art and literature and business up at the state college. I should have thought something strange was happening on the basis of that alone, but I didn't pick it up for quite some time. Actually," she said, looking around, "not until after it was too late."

"Too late?"

"He bought these clothes, the computer, the artwork, all these books. He began spending long hours in this room and then he started going away for weekends. I had no idea where he was going or what he was doing, but I wasn't going to chase after him. He was no child; he was more than twenty-five years old."

"Where did he go?"

"I don't know all of it. I think he went to the Cutler stores from time to time, well disguised, I imagine, and then..."

"Then what?"

"He started..." She bit her lip. "He started going where Ron might have gone and doing things Ron might have done. He never told me outright. I picked it up by the things I found about...stubs, theater tickets from New York plays, airplane tickets, bills. Gradually I pieced things together."

"My God. You're telling me your son Paul tried to become his twin brother Ron?"

"As I said downstairs, I thought it had begun to diminish. He seemed more and more like his old self and did fewer and fewer things that were out of character. And then...you came to my door."

Jillian looked about the room, not sure whether she was terrified or fascinated.

"But why do you think he did it? Out of a sense of inferiority?"

"I did confide in a doctor and he thought, from what I had described, that Paul did feel a need to prove himself to himself. I thought once he had done that to his satisfaction, he would stop. So I let it go on. That's why I told you downstairs that I thought what happened to you was my fault. I'm sorry."

"Then it's true," Jillian said in so low a voice it was more like a thought spoken aloud, "the man who fell in love with me and with whom I fell in love does not exist. He might as well be a ghost."

"I don't blame you for being angry; it's cruel. I'd be angry."

"I don't know if I am angry. No," she said, "I don't feel angry. I feel like I'm in a daze, but I don't feel I should hate anyone, least of all you. And, in a way, I feel sorry for Paul."

"That's very kind." Gloria stood up. "Maybe now, since he didn't get in touch with you, maybe now it will end. Maybe giving you the ring was a step too far and that step shook him up enough to get him back. I hate to say this," Gloria Kane added, "but the best thing now might be for you to go away from here as quickly as possible. If he saw you, it might revive the... the... problem."

"Yes," Jillian said, but she wasn't sure she wanted Gloria Kane to be right.

GLORIA KANE STOOD in her doorway. Jillian didn't know what her final words to this woman should be. She wanted to offer her some words of comfort, but everything she thought of seemed inane, if not out of place. Would she tell her not to worry, that anyone who could be as charming and intelligent as Paul could be would find his way out of this? Was she a fool for not being angry? Something else occurred to her.

"Tell me, didn't your son ever have any serious relationships with women before this?"

"Oh, yes. He was practically engaged right before Ron's death. A very nice girl, Audra Rifflin. She worked for us at one time."

"What happened?"

"He just stopped seeing her. It was almost as if he'd completely forgotten about her. Whenever she called or I mentioned her, he had this blank look on his face. No emotion, no concern. There was no longer anything special about her."

"What about now? Recently, I mean?"

"About a year ago, she married someone else and moved away from here."

"Oh."

"That's why I thought... when he was taking these mysterious weekend trips, he was seeing someone."

"He was," Jillian said.

"Yes, but as a different person. You have to understand, Jillian—my son, Paul Kane, has never met you."

The cold feeling that came over her was enough to move her quickly to the car. Gloria Kane watched her pull away to satisfy herself that Jillian was gone. She had succeeded in making her feel like a leper, but thinking about it objectively, Jillian concluded that she would have probably acted the same way had she been Paul's mother.

It wasn't until she was headed out of Oneonta again that she decided she didn't want to think about it objectively. Why should she be objective? She wasn't some outside observer; she was a participant in something so dramatic and so intense it nearly changed her life. It could still change her life. How would she react to another man? What was that Biblical line she liked so much: "If you should die, I will hate all womankind." Well, why not think of it from a woman's viewpoint, as well: "If you should die, I will hate all men."

Ron Cutler had died twice, only the second time he had taken part of her with him. Did he take the part of her that enabled her to love another man? That enabled her to give freely of herself? To sacrifice, to compromise, to surrender that part of her ego that would enable her to have a significant relationship? Look what had happened to Mrs. O'Shane's aunt, standing on the widow's walk until her dying day, watching for her lover's return, for to admit the death of him was to admit the death of an essential part of herself.

Was it old-fashioned? Was it a weakness to commit so much of yourself to another human being? Surely some of her friends, learning about this story, would tell her that they would have pressed their feet down hard on their accelerators to get out of this city as quickly as they could. No man is worth such a sacrifice.

But who was the man whom she'd met and loved? Was he simply a part of another man's illusion or were there things about him that went deeper, things that reached down into the truth of who he was, whether he realized it or not? Could she really just leave without knowing that?

She paused at the last traffic light before the highway leading out of Oneonta. A man in his car beside hers was looking at her oddly because she was smiling idiotically. She was smiling because she realized that subconsciously she had made the decision back at the Kane residence when she had forgotten to return the ring. It was still in her pocketbook. Ron—or Paul, as she would now have to know him—had told her he wanted it to haunt her. How right he was.

She pulled over to the side, waited for the traffic to pass, and then turned around, really not knowing what she would do next. She had to admit she was afraid, but her memories of the words and the music and the warm embraces were enough to insulate her from those fears.

CHAPTER FOURTEEN

JILLIAN WENT BACK to the Kane Construction Company building and parked across the street where she had parked earlier. A quick perusal of the parking lot told her that Paul Kane had not returned with the truck in which he had left. Of course, he could have been dropped off at his house, but for the moment she didn't know where else to go or what else to do.

The longer she sat there, the more foolish she felt. Fortunately she didn't have to wait long. The truck appeared and Paul got out with the other man. She watched him walk into the office. Was it her imagination, she wondered, or did he seem to walk differently, have a different rhythm to his gait and a different posture? His stride looked longer, his steps more aggressive. A few minutes later he emerged by himself and got into a gold Mazda RX-7 that had been parked toward the rear of the lot. She watched him pull out of the parking lot, turn left, and head back toward the city.

As she followed at a safe distance, she thought about those aspects of Ron Cutler that she had considered paradoxical. Her instincts had made sense after all. What had she called him, "a hands-on executive?" She laughed to herself. No wonder he had that rolled-up-sleeve appearance; no wonder he was so comfortable around the old Jeep in Provincetown and could talk to laborers and fishermen so easily.

Now she realized that during their first lunch meeting in the Korean restaurant on Vanderbilt, when he had tricked her into analyzing him aloud, he was really testing himself, just as she had thought. He was looking for reassurance, but was he doing it consciously? Was he continually aware of what and whom he was portraying, or was it as his mother thought...an obsession better described as schizophrenic? And what if he was? she thought. We're all a bit schizophrenic at times. Of course, not to this extent. But how many of us have the twisted and mysterious background Paul Kane had?

She realized she was defending him, rationalizing and looking for ways to accept what had happened, but she couldn't help it. Despite what had happened to her and the strong possibility that she was merely another adventure for Paul Kane, she still felt sympathetic toward him. What would it have been like for her to discover after twenty-odd years that she had a secret twin, one that had obviously had more advantages from the start? Wouldn't it just be natural to wonder what she would have been like had she been the one who had gone to the wealthy family?

And how did Gloria decide which child to give John Cutler? Did she toss a coin? Or did she simply decide that he would get the first child to be born? She did say that she had originally intended to give him both children eventually, for a price, so the method of choice was obviously not very important at the time. Still, one had to think about the turn of the wheel of fortune.

One of the twins would go and one would stay; one would be brought up around luxury and one would work side by side with a tradesman; one would go to an Ivy League college and one would go no further than high school. The prince and the pauper, she thought; and yet somehow, after all the development years were over, the poorer twin would have something significant to show for himself. He was not really a pauper, certainly not financially, and perhaps the distances that had existed between them were not as wide as first thought.

Why is it necessarily true Ron had the better life? In fact she had to wonder now whether or not she would have fallen in love with the real Ron Cutler.

Paul didn't drive into the city proper. Instead he made another left and headed in the direction from which she had come. He drove for nearly two miles before pulling into the parking lot of a small tavern with the tongue and cheek name, the Dew Drop Inn. She slowed down until he was out of the car and inside. Then she pulled up along side the Mazda.

It's down to it, isn't it? she thought. If she had her druthers, she wouldn't have picked this place for the confrontation, but it was where he was, where it had to be. She got out slowly and closed the car door softly, as if she didn't want to warn anyone she had arrived. Then she started for the front door of the tavern. She had no idea what she would do or say once she went in, but her legs were carrying her forward. She was moving irrevocably toward another moment of truth.

It wasn't a big tavern, just one rectangular room with a long bar and a dozen tables with a half dozen booths, but it was obviously a very popular place at this time of the day because it was jammed. It was primarily a male crowd, but she was happy to see a number of obviously single women at the bar and at a few of the tables. No one took great note of her entrance; they were all pretty much involved in their conversations. Ironically the song coming from the music box was Tammy Wynette singing "Stand by Your Man."

Paul Kane had already made his way to the far end of the bar and had his back to her. She noted there were no waiters or waitresses, just two men behind the bar. People carried their mugs of beer and drinks to their tables themselves. From what she could see, these people were all blue collar workers, although she did see half a dozen men in shirts and ties. By now their ties were loosened.

Although the tavern had no real air-conditioning, the three large ceiling fans were going at full speed and creating a pleasant flow. When she had driven in, she had seen that the tavern was surrounded by tall hickory and maples and was thus nestled coolly in the shadows of their leaves. The place did have the atmosphere of an oasis.

There wasn't very much room at the bar, but when she approached, two men separated to give her some space. She nodded and smiled and then ordered a cold beer. She was happy to see the bartender pull a mug out of a freezer and fill it with draft beer. She thought it was the most refreshing thing she had ever had.

For a few moments she stood sipping on her beer and watching Paul down at the other end. Then she started around, making her way slowly through the crowd. Her heart was beating so rapidly she thought she might grow dizzy and draw everyone's attention to her as she gasped and fainted. She caught sight of herself in the mirror behind the bar and saw how flushed and excited she looked.

She hadn't done anything with her hair or makeup before she had gotten out of the car to come into the tavern. Considering what she had been through so far this day, it was not surprising that she had so wild and maddening an expression on her face. For a moment she thought she, too, had become something of a schizophrenic and was now looking at her other self. Had this journey taken her to a part of herself that she had never known?

She paused a few feet behind Paul and waited, hoping he would simply turn around, hoping that he would feel her presence. He was in a very animated conversation. From what she could hear of it, he was talking about some building project with which he was presently involved. He was complaining about the engineer's design.

She closed her eyes to listen more intently to the sound of his voice. Was it a different voice? Could the voice itself have changed? Did she imagine the difference in the tone and rhythm? Was there another accent?

She was really only inches behind him now; she could reach out and touch his shoulder. He would turn around and see her face to face and there would be no way to avoid the confrontation. Would she say, "Hello, Paul" or "Hello, Ron"?

Out of nervousness, she raised the mug to her lips and closed her eyes as she swallowed more of the cold beer. Just at that moment Paul Kane's gestures expanded as he described his construction problems with more animation. Jillian had brought herself right beside him so that when he brought his right arm back to demonstrate the length of this steel girder, he struck her on the upper arm, jolting her so hard that the beer jumped out of her mug, over her face and down her neck and blouse.

Her cry was subdued, but Paul spun around quickly, his friends laughing. Jillian stepped away from the bar. However no one but Paul and the people he was talking to had seen what had happened. The conversations and activity around her continued unabated.

"Oh, jeez, I'm sorry," Paul Kane said.

Jillian turned and looked up at him. It was as though Ron Cutler were resurrected and then died right before her. She saw the flash of recognition in his eyes; she saw his face change, his lips begin to form her name, and then she saw it all become suppressed as Paul Kane struggled to bring his true identity to the forefront. It happened with the speed and the drama of a film dissolve. She wanted to cry out to stop it from happening, but the change occurred too quickly. In a moment the recent past dangled before her and was gone.

"I'm really sorry," he said. "Can I get you a napkin or a paper towel?"

Jillian put the mug of beer down on the bar. She couldn't speak. The tears that had come into her eyes were beginning to flow over her eyelids. Her mouth quivered, but she was unable to deliver a sound. Instead she turned quickly and fought her way through the crowd, rushing to the doorway and out. She didn't stop running until she had reached the car.

There she paused to catch her breath and control the sobbing that had begun even before she left the tavern. It was too much; it had all been too much. She should never have attempted it. It was like looking into the dead face of someone you loved and finally realizing that he would no longer whisper your name or kiss your lips, or hold you against the warmth of his body. Not even all the tears in the world could wash away the truth and the finality of death. There was nothing left to do but fight off the memories. All they could bring her now was pain.

That line she liked so much from one of the Rossetti poems came quickly in the role of confirmation. "Beauty without the beloved is like a sword through the heart."

Would she ever look at the ocean again and not feel the sorrow? Could she see a sailboat and think about anything else? What would it be like to see a man and a woman walking hand in hand on a city street?

There was nothing left to do but go back and throw herself so completely and so intently into her work that she thought of nothing but the work. She wanted to come home exhausted every night and fall into her bed. At least for a while it would be a way to face reality.

Jillian took the handkerchief out of her pocketbook and wiped her face. The sobbing had stopped but the pain in her chest remained. She swallowed hard and took a deep breath. Then she opened the car door, realizing she was on her way out of Oneonta anyway. She would simply keep going. But before she could get in, he called her.

"Miss."

She turned. He was in the doorway. Someone walked out and he stepped forward with him. It was strange, but when she looked back at him standing there in front of the tavern, she really felt she was looking at someone new. The traumatic confrontation in the tavern had produced the effect of a mental cleansing. When she said nothing, he continued toward her.

"I'm really sorry about what happened back there."

"It's okay," she said. When she sniffed, he smiled.

"No, it's not." He leaned back, sitting against the side of her car, and folded his arms across his chest as he looked out across the parking lot. "I've got a habit of getting so wrapped up in my conversations...I get dramatic as hell...talk with my arms. My friends say it proves I have Italian blood."

Jillian smiled through her tears.

"Do you?"

He shrugged.

"Who can swear for his ancestors? Anyway," he said, turning back to her, "were you here to meet someone?"

"Yes," she said after a moment.

"Oh. Too bad."

"But he's not here," she added.

"He stood you up?"

"You might say that," she said, hoping this conversation filled with puns and symbolism would trigger a return of recognition and love.

"Well, that's just too bad for him. How about letting me make up for my clumsy ways?"

"What did you have in mind?" she said. It was strangely fascinating to talk to him this way, but she couldn't help doing it.

"Dinner?"

She smiled and turned away.

"I know this great Italian restaurant," he went on. "It's not fancy and showy, but it's authentic. It's owned and operated by an Italian family and everything tastes homemade. You won't believe the pasta."

My God, she thought. Déjà vu. Is he deliberately doing this?

"I don't know. I don't live here. I was just passing through. I came to see someone, but..."

"But he's not here; you told me. Why waste time thinking about it?"

She looked at him. His eyes twinkled with charm, but it was an impish charm. Was this the same look he had when he came to her as Ron Cutler? She couldn't remember; she was getting so confused. Don't do this, she told herself, don't do this to yourself, Jillian. But could she help it?

"I really haven't even checked into a hotel."

"You're not going to go on the road now, are you? It's getting late. Look, a friend of mine owns the Plaza right in town. Let me get you a room on me."

"Oh no, I couldn't..."

"It's no big deal. He won't charge me anything, anyway. I do work for him from time to time, and most of the time I don't charge him."

"It's not the money."

"So then do it. Come on, do something spontaneous. What's life all about?"

"I don't know what life's all about," she said.

"Then let me help you find out."

She laughed and shook her head. Why not go with this a little longer? It was late; she wasn't in the mood to drive all the way back to New York.

"The Plaza, you say?"

"Yeah. It's right in town. A very nice hotel. Really, it's no roach city."

She studied him for a moment. Could a change in personality, in identity, actually change someone's physical characteristics? Was there a difference between the smiles he gave as Ron Cutler and the smiles he gave as himself? She couldn't remember if the right corner of his mouth rose that way after he said something intently and waited for her decision.

There was no getting away from it. She wanted to know more. She couldn't just walk away.

"Okay, I'll do it," she said.

"Great. You know how to get back into town, right?"

"Yes."

"Just go right to the hotel. I'm going to call him from here so that by the time you arrive, you'll be checked in. I'll pick you up at eight, all right?"

"Yes," she said. "Eight is fine."

"Good." He started away. "Wait a minute," he said, coming back. "This is unbelievable."

"What is?" She looked up with expectation.

"I don't know your name and I didn't tell you mine."

She just stared at him for a moment, searching his face for a sign of falsehood, but he looked frighteningly authentic. At this moment there really was no Ron Cutler in him.

"My name is Jillian. Jillian Caldwell," she said. She spoke like one in a dream.

"Hi, Jillian. I'm Paul Kane. See you at eight. The Plaza. Just go right to it."

She watched him go back into the tavern. Then, truly moving like one in a daze, she got into her car, backed out of the parking lot, and headed toward the city and the Plaza Hotel.

As soon as Jillian arrived at the hotel, she saw she was expected. They treated her like a VIP. She didn't even have to sign in; that had been done for her. She felt foolish having a bellhop carry her small overnight bag, but the desk clerk insisted he do it. The room was a delightful shock. They had given her a suite, and one of their deluxe ones at that. What she couldn't believe were the bowl of fruit and the vase of roses that awaited her on the table in the small sitting room. In the short time it took for her to arrive, they had gotten it in there with a card from Paul.

The card read, "Hope you enjoy. The clumsy one." She smiled and turned to give the bellhop a tip, but he shook his head adamantly.

"No, that's been taken care of."

"Even that?" she said, but he didn't understand her surprise. He shrugged and left quickly.

Seeing the time, she hurried to the bathroom to shower and prepare herself as best she could. Without consciously doing it, she had packed her cotton-challis floral skirt and her heavy-silk mauve-gray blouse with pleated sleeves, the exact outfit she had been wearing the first time Ron Cutler had walked into her office. Was it simply a coincidence or had fate taken control?

While she was working on her hair, the phone rang. It was Paul.

"Everything all right?"

"A little much, but certainly all right. Thank you for the flowers and the fruit."

"I would have brought flowers personally, but I probably would crush them before I got there. Is it all right if I'm on time? I'm starving tonight."

"Of course. Why shouldn't it be right for you to be on time?" She recalled the discussion they had had when he had arrived right on time at her New York apartment.

"Great," he said. "I'll meet you in the lobby in ten minutes."

It wasn't until she had actually left the suite and headed for the elevator that her panic began. Was she doing something terrible? Could she trigger some horrible reaction and cause irreparable mental damage? Why couldn't she have just accepted the end and gone back?

She hesitated to push the button calling for the elevator. She should have gotten more advice about this; she shouldn't have taken on so much so impulsively. Maybe she should call Gloria Kane and tell her what was happening, she thought; but then she recalled how the woman acted at the end of their conversation and how anxious she was for Jillian to go. She wouldn't like this; she wouldn't like it at all.

She paced about in the hallway for a few moments. How could she get out of it now? She could pretend to be sick. Maybe that would work. Then, sometime during the night, she would just leave. The idea actually seemed feasible. She looked back toward her suite anxiously. All she had to do was call down to the lobby and give him the message. What would he do? She could even promise to see him tomorrow if he got insistent.

The option was becoming her choice just as the elevator door opened, but when she turned, she saw him standing there.

"Good," he said. "Caught you before you came down. Thinking about it, I realized it wasn't the gentlemanly thing to do to ask you to meet me in the lobby."

"That's really not so terrible," she said.

Paul wasn't dressed in the kind of clothes she envisioned Ron would wear, but he looked comfortable. He wore a dark blue, short-sleeved shirt and a pair of light blue jeans with blue socks and black loafers. He had the sleeves of the short-sleeved shirt rolled back an additional two inches. There was no jewelry around his neck, nor any rings on his fingers.

"You look great," he said. "Glad you had a change of clothes after the mess I made of your blouse."

"It'll survive."

He laughed.

"It'll survive. I like that. Come on," he said, reaching out for her hand. "Let's ride this wagon down."

With obvious hesitation, she lifted her arm toward him. He seized her hand the moment it was comfortably in reach and tugged her gently toward him. She nearly tripped and fell on him.

"Whoa," he said. "I guess I'm not the most graceful escort you've had." He pushed the elevator button and the doors closed. For a moment she recalled going down the elevator when they had left Nelsen Grant's that first day. How talkative she was then. Now she was afraid of the effect of every word. "I hope you like this place," he said. "It ain't fancy."

"What makes you think I like fancy places?"

"Jillian. Can I call you Jill?"

"Please do."

"Jill, you just look to me like a woman who's been to fancy places."

The elevator doors opened to the lobby. Standing there and smiling stupidly were the desk clerk and two bellhops.

"Have a good evening, Mr. Kane," the desk clerk sang as they walked through. The bellhops laughed.

"Funny guy," Paul said.

The Mazda was parked right in front of the hotel. He opened the door for her and she got in. She noticed that he was parked in a no parking zone, however. When she pointed that out, he shrugged.

"Cops know me," he said.

"I guess this is a small city," she said, more to herself than to him.

"You're from New York, right?"

"Yes, I am," she said. He pulled away quickly and shifted with the expertise of a race car driver. She remembered the way he had driven the Jeep in Provincetown.

"Do you get to New York much, Paul?" She couldn't help it, but she felt like she was teasing him. She was fascinated with every answer he gave though.

"No, not much. You're pretty far away from New York," he said. "Whoever you were supposed to meet must be something special, huh?"

"Yes, very special."

"Oh," he said. She thought that his eyes blinked more rapidly. Was it coming back to him? He was more like a man who had suffered amnesia, she thought. Yes, that's it, a man who has lost his memory and when that memory begins to return...what then? "Well, he couldn't be too special if he stood you up, Jill." He turned and smiled at her, but there was yet no recognition in his look. "I'll have to thank him if I meet him," he added, and laughed. She almost laughed herself.

My God, she thought, this is insane. This is so weird. She turned to look out at the city, but they were already on a quiet, country highway. Moments later they pulled into the parking lot of Madeo's Italian Restaurant.

"How's this for a restaurant name?" he asked her.

"Madeo's? What does it mean?"

"Nothing. It's the family name. Told you this was authentic stuff."

He had had the same attitude about the restaurant he had taken her to in New York. Indeed she felt a resemblance. Just like the New York restaurant, Madeo's was cozy and warm. There were no booths, but the tables were a good distance from one another so that the patrons had a sense of privacy when they dined. The room was nearly full.

A tall, elderly man with a gray mustache and goatee greeted them. He had a thin, narrow face with a dark brown complexion and black eyes.

"Good evening, Paul." He turned to Jillian. "I can see why you wanted your special table."

"Special table?" Jillian looked about. What table could possibly be special? she wondered.

"Now don't give away any of my secrets, Joe. This is Joe Madeo, the owner," Paul explained. Jillian extended her hand to meet his and the restaurant owner took hers to his lips.

"He's a charmer," Paul said. Madeo raised his eyes and smiled.

"This way, please," he said, and led them through the restaurant to a table situated near a rear window. He held the seat out for Jillian.

"Thank you."

"It's the table with a view," Paul said, "even though there's really nothing much to see."

"The specials tonight include pasta e fagioli soup, saltimbocca alla romana, chicken Madeo, and my wife's rum cake for dessert," the owner recited.

"Your wife is the chef?" Jillian asked. This really was family owned and operated. Was she falling back through time?

"And my daughter is the cashier and one of my sons will be your waiter."

"If his mother could work, she'd be in the kitchen, too," Paul said.

"She can work, but I can't pay her what she wants," Joe said. Jillian and Paul laughed. "Cocktails?"

They ordered their drinks and watched him go.

"You're going to be amazed at the food here. Don't let the simple decor fool you," Paul said.

"Things are often not what they seem," Jillian replied.

"You sound like you know. Tell me about yourself," Paul said. He offered her some of the homemade bread.

"No," Jillian countered. "You tell me about yourself. What do you do, Paul Kane? Tell me..." She paused as the waiter brought them their drinks and took their orders. "Tell me about your family," she insisted after the waiter left. "I want to know it all."

And so he began. She wondered if it was cruel to make him repeat what she already knew. He told her about his brother Michael and his mother and their business. He talked a great deal about his father and he described some of their projects. He spoke with pride, but she sensed an insecurity because he paused after certain things to see if she agreed or appreciated what he was saying. This wasn't the man of confidence she knew as Ron Cutler, but in a way she felt more warmly toward him because of his vulnerability. He needed her reassurance. Did she ever feel that when he spoke to her as Ron Cutler? She couldn't remember.

The food was as good as she imagined it would be, and the wine Paul chose, although not anywhere as expensive as the wine they'd had in New York, was just the right distance between being too dry and too sweet. During the course of their meal, people who knew Paul came over to their table freely and made conversation. She could see he was well known and well liked. Also, she sensed that being recognized affectionately buoyed him. He grew more exuberant and animated as the evening went on. His energy was infectious and despite her mental and physical fatigue, she found herself becoming more outgoing and relaxed. For a few moments she forgot where she was and what was really happening.

"I want to tell you something," he said after they had had their coffee and Mrs. Madeo's famous rum cake. "I'm damn glad I was clumsy today at the Dew Drop Inn."

"I am, too," she said. "It made things easier."

"Easier? How could that be?" He smiled with confusion, but she also saw a suggestion of pain and anguish. Was the wall he had created between who he was and who he pretended to be beginning to crumble finally? She hadn't pressed hard for that to happen, but she was moving in that direction. "Oh, you mean easier to get over being stood up. Yeah, sure."

"Yes, easier to get over being stood up," she said, pronouncing each word slowly and deliberately and staring hard at him as she did so. The tinge of anxiety began to expand. He looked flustered for a moment as he went for his wallet and pulled out the money for the dinner.

"I'm always amazed at how cheap this place is. If you got this same meal in New York..."

"Yes, how much would it be?"

"A lot more. That's for sure."

"You've had it there, then?"

He looked at her, but he didn't reply. Instead he put the money down and stood up.

"I'm too full to move," he said. She didn't stand. She sat there looking up at him. "Maybe we can go for a walk. I'll show you the highlights of downtown Oneonta."

"All right," she said, and they started out.

"Everything okay?" Joe Madeo asked as they approached the door.

"It was wonderful," Jillian said. She looked at Paul. "There's a little restaurant in New York, family owned and operated like this. Their food is wonderful, too, but even though it's in the world's most famous city, it's not any better than your restaurant."

"Why thank you. I like her, Paul. Don't let her leave."

"I can only spill so much beer," Paul said.

"Huh?"

"Private joke," Paul said. "Good night." They said nothing to each other until they were back in his car.

"You're serious about the walk through town, right?" he asked.

She reached across the seat and put her hand over the hand he held on the gearshift.

"No," she said. "Don't take me there. Take me somewhere where there is a view and we can be alone."

They stared at each other for a moment. Only the illumination from the restaurant sign provided any light. She could barely see his eyes. It was like looking at the shadow of a man. During the moments of silence that passed, she felt as though a curtain had fallen between them. She wondered if he felt the same way, for he said nothing in response. He merely started the engine and shifted the gears. In seconds they were back on the highway, driving deeper into the darkness.

She sat back with the knowledge that she had forced her way across the boundary separating Paul's world of illusion and world of reality. There was no turning back. As if in confirmation of that fact, the darkness sliced away by the headlights of Paul's car rushed in behind them. She turned to him. His face was illuminated by the lights of the dashboard. It threw his reflection on the inside of the windshield, but for a moment it looked more like the face of his twin brother looking in.

CHAPTER FIFTEEN

PAUL HEADED UP A HILL and continued past houses until they were riding on a road in an area that was still undeveloped. He made a sharp left turn off the macadam and shifted down to ride a gravel roadway that led them to a large clearing. There he stopped and turned off the engine. The headlights closed and she and Paul were dropped into a darkness made more friendly by the starry night sky visible through the car's sunroof. She hadn't realized there were so many stars shining so brightly. Even though there was no moon, the sky seemed luminescent.

"Where are we?"

"You wanted a view and you wanted to be alone. This is the best spot for it." He opened the car door and stepped out. She did the same.

She followed him to the edge of the clearing from where they could see over the small hill. It was a breathtaking view of the valley below. Because of the clear visibility this evening, they could see far off to where lights twinkled on the surrounding mountains. She stepped up beside him to take it all in.

"This is a very beautiful place."

"I own it," he said, looking out.

"You do?"

"Over two hundred acres. My father liked this place. He always talked about it, but he never did anything, so one day I bought it. I was going to give it to him for an anniversary present, but he died before I could."

"That's too bad," she said. "Your mother knows about this, though, doesn't she?"

"Yeah, but it's not the same thing. It would have been something if my father was alive; she would have loved it. Now she has no interest. Why should she?" he said before she could ask why not.

"Are you going to sell it?" she asked. He turned to her. Now that her eyes were used to the darkness, she could see his expression more clearly. He reminded her of the way he looked when she had awakened at the Portuguese House and found him standing on the widow's walk staring out at the night.

"No, I would never sell it. I have hopes of one day building my house right on this spot. There would be a big picture window right about there." He stepped to her right and indicated the spot. "It's a great place for a living room or a dining room. Just about any room on this side of the house would have a great view. I'd want the master bedroom over there," he said, pointing to the far right.

"The kitchen should be right here," she said, stepping forward. "We're facing east, right? There would be sunlight coming in during the morning making it cheery."

"Yeah, I'd put the kitchen there."

"That would be wonderful," she said.

"Would it?" He sounded distrustful, skeptical of her enthusiasm.

"I think it would. It's not that far from civilization and yet it's so private and breathtaking."

"Civilization?"

"Other houses, other people."

"Oh, I forgot. You're a city girl." There was a tone of derision in his voice.

"Meaning you don't think I could be happy here?"

"Could you?" He turned to her expectantly, but she said nothing for a moment. Then she folded her arms across her chest and looked out at the twinkling lights of the small village that loomed on the horizon.

"I don't know. I am a city girl now. You're right. But I don't know if that's what I really want. I'm not sure about too many things anymore."

"Really?" He came back to her.

"Yes, really. You're not the only one who's confused about things. No one has a monopoly on that."

He said nothing for a moment. Then he walked back to the car and sat against the side, just the way he had sat against her car in the Dew Drop Inn parking lot.

His gestures, his posture, his expressions, they are different, she thought. It was a little frightening. She was with someone who was really more of a stranger than she thought he would be, and yet there were things about him that were familiar, things she liked. She realized that was all part of the paradox.

"Why did you want me to take you to where we could be alone?" he asked as she started back toward him. "Not that I mind being alone with you. Are you what they call the new woman?"

She laughed.

"You don't mean to say there are no aggressive women here, do you?"

"No. I'm just kidding. Seriously though, the way you asked back there..."

"Being here, alone with you, makes it easier to say things," she said.

"What things?"

"Things we both know have to be said."

"I don't know what you mean." His voice sounded shaky. He unfolded his arms and pressed his hands down against the car. Should she push on? She wasn't a psychiatrist.

"I knew your twin brother," she said. She waited to see if he would deny Ron Cutler ever existed, but he said nothing so she continued. "He looked just like you, but he was different in many ways."

"What ways?" he asked quickly.

"He was a little more confident of himself at times, maybe. Maybe a little more ambitious. He had a different background, a different sort of education and upbringing."

"He was better than me. Is that what you mean?"

"No. I said different in many ways, but not better. You each have your strengths and I'm sure you each have your weaknesses."

"Why tell me all this? Why did you come here? To compare us with each other?"

"No."

"Then why did you come? It wasn't such an accidental meeting, was it?"

"No. I followed you to that tavern."

"Why?"

"I thought I would find him there," she said. She was standing only a foot or so in front of him, but even though her eyes were accustomed to the darkness, she couldn't see his eyes as sharply as she would have wanted to. She realized he couldn't see hers distinctly, either. The darkness made it possible for her to talk to him this way, and she suspected it also made it possible for him to endure it.

"You thought you'd find him there? When did you know my brother?" he asked suspiciously.

"He was there, wasn't he?" she said rather than answered.

"No." She heard the defensive tone in his voice. "He wouldn't go to a place like that. Nightclubs, cafés, sophisticated bars, those were his style. Why did you come here? You know more about him than I do."

"We were supposed to be married," she said.

"Really?"

"He never told you about me?"

"My brother and I never met," he said. "We were separated at birth. He had his life and I have mine. Anyway," he said as if he just realized it, "you didn't seem that disappointed about not finding him."

"I was for a while, but you helped me to forget. You're really a very nice person, Paul Kane. I can see that people like you. They sense you're a sincere, interesting man."

"Is that what you think?"

"Yes, I do."

"Interesting?"

"Very much so."

He just stared at her for a moment. Then he leaned forward and stood away from the car.

"Ron's the one who had the interesting life. Ron was glamorous and famous."

"You underestimate yourself, Paul."

"Is that so?" They were inches from one another now. She saw a smile form on his face. "I think if I were my brother, I'd probably kiss you at this point," he said. She thought it was his first Ron Cutler line.

"Then do it," she whispered. She was so nervous, she barely had the breath with which to pronounce the words.

He stepped toward her, took her in his arms, and brought his lips to hers softly. His first kiss was tentative, but she didn't move back and he brought his lips to hers again; this time he moved like a man who had just recognized something wonderful from long ago. His kiss was a search, a journey into the maze of his mental confusion. As he pressed harder and held her tighter, she felt his need to understand what was so familiar about the taste of her lips, the scent of her hair, and the warmth of her body.

"Jillian," he said. It was Ron's voice. He pronounced her name with the same rhythms and intonations he used when he was in the guise of his brother. She touched his cheek.

"Yes?" She held her breath. Would he respond as Ron Cutler? Was it wise for her to make him do so? They kissed again. Then he suddenly broke away and turned from her. "What's wrong?" She reached out to touch his shoulder, but he didn't respond. Was this part of the terrible reaction she was afraid would occur?

"You're teasing me. You came looking for Ron."

"I said I was looking for him. He never called. I waited and I waited."

"Maybe he couldn't call," he said.

"Why not?" He didn't respond. "Why didn't he call? What made him stop? Why didn't he want to see me anymore?"

"I'm sure he didn't want to stop seeing you."

"Then why did he? Tell me," she said in a more demanding tone. She would see this to the end, even though she was out here in the dark, alone with him, some distance from other people. She had a faith built out of the strength of their love. Nothing bad could come of such passion.

"Because he..."

"What? Tell me. Say it. You've got to say it." She seized his upper arms. "Say it." She shook him. "Paul Kane, tell me why Ron Cutler never called. Tell me," she demanded again, turning him toward her.

"Because he died," he said. "My brother's dead," he whispered, and she pulled him to her, wrapping her arms around him and embracing him so tightly it was as if she would never let him go again.

THEY SAID NOTHING MORE. They both understood that the pain of the first revelation went deep. Her heart was beating madly against his chest. She wasn't sure what forcing him to admit to his brother's death would do. She felt certain it meant he would no longer take on his identity. She sensed that something had brought the truth home to him before this, and when that had happened, he had stopped seeing her just as he had stopped doing all the things Ron would have done. Of course, it could mean that he would have forgotten all the things he had done as Ron Cutler, which meant she was wiped clean from his memory.

With his arm still around her, he walked her around the car to the passenger side and helped her get in. Then he got in and turned the car around. Still, with neither of them speaking, he drove back down the hill, back toward the city and the hotel. When they pulled up in front of it, he just sat there.

"What are you going to do now?" she asked.

"Go home, I guess."

"I don't want you to."

He looked at her.

"What do you mean?"

"I don't want to be alone," she said.

"But...I'm not Ron Cutler," he said. "You said you came here looking for my brother. He made promises to you years ago. I don't know what you expected to find now, but he and I...we're two different people; or at least we were until he was killed."

"I know."

"Then how can you...how can you want me to stay with you? Is it just because I look like him?"

"I don't know; I'm not sure. All I know is I want to be with you and I want you to be with me. Can't you stay with me a little longer?"

He said nothing more. They got out of the car and went into the hotel. When they got to the suite, she went to the small couch and sat down. He stood there looking at her.

"I met your mother," she said. "I went there looking for Ron and she told me about you and all that had happened." His eyes widened with surprise. "I met your father, too, your real father, John Cutler."

"I never met him."

"I know that. I think it's time you did, before it's too late for both of you."

"I almost did a few times. I almost went right up to him and confronted him, but I couldn't do it."

"You can do it now, Paul. Your brother's ghost is dead. You can do it."

"Look, you don't know me. You knew my brother, but that doesn't mean you know anything about me. We had no contact with each other; we shared nothing but genetic backgrounds. I discovered his existence only by accident. There's no sense in even talking about this anymore. You came to the wrong place. I can't give you what you want. He could have done it, but he can't now. Thanks for the company," he said, and started toward the door.

"Wait!"

He turned and she studied him. He was telling the truth. At this moment there was no Ron Cutler in him. Would she accept it? She debated telling him what he had done. Was it good psychological technique to confront the person directly? As he was now, he probably wouldn't accept it anyway, she thought. How could she convince him? Should she convince him?

The truth was she wanted him to return to his illusionary existence because she wanted his love. He didn't love her as Paul Kane; he loved her only when he was Ron Cutler.

"It wasn't your brother I came to see," she said, "it was you."

"What?"

"It's true. I didn't know it myself until I got here."

"Look, you and I never met before. So what are—"

"But we have met before, Paul. I don't know if it's right or wrong, selfish or not, for me to do this, but I can't help it. I just can't let you walk out the door forever. I just can't let all that has happened between us be part of some illusion, an illusion to forget."

His smile began to crumple and there was a wild, frightened look in his eyes.

"I don't care what your reasons were, but I want you to know that I cared about you then, not because you were rich or sophisticated. My feelings went deeper and I know—I hope—yours did, too. For whatever it's worth and wherever it takes you..." She got up and went to her pocketbook. He had backed up to the door, but he didn't move. He watched her like a trapped animal, his eyes still filled with tension.

She stepped up to him. Her face was soft and loving. He seemed to relax some, his shoulders lowering, his lips less firmly pressed against each other. She took his hand into hers and then pressed the ring into his palm.

"You gave me this at a beautiful moment in a beautiful place, Paul," she said, without uncovering the ring. "Take it back and let it now haunt you until you remember not the illusions, but the love, and when that happens, if that happens..."

She couldn't finish. She turned from him and fled to the bedroom. Moments later she heard the front door of the suite open and close.

And then, like the phantom lover he had been, he was gone.

Epilogue

JILLIAN DID what she had intended: she returned to work with a fanatical intensity helped by the fact that the Benton walkathon was quickly capturing national attention. One of the major networks had made the walkathon a tag item on its nightly news, showing a map of the country and the Bentons' progress. Coordinating the walkathon's itinerary with local television, radio, and print media coverage along its way had become one of Jillian's major responsibilities. Nelsen worked out a budget with the Pooley people to employ two assistants to work under her. Magazines such as *People*, *Newsweek*, *Us*, *Time*, and even *Cosmopolitan*, emphasizing Mrs. Benton, published features and used the Bentons on covers. Twice during her first week back, Jillian flew out to meet the Bentons and personally coordinate the publicity coverage.

Then word came that Nelsen Grant had won the New York City campaign. Staff had to be expanded even more. Jillian found herself working into early evening, eating late dinners, driving herself to the point of exhaustion every day. Sleep came as she hoped it would—a few moments after collapsing in bed.

All the work was interesting and exciting, but when she did stop to think about it all, she recognized that something was missing. Maybe she was burning herself out with all this intensity or maybe she was finally experiencing the emotional collapse she had feared. Whatever the reasons, she sensed an underlying emptiness. It was as though all of this were built on a false foundation. Someday, any day, something would happen, something would be said, and all of it would simply fall apart around her.

During these thankfully rare moments of introspection, she was always on the verge of tears. One time the tears actually appeared, but a visit from one of her assistants prevented her from doing any real crying.

She was glad her parents had had little or no opportunity to see her during those first few weeks. She was sure her mother would take one look at her and know something serious was wrong. Her eating habits had changed and she knew she had lost a few pounds already. Her weight losses always showed themselves in her face first. Her cheeks became a little drawn, the lines a little deeper.

When her mother called, Jillian put on a good performance. She babbled so quickly and so excitedly about all she was doing that her mother had no chance to pick up the underlying note of depression. If she did sound down, she blamed it on her work and her mother went into a lecture about driving herself too hard and risking her health. Jillian agreed, made promises, and hung up, grateful that that was all that had resulted.

Of course, Betty Dancer called her on the Monday after she had returned from Oneonta. Jillian was prepared for it. She had rehearsed the conversation while driving back to the city. She had made up her mind not to tell it all, at least, not the actual all.

"It's over," she told her. "It wasn't what I hoped it would be," she added, nearly laughing at the understatement herself.

"Oh, Jillian, I'm so sorry, but I guess it's better you found out when you did. What happened? He lacked the courage to back out himself?"

"Something like that," she said. In conversations like this one, Jillian realized, it was acceptable to be vague.

"So you gave him back the ring," Betty muttered. "Oh, well," Betty continued, falling back into her usual caustic self, "maybe in a year or so when you're sufficiently over it, we'll be able to develop it into an episode for the show."

"Thanks a lot. I knew you'd be sympathetic." They both laughed and Jillian promised to meet her for lunch as soon as she had an open date, but because of all the work at the office, that lunch date didn't take place for weeks. Whenever Betty called, Jillian went into her tale of activity. Betty said she was exhausted just listening to it.

She made one exception. Uncle Phil came into town and called her at the office. He tempted her with lunch at the Russian Tea Room. It was as crowded as ever, but because she was with Uncle Phil, she didn't seem to notice the noise and activity around her. He sensed a change.

"Your mother called me," he confessed.

"I knew it."

"She's worried you're overdoing it and made me promise to see you and bring back a report. Are you overdoing it?"

"Yes."

"You going to keep overdoing it?"

"For a while."

He studied her a moment.

"Bad love affair?"

"How'd you know that?"

"Happened to me a few times," he said nonchalantly, and looked at the menu. Then he smiled at her over the top of the menu.

"How long does it take to get over it?"

"This is your first?"

"I've broken up with boyfriends, but I never had the personal commitment like I did this time."

"Then it's going to take some time," he said, "but you'll be all right. Remember what I once told you about your ancestors—they had grit. You're a survivor, Jillian."

"I hope you're right."

"Look, I make a good part of my living gambling on things. I know a sure thing when I see one."

"Thanks, Uncle Phil. Thanks for caring," she said. Then, despite his promise to her mother not to, he got her talking about her work. It didn't do any damage. She left on a high note, rejuvenated by the warmth and the comfort her uncle Phil provided. On the sidewalk just outside the restaurant, he offered her one last piece of advice.

"You want to end the pain faster," he said, "find someone new."

She wanted to say that part of the pain was that she had, but she subdued the thought and kissed him on the cheek instead. He told her he'd call her in a week or so and maybe spend some real money on her for dinner.

"Without Mom's knowing?" she quipped. They both laughed and parted.

One night, deciding to walk more than usual after work, she went over to Fifth Avenue and window-shopped her way home. She paused at a display in a travel agency advertising a trip to Cape Cod. They showed a picture of Pilgrim's Tower in Provincetown and a strip of beach. As she reminisced, a strange thing happened in her memory. The man sitting beside her in the Jeep looked, dressed, and acted more like Paul Kane than Ron Cutler. Maybe it had been because of the way she had permitted her work to absorb her every thought, but the memory of Ron became vague and confused with the memory of Paul. It was as though the battle for identity were taking place in her memory just the way it was taking place in Paul Kane's mind.

She walked on thoughtfully, concluding that Uncle Phil was probably right—she should slow down on the work end and get back into social circulation. It was time to meet other men and have other experiences. Time itself was not sufficient enough of a panacea for this illness. She needed other distractions besides the distraction of work. The way to do it was to call some of her girlfriends and see what they had planned to do. She had been avoiding them all during the past few weeks. The time had come to be romantically resurrected, she thought, and laughed at the image of a broken hearted lover rising slowly from the grave of her own misery.

By happy coincidence, when she got home she found a message from Miriam Levy who wanted to invite her to a luncheon at the Sheridan, where "you will be surrounded by dozens of male models."

She called her back and agreed to go. It was scheduled for the following Wednesday.

But she never went.

In the beginning she thought the reason for not going was a horrible mistake. The debate she'd had with herself put her into distracting mental turmoil that followed her to work and remained with her each and every day. Gradually though, she found the distraction to be a healthy one. She had been devoting herself too fanatically to the work. It was good to have something else with which to occupy her mind, even if it was this.

On Thursday night while she was in bed trying to read herself to sleep by going over the copy for some new ads for the New York campaign, the phone rang. She lifted the receiver in a reflex motion and put the earpiece to her head without taking her eyes off the page in front of her or her mind off the words printed there.

But the sound of the voice tore her attention away from the work. She sat up quickly, unable at first to say hello.

"Hello, Jill?"

"Yes?"

She waited. Her heart beat so fast she had to swallow to catch her breath. Who was he?

When the answer came, she realized it was all over.

But she also realized it was about to begin again if she would let it.

She decided she would and even after the debate she had with herself during the days afterward, she stood by that decision. In the end she was very happy she did so, for this was no longer an illusion.

"It's Paul," he said. "Paul Kane."

It was a misunderstanding that could cost a young woman her virtue, and a notorious rake his heart.

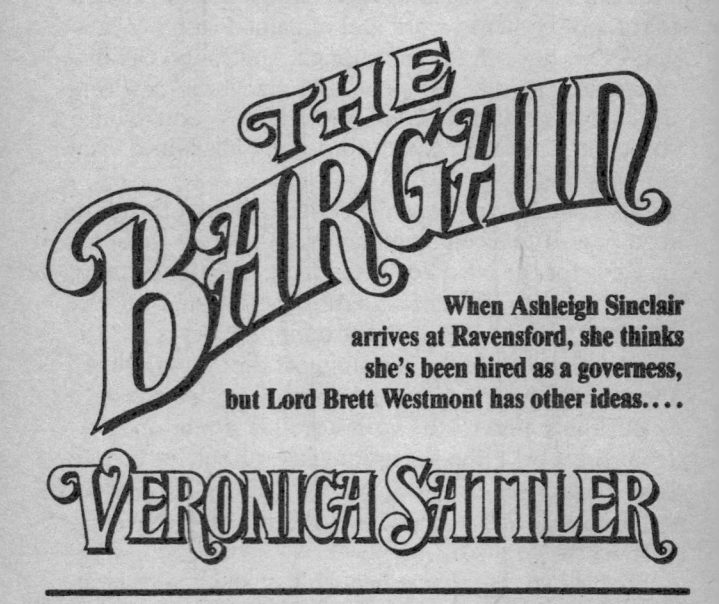

THE BARGAIN

When Ashleigh Sinclair arrives at Ravensford, she thinks she's been hired as a governess, but Lord Brett Westmont has other ideas....

VERONICA SATTLER

Available now at your favorite retail outlet, or reserve your copy for shipping by sending your name, address, zip or postal code along with a check or money order for $5.25 (includes 75¢ for postage and handling) payable to Worldwide Library to:

In the U.S.	In Canada
Worldwide Library	Worldwide Library
901 Fuhrmann Blvd.	P.O. Box 609
Box 1325	Fort Erie, Ontario
Buffalo, NY 14269-1325	L2A 5X3

Please specify book title with your order.

WORLDWIDE LIBRARY

BAR-1R

He could torment her days with doubts
and her nights with desires that fired her soul.

Ride the Eagle

VITA VENDRESHA

He was everything she ever wanted. But they were opponents in a labor dispute, each fighting to win. Would she risk her brilliant career for the promise of love?

Available in October at your favorite retail outlet, or reserve your copy for September shipping by sending your name, address, zip or postal code, along with a check or money order for $4.70 (includes 75¢ postage and handling) payable to Worldwide Library to:

In the U.S.

Worldwide Library
901 Fuhrmann Blvd.
P.O. Box 1325
Buffalo, NY 14269-1325

In Canada

Worldwide Library
P.O. Box 609
Fort Erie, Ontario
L2A 5X3

Please specify book title with your order.

WORLDWIDE LIBRARY

RID-1

An enticing new historical romance!

Spring Will Come

SHERRY DeBORDE

It was 1852, and the steamy South was in its last hours of gentility. Camille Braxton Beaufort went searching for the one man she knew she could trust, and under his protection had her first lesson in love....

Available in October at your favorite retail outlet, or reserve your copy for September shipping by sending your name, address, zip or postal code, along with a check or money order for $4.70 (includes 75¢ postage and handling) payable to Worldwide Library to:

In the U.S.	In Canada
Worldwide Library	Worldwide Library
901 Fuhrmann Blvd.	P.O. Box 609
P.O. Box 1325	Fort Erie, Ontario
Buffalo, NY 14269-1325	L2A 5X3

Please specify book title with your order.

WORLDWIDE LIBRARY

SPR-1